Fateful Friend

Book 4 of the Masterson Files

By

Andrew Allen Smith

Fateful Friend

DEDICATION

To Doctor Steven Speet, without whom this book may never have finished, and to Alex and Kenzie, who made a bad time bearable. Life is a series of intertwined adventures, and I am thankful for many more.

Prologue

The concert had been fantastic. Kira Calloway and Beth Turnbull had an exciting time but for them, the night was just beginning. They had gone back to the hotel with friends and had just started partying when their friend Lisa had gotten sick. It was a terrible mess. She was covered with recycled alcohol and hot dog. The chain of events forced the girls to go get some type of detergent and soda crackers to keep it from being an even more miserable night.

That did not stop Beth and Kira from still having fun. They turned up the music loud in their little Subaru and headed into downtown Indianapolis looking for a drug store, a convenience store, or any store for that matter. They needed to find the items so the other girls could clean up the mess that Lisa had made of their hotel room. Beth and Kira would handle the easy run since they had a good car. Everyone else's car was either old, older, or less than drivable on a good day.

They listened to the music blaring and sang along at the top of their lungs, sliding through the warehouse district towering around them. The giant buildings looked like massive sentinels, watching over them from afar. They swallowed up the night while creating spots of fake daylight with high power halogen bulbs.

As the two girls sang and almost screamed, Beth saw the sign for the interstate, "Turn here. There has to be something near the main roads."

Kira's reflexes were quick and flawless. She turned the car with grace and speed so as not to miss the intersection. She did not miss, but also did not see the double median. The Subaru hit it square, both tires grinding as both girls heard a large pop, and with a rapid suddenness felt the all too familiar feeling of a flat tire.

"Well that sucks," yelled Kira, almost laughing. "I guess we get to change the tire."

"You are such a jerk," Beth said as she opened her door and got out.

"That I am," Kira agreed as she turned off the car and opened her door. There was silence in the night now. A dark silence surrounded them that seemed oppressive and cold.

Kira leaned down to inspect the tire in her tight jeans and chucks. The oversized t-shirt she wore was falling off her shoulder and she pulled it back up in a gesture that could only be considered absentminded.

Beth came over to her side of the car. "Bad news, the other side is flat too."

"Maybe we should not have turned," Kira said as she stood and punched Beth in the arm.

"Oww! What was that for?" Beth asked.

"For telling me to turn," Kira laughed.

Kira smiled at Beth, "I will call my dad, he will find someone close and get this fixed. We will be back on the road in nothing flat."

"It is 2 o'clock in the morning," Beth stammered.

"He will be up, he always is. He talks to people all the time about staying alive after the government falls and all that crap. It is fun to listen to," she paused, and a wry smile crossed her lips, "for about 5 minutes." Kira laughed.

She took out her cell phone and dialed a number.

"Hello," came a voice.

"Dad, we blew a tire," Kira said.

"What are you doing out this late? I told you to stay in the hotel after dark," her dad said on the phone.

"Dad," Kira whined, "It is no big deal. We had to go out and get some things for the room."

"It is a big deal," her Dad said, "I'm too far away to help."

"I know dad, but can you call a wrecker for us? I don't know who to call, and, well... two tires are flat."

"How did you blow two tires?" her dad asked with a tone that only fathers seem to know.

"Gracefully?" Kira replied while Beth giggled to her side.

"Have you been drinking?" her dad asked.

"No," Kira said, "Well, I had half a beer, but that was hours ago. Can you help Dad?"

"Who is that?" Beth asked.

Kira turned to see a car driving up. It was a big Jeep CJ, and as it got closer the lights blared at them. "Dad, someone is here," Kira announced.

"What's going on?" her dad pleaded.

"Need help?" came a bodiless voice from behind the lights.

"No," Kira yelled, "We are waiting on the wrecker."

"Sure?" the voice said with a questioning tone, "They rarely come here at night."

"I'm sure," Kira yelled back.

She heard her Dad's voice on the phone even though she did not have it near her, "What is going on?"

Beth looked at Kira, "You know, maybe we should..."

"Shut up," Kira said.

"Looks like a bit of unsure dissension," the voice observed, as three boys jumped out of the car. "Maybe a wrecker is not coming."

The three boys looked as though they were part of a serious athletic team. Each was muscular and walked with a steady pace as the approached the two girls. "Maybe we should party instead of looking for a wrecker," said the leader in his jeans and blue t-shirt. "Maybe we really should party like we were wreckers." He said the last with a strain and a groan as he grabbed Beth by the hair and pulled her close to him.

Both girls screamed. The other two boys grabbed Kira letting her phone drop to the ground. Kira heard her dad's voice screaming as she watched the lead boy lick the side of Beth's face.

Beth kicked and screamed. Yelling, "No!" in a very loud voice.

The boys all laughed.

Beth twisted, and the lead boy twisted with her, "No, no, no. You will not be getting away from me," the boy yelled, his blonde hair messed by the rough work. But Beth was not giving up. She somehow got enough leverage to kick the boy in the groin and he doubled over for a second as air rushed from him. When he stood, a pained look covered his face, then anger flashed, and he backhanded Beth against the car.

Beth fell back, landing against the car, but free. But the boy did not stop. Overcome by pain, which seemed to inflame his rage, he grabbed Beth by the throat. With his free hand, he began hitting her in the face, over and over. As he did, he swung harder and harder until Beth slumped to the ground.

Kira heard her dad's voice on the phone. He was yelling to her.

Seeing Beth on the ground unconscious, one boy panicked. "Jimmy, you shouldn't have hit her so hard."

"Shut up you idiot! Why did you say my name?" Jimmy demanded. The boy turned his attention to Kira, leaving Beth on the ground. "Hold her down," he said, pointing to Kira, "She's mine."

"Jimmy," the first boy said, "I don't know, maybe we should go."

"You aren't going anywhere," Jimmy screamed in a frenzy.

The third boy spoke up, "Jimmy, Coach will…"

"Shut up and hold her down," Jimmy repeated. The boys looked at each other with unsteady gazes. Still, they stopped and held Kira to the ground.

Kira struggled, but the boys were strong. Very strong. As she struggled, she saw sinews flex and knew she would not easily be going anywhere. Kira thought of her Dad with his constant worries and it all seemed to fall into place. She thought in the back of her mind that it was too late, but she should have listened. She tried to move but felt her legs being forced apart. Her screams were muffled as Jimmy started kissing her with anger, forcing her to gasp for breath as his rough face rubbed on hers.

Kira struggled with renewed vigor. She heard her father's voice close and saw the phone near her. "I don't care if we are found out, she is my daughter! Do it! Do it now!" She could not understand the words even though she heard them clearly. She tried again to kick only to be held even more tightly. For a moment, she considered how an Anaconda would wait for the panic only to get tighter and tighter and she thought she knew how an unwilling prey would feel. The panic overwhelmed her.

Kira screamed and heard tires screeching. As the two blended, they became a cry for help even greater than she could have done on her own. The night air seemed stiff with anticipation and after the screech, the silence closed in on them all.

"Get off of her," she heard a thick, deep voice yell.

"Get out of here," Kira heard Jimmy say as he stood. She was thankful the onslaught had stopped and felt her senses returning. As the other boys let her go, she scrambled backward away from them, away from it all. Kira picked up her phone as she looked at Beth, still slumped against the car, unmoving.

"You boys best get out of here," she heard the deep voice say.

"There are three of us," said Jimmy, "Leave now."

"Police are on the way, and all I have to do is hold you," the new voice said.

"C'mon, let's get out of here," the third boy said.

Kira heard scrambling. There was a measured uncertainty in the steps they had now as they fumbled and were uncoordinated. It was nearly unsettling that she could not see beyond the darkness.

She saw the boys drag each other to the Jeep. The engine came alive with a growl that made Kira jump, the tires wailed and they car sped off into the distance.

"Dad," Kira said, "Beth, well, dad, she, well, she isn't moving."

"Are you ok?" her dad asked frantically.

"Yeah, someone stopped and ran them off," Kira said, her voice filled with sobs.

Kira looked up and saw the massive black boy before her. He reached down his oversized hand and smiled the most perfect smile Kira had ever seen. She felt serene and safe inside where only a moment ago panic had gripped her very soul.

"It's ok, Miss," the boy said, "They're all gone, there is an ambulance coming. I called when I pulled up and saw your friend. The police are coming too. Can you stand?" the boy asked, "Are you ok?" he asked her in a soft well-measured voice.

"I think so," Kira said nervously, "but Beth."

"They'll be here soon."

Kira heard the sirens.

"See," the boy said in his soft tone.

Kira reached up her hand and took his.

"My name is Jackson." The boy said, his eyes smiling at her, calming her. The sirens were getting closer, their screams echoed in the industrial area like wolves tracking an elk.

"Jackson, I'm Kira," she said and suddenly her face was splattered with warm liquid. Jackson slumped forward to the ground. Kira saw the bloodstain appear and begin to spread in the cloth of his shoulder, the growing red spot became a large pool. She looked around, stood and began screaming. In moments she did not know where her screaming stopped, and the sirens started as they blended into one giant crescendo as the lights played across the dark night sky.

Chapter 1

The scene was out of a movie with a chaotic script. Dozens of police officers combed the area while three ambulances were working on different people. The Detective in charge, Sergeant Walter Franks, took a few moments to clear his head while he spoke to Kira. Around him, photographers were taking pictures of numbers all over the ground as evidence was being collected from nearly everywhere. A half dozen news crews milled around the edges of the police line and a small crowd of people looked on even though it was the dead of night.

"Let me get this straight. This guy," he looked down at his pad while a female officer stood behind him, "Jackson, he was not involved in any of this?"

Kira sighed, "He ran the people off, there were three boys. They were big, but Jackson scared them away."

"So why did you shoot him," the detective asked.

"I didn't shoot him," she cried again, "I was on the ground when he was trying to help me up, and he just fell on me."

"But you are covered in his blood," Franks countered with a brusque stab of his pen. "We will not get anywhere until you tell me what really happened."

Kira sobbed, "I told you, the three guys attacked us, Beth was knocked out, and they were going to hurt me. They had me on the ground and well... Jackson drove up and scared them away."

"Yeah, one guy scared three others away and you shot him," Franks countered again.

"I didn't shoot anyone," Kira yelled, "My dad was on the phone the whole time, ask him. I didn't shoot anyone! Is this how you treat people who are almost raped? If I *was* raped would you have to beat me?"

Kira's face turned red as she yelled, and she started pacing. The female officer stepped forward and said, "It will be ok. He is just trying to get to the truth."

Kira glared at the woman, "It'll be ok when he stops accusing me of doing something I had nothing to do with."

"Let's start over," the Sergeant began, "So you were at the concert. Then you went to the hotel and…"

A uniformed officer walked up and whispered to the Sergeant for a moment. Shaking his head, he pointed, then looked at Kira. He then looked back at the Sergeant and made a few more statements.

"Are you sure?" Franks asked.

The officer nodded, "It will take getting back to the lab to be certain, but this is not close range at all."

Franks looked at his paper, considered for a moment and scanned the area. Warehouses spread out for blocks upon blocks. There were dozens of vantage points, dozens of places, near and far. He looked at the officer, then at the woman next to him.

"Kira, take Officer Phelps here," he pointed at the female officer, "and lay her on the ground exactly where you were."

Kira looked at him with a suspicious frown. "What?"

"Humor me," Franks said.

Phelps walked to Kira and Kira lead her in front of her car, pointing to the pavement. Phelps stood over the spot.

"Go ahead Phelps," Franks said, "Lay down on the ground."

"Sir, there is blood all…" Phelps started.

"I really don't care, lay down or get off my crime scene," Franks snapped.

Phelps laid down and Kira looked at her, "Yeah, that's about it."

"No, no, is she exactly like you were?" Franks asked.

"Well, close," Kira said concentrating.

"Think Kira," Franks prodded.

Kira knelt next to Phelps and moved her to the right a little. She looked at the blood. The little yellow tags were everywhere. Remembering where the bumper of the car was when she was on the ground, she moved Phelps, so her head was in the same place.

"This is really close," Kira said.

"Ok Bill, lean over her," Franks said. "Kira, look at Bill over top of her. Where was he when you saw the blood?"

Phelps protested, "Sir, this is got to be hard on her. Don't you think we can..."

"Yes, we'll talk more. I just want to see something," Franks interrupted.

Bill leaned down and Kira posed him for a moment. "He was here when he fell over."

Franks walked around and looked at all angles. Finally, he looked at Bill and pointed in the distance to a group of buildings about 700 yards away.

"That would be one hell of a shot," Franks said out loud. "Get some men over there to look at it."

Bill stood up and helped Franks pull Phelps to her feet.

"Kira," Franks said, "I'm sorry for putting you through hell, but we have to explore every option. Is anyone on their way to get you?"

"My dad, but he is in Lexington and it will be a few hours before he makes it," Kira said. "I should call about my car."

"We have a wrecker on the way, they will fix it," Franks replied.

"Beth?" Kira asked.

"Your friend is on her way to the hospital; I can get you a ride. The boy who was shot is already there. Phelps can take you if you want and we will get your car there later. When Beth wakes up, we'll have some questions for her." Franks said.

Kira teared up, "Why did this have to happen?"

"There are a lot of bad people in the world, and sometimes they are worse. We'll find everyone involved. Don't worry. You'll be safe with Jenny."

"Jenny?" Kira asked.

Phelps answered, "Jenny Phelps, I'll take you."

Kira walked to the car while Bill Mitchel and Walter Franks watched. An officer walked up and Mitchel talked to him for a moment before the man scurried off. As the bright Chevy truck drove away, Franks looked at Mitchel. "Why did we buy those bright undercover cars? Seems like a waste."

Bill looked at the distant buildings, "You know if they shot from one of those buildings it was a blind shot at about 700 yards at least. At an angle to hit him as he was reaching for her, I bet he wasn't the target. It may have been a loose round."

Franks studied Bill, "Really? Think someone was trying to shoot her? It would be a little too quaint to be an accident."

"Maybe it was random," Mitchel said as he stared into the distance. A patrol car with lights flashing sped toward the warehouse area.

"Maybe," Franks mused. "Then again, maybe it was very deliberate."

"Racial?" Mitchel asked.

"Do I look like Dion Warwick?" Franks asked. "I'm not psychic, I need facts."

"Fact is, how many of us could make that shot? Two, three, none? Who would want to or would be out here tonight? Fact is, why would anyone care?" Mitchel asked in rapid succession.

"Good questions," Franks stated dryly. "But again, I am not part of a group of psychics. Get the lab on the bullet and try to work out a trajectory. We guessed. I need locations and some real data. Get this crime scene closed, we've been here an hour and not found anything new. We look like a parade and the news crews are getting antsy."

"Ok," Mitchel said, "Will do."

As Franks walked back to his car, the news crews chattered at him like hungry squirrels, "Franks, give us something."

Franks stopped at his door, walked over to the police line, "Sure. We of the wonderful city of Indianapolis did not welcome these people in a very nice manner. We will be releasing a formal statement in the morning at the station."

"Who was it?" A dozen other questions rang out, directed at Franks.

"No more right now," Franks stated. Returning to the sleek cruiser, he got inside. The Crown Victoria was still a great car for officers, and right now he was happy because it was nearly quiet even with all the yelling going on outside. Franks looked out the window at the buildings in the distance and wondered about who took the shot. He looked down as he thought about it, "That was one hell of a shot." He said out loud, shaking his head.

Franks started the car and began the drive to the station.

Chapter 2

The Indiana University Health Hospital Emergency room was one of the best in the country. Jackson Sheldon was brought into the hospital and taken directly to the Emergency room. A clatter of attendings and skilled nurses determined that he would need to have surgery right away. Their fast treatment protocols saved his life.

As Jackson was taken to the operating room, his father arrived at the hospital.

"My son is here," he announced to the front desk as he walked into the well-built reception area.

"Yes, of course," the volunteer at the front desk stated. "What is his name?"

"Jackson, ma'am," he stated, "Jackson Sheldon."

"Yes sir, and what is your name," the woman in the pink scrubs asked with patient grace.

"My name?" he said, "Oh, my name is John Sheldon. I am his father. Is he ok?"

The volunteer typed with a clickety-clack on the computer. "John," she said, "I can't tell you anything because I am not a doctor, and well... I am not allowed to say anything beyond what is on his chart. It says he was admitted to the ER about 45 minutes ago, and then he was taken to the 6th floor."

"What's on the 6th floor?" John asked.

"Surgery," the pleasant woman stated. "But don't worry, our surgeons are the best if he is in surgery. Check-in at the desk up there and they will tell you everything you need to know." She handed him a card with a clip on it. "This is your visitor's pass to the 6th floor. Take the elevator and when you get off turn right. The desk will help you from there."

John looked puzzled as he took the card from her, a million thoughts coursed through his mind.

"Don't worry," the volunteer said, "He's in good hands. Find out what is going on first."

John stammered for a second, then caught himself, "Yes ma'am." John started to walk towards the elevators, and stopped to turn around, "Thank you, ma'am." He said with a more direct, softer tone. "I appreciate your kind words."

The woman smiled, "Get up there."

John turned back and walked to the elevator. He wrung his hands and looked down at them. His hands were worn and calloused, his skin dark with pink where he had burned them so long ago. John was a big man, almost seven feet tall, and his early years had given him a heavy body. To most, he would be intimidating, but he did not try to be. Instead, he was easy going and patient. His friends described him as a gentle giant, and his son was all he had left in the world.

John stepped into the elevator and ducked a little even though he did not have to do so. It was a habit to keep his head as he had hit it on numerous occasions while trying to get into places. He used to guess he was smaller than he was. Now he simply paid attention. It was safer ducking a few times when he wasn't sure and always ducking at doors and places where the ceiling lowered. It had saved him a lot of headaches.

As John moved to the back of the elevator, a few women got on and pressed buttons and he realized he had not done so. "Six please," he said. The front woman mindlessly pressed six while not missing a beat in her conversation.

"Did you see the group in the cafeteria," the woman droned on, "They need to clean up a little. I mean... why would you wear pajamas to a hospital unless you're a patient?"

"I know, right," the second woman said as the elevator began to go up. "I mean, we work here at the hospital for a living and don't need to see that."

John looked down at his flannel shirt and worn jeans, wondering what they would think of him. He had better clothes. But when the police called, he grabbed what he had been wearing the day before. And well? It had been a day around the house.

The elevator stopped at three, and the two women got off. John was happy that they left as he didn't want to make them uncomfortable. He was now alone, still wringing his hands and thinking about his son. The elevator door began to close, and a hand shot in. The door opened again.

"Sorry," said a spry young voice. The small girl looked up at him, "Wow, you are a big guy," she said with a giggle. "Do you know where you are going?"

"Yes' ma'am," John said, "Six."

"Me too," the girl laughed, "I have to take care of the surgeons, you know they are all babies at heart. They are so smart they just aren't smart. Sometimes I think if I didn't feed them, they would just waste away. I have to get some things ready for them when they get out of surgery, but it may be a while for the ones I report to. They are in a big case, police and all." The door closed and the elevator kept rising. To John, it was taking forever.

"Yes ma'am," John said to the girl. She was small, close to only five feet tall. She had little blonde curls hanging out of a tight ponytail that was barely down to her shoulders.

She looked up at him, straining her neck a little. Her scrubs were blue and white with a small emblem on them. While her brilliant green eyes looked up at him with a mischievous look that he had not seen in a long, long time, "Ma'am? I am not a ma'am. I am Lindsay."

"Thank you, Lindsay," John replied as the door opened to six.

Lindsay stepped out before him. "Where do you need to go?" she asked, looking back.

"My son is on this floor. They told me downstairs he was up here from the ER," John said in a soft tone, trying to hide his emotions.

Lindsay turned around, she took John's calloused hand, her diminutive porcelain white hand a huge contrast in his massive black hand. "C'mon, let's find out what is going on."

Walking to the information desk, Lindsay led him while he was still in a near shock stupor. "Madalyn," Lindsay started, "Can we find where John's son is for him?"

Madalyn looked at Lindsay with mild annoyance, "A last name would help."

"Oh," Lindsay giggled, "What's your last name?"

"Sheldon, ma', uh, Lindsay," John stammered, "My name is John Sheldon, my son is Jackson Sheldon."

Madalyn looked up at him with a new look, "Your son is in surgery right now." She seemed concerned.

Lindsay looked at her, "But you didn't look." She said.

Madalyn looked at the younger girl, "He is the one who has been shot."

"Shot?" John asked, suddenly more in control. "Who shot him?"

"John," Lindsay said, "We can find out what is going on, the police will be here if he was shot. We just need to ask."

Madalyn studied Lindsay, wondering why she suddenly had this interest in someone she obviously didn't know.

John looked at Madalyn, "Thank you, ma'am." He said softly but his tone was far more concerned than a moment ago He followed Lindsay to a small room. Inside, an officer was there waiting.

"Excuse me," Lindsay questioned the officer, "This is John Sheldon. His son may have been shot. Do you know what's going on?"

The officer stood and studied the mountain before him. "Are you John?" the officer asked in a polite tone, born of dealing with people in a variety of serious situations.

"Yes, sir," John said, "John Sheldon. My son was shot?"

"We don't know everything, but it appears he was shot. We're here to protect him as necessary. He is in surgery now and the doctors have not come out. There is a detective on the way with one of the two girls."

"Girls?" John asked.

"Yes," the officer continued, "You'll have to ask the detective for more details."

Lindsay watched John. His arms looked like bridge cables and she could see the tendons flexing under his red flannel shirt as he wrung his hands. "John," Lindsay said, "The doctors here are really good. Let me go see what I can find out. You stay here."

"Girls?" John asked again and smiled a little.

Lindsay smiled, "I'll be right back." She walked to the back of the hall and scanned her card then disappeared through the crisp automatic door.

"John," the officer stated, "I'm sure you'll have some answers soon."

John sat down in one of the chairs and looked awkward in the small waiting room. He was too big for both the chair and the room. The four other people in the room eyed him with caution and uncertainty.

"He was going downtown to meet friends; he tries to keep everyone out of trouble. He doesn't drink or do anything bad, and he was with girls?" John said with an incredulous tone. "I just don't know."

"I don't think they were with him," the officer said, "but the detective will know."

"I promised my wife as she lay dying, I would take care of him. I just don't know," John said, wringing his hands together.

"I understand," the officer said.

Lindsay walked back through the door and straight to John. John stood as she approached. "He's still in surgery, but the nurse on station said it looks good. I'll go back in and bring the doctor out to you when he is through. Don't worry John, the doctors here are the best. They'll take good care of him."

John looked down at his hands and Lindsay looked up at him. The tears welled in his eyes and Lindsay put her hand out to him and laid it on his massive arm. He looked at her with those tear-filled eyes and there was something else there too, worry, passion, concern, and something else.

Chapter 3

Sarena Prince didn't like her job sometimes. It was difficult to consider the world as a good place, and often she was brought in when the world was a bad place. Sarena was one of the youngest FBI agents in the Midwest and had been considered not only good at what she did, but an expert at it. She had been put in charge of multiple difficult projects that others just didn't want to touch. She had enjoyed them except that each one seemed to draw her deeper and deeper into strange situations. Her specialty revolved around weapons and tactics. With her Princeton Education she seemed to fit, but it was the mathematic genius that her Grandfather passed to her that made her most useful. She had an uncanny knack to be able to run angles without massive machines and simulations. She could literally see a bullet trajectory and calculate the distance in her head with an efficacy that was considered uncanny.

This uncanny ability was the reason Sarena had been called by her younger brother on the Indianapolis police force and asked if she could come to a scene in the warehouse district downtown. She had made her point that this was not an FBI case and she could get into trouble, but Anthony almost begged, "Please, this is a tough one. I am sure the captain will request you officially."

Frustrated and a little angry Sarena pulled on a pair of jeans and a white cotton shirt, throwing a leather jacket over it. At almost 5'11", she chose her clothes sensibly. Sarena tied her hair in a makeshift ponytail. Glancing in a mirror as she was walking to the door, she noted her long brown hair looked OK in a ponytail, but it was a little off. She had no time to redo it. "They wanted her brain, not her hair," she thought to herself as she left.

The trip from her house to the Warehouse district was quick in her White Camaro. Driving in a rapid manner, she considered what could be so difficult that they would need her help in such a hurry. It was not like the skilled individuals in the Indy Police department to ask for help in such a manner. They had more than their share of experts and were as adept as she was in dealing with the day-to-day rigors of police work.

Sarena sighed at how difficult it would be to deal with her brother if she had not come. Anthony had not gone through school and had instead fought his way through the police academy. It didn't come as easily to him as he was constantly scattered, but he worked hard and was well respected as an officer. Some of his peers were not so nice. They would rib him as the brother of the FBI genius that was always going farther than they did or point out that she outranked him or worse she could outshoot him. In truth Sarena was ranked number one on the tactical training team. She frequently shot far better than the snipers on active duty SWAT. Anthony avoided asking for favors and tried to do everything the right way. It was a major move for him to ask for help from her at all.

Sighing again, she pulled into the warehouse district, seeing the familiar red and blue flashing lights in the distance. As she drove forward, she noticed the throng of reporters that circled the area like hungry piranhas and grimaced. She was not here on official business. It would not be good to be noticed.

A familiar face beckoned her forward and she moved her car under the tight yellow tape into the heart of an investigation. Sarena took a deep breath and stepped out of the sleek white car.

"Sarena," her brother greeted her, "I'm glad you came."

"Anthony," Sarena said with her head bowed slightly to avoid attention or worse, photographic proof she was there, "I'm not sure this is a good idea. You know that there has to be authorization for something like this."

"I know, I know," Anthony said, "but we are against a wall already. And well... I was talking to the lead detective... he said I should call you and see if you would come in."

"OK," Sarena relented, still barely whispering, "Who is this genius?"

"Franks," Anthony said, "He said you were the best and he would..."

Sarena paced a little before looking her brother square in the eye, "You called me out here for Franks? He is in trouble all the time. He can't seem to follow an order and gets results by breaking rules. Do you think I should be involved in that?"

"Rena," Anthony said, "Give him a chance to explain. He said he would get the authorization for you."

Sarena looked deeply into her brother's chocolate brown eyes, "You know, I used to look down on you."

He smiled, his white teeth glinting in the darkness, "Yeah, I grew up."

"Damnit, I'm going to regret this," Sarena fumed, "Where is he?"

Anthony gestured to the side and Sarena saw Franks nearby in front of a car. He was kneeling, looking in the distance. Then shaking his head as he looked in the distance again and talking on a cell phone. As he spoke into the phone, he scratched his head. Glancing over, he saw Anthony with Sarena. He brushed off his pants and walked over to them.

"Sarena," Franks began, "I am so glad Anthony convinced you to come. I know this is a little irregular, but we're stumped."

Sarena took in the man. Franks was a little disheveled and his shirt, though crisp in places was untucked and unruly. He would have been dressed well in the jeans and button down if not for this look. Franks held out his hand to her and she shook it, not in a passive manner, but with strength and confidence like their father had taught them.

"Nice handshake," Franks commended. "So, we are having an issue and Anthony has always said you are the best."

"What issue?" Sarena asked with a sarcastic tone.

"Well," Franks knelt over the blood stains, "We are pretty sure the boy who was shot was about here. We keep trying to line it up but can't determine where the shot came from. We started with the idea it was those warehouses in the distance, but there was not an easy clear shot. They weren't high enough. We came forward, and the angle seems wrong. We went back further and well." Franks paused and tucked in his shirt a little with no visible effect, "it doesn't seem plausible."

"Why is that?" Sarena asked, looking at the area closely then scanning the horizon.

"Well, I am here, and our victim said the boy was shot when he was kneeling... about like this." He stood, reaching down toward the blood stains," but the bullet clipped him in the shoulder at about a 30-degree angle off center. Which seemed to point out the distance shot to those warehouses. But he is a tall kid. We can't get the angles to work."

Sarena looked further in the distance, "How about the offices behind the warehouses."

"That's over a mile," Franks mumbled.

"The angles would work, but I would have to know how tall the kid actually was and how the bullet struck. Why not just canvas the warehouses?" Sarena asked.

"We did," Franks explained, "They are on overtime and were full, automated cameras and all, nothing moved out there, not even an animal."

"Doctored footage?" Sarena asked.

"The facility is DOD parts development, so it is doubtful. Five guards on rotation, nothing moved there," Franks reported.

"Did they hear anything?" Sarena asked.

"Not a sound," Franks confirmed.

Sarena looked around the crime scene, "Did you get pictures of everything?"

"Of course," Franks said, "Why?"

"I need to see the victim himself, and I need to understand what happened a little better," Sarena replied.

"We have statements," Franks said to her.

"Thanks, but I'll ask my own questions. You asked for me, let me see what I can do." She walked back to her car; Anthony fell in with her.

"Where is the kid that got shot?" Sarena asked her brother.

"ICU probably," Anthony replied. "He was in surgery."

"Get me out of here," she ordered as she got into her car and closed the door.

Anthony raised the barrier and pictures and tape rolled from a dozen news sources. Sarena was glad to be out of the media mess but she knew this was going to be a long night. She glanced down at her phone as she drove toward the hospital. Sighing, she dialed a number and waited for a response.

"Sir," she reported, "We may have another possible fit for your file."

Chapter 4

John looked down at his son laying in the bed. He had not been out of surgery long. The doctors had been very positive, telling him the bullet went through and had missed all the major organs, minor organs, and had really just shaken his son from the impact.

John was not pleased. He had seen combat and knew firsthand what a shock like this could do to a person. It could turn a man into a scared child, or it could make a man focus on things he should not be focusing on. Worse, it almost always made a person worry about every moment.

He watched Jackson. His son lay there before him, unconscious and John wondered how this could have come to pass. Jackson was the future. Jackson was ready to become All State, a football scholarship, college, and then a good job. He would not have to be the grunt John was. He would not have to go to war, fight each day and work his fingers to the bone.

Hearing a sound behind him, John spun quickly, on edge without knowing it. He saw the small frame of Lindsay walk into the room.

She smiled at him. "Sorry," she said, "I didn't mean to scare you."

John looked at her, then back to his son, "I'm sorry, I wasn't paying enough attention. It is funny how you get caught up in your thoughts when your son is lying in the hospital in front of you. I wonder what I could have done differently to keep this from happening. I wonder what Jackson was doing out there. I wonder what was going on?"

There was a rap at the door, "Excuse me," a timid voice came, "Is this Jackson's room?"

Lindsay turned, and John could see a young girl. She was pretty, but disheveled. Something was going on in her eyes and they were glossy, like someone who had been crying.

"Yes ma'am," John said, "I'm his father, John. Who are you?"

"Sir, my name is Kira," she stuttered and looked over at Jackson, "and Jackson saved my life."

John cocked his head a little at the girl and her tears began pouring out. She turned to go back out the door, mumbling, "This wasn't a good idea."

John walked out towards her, "It was a good idea. What are you talking about? Tell me more."

Kira looked down at the ground. She felt silly for crying so much when she had no reason to do so. She had broken down so easily when talking to John and after seeing Jackson lying there. She just didn't know what to do with it. Kira turned to face John. "I told the police everything. At first, they didn't believe me, then they had me pose people and said something about a really long shot."

"Slow down," John said as the girl began pacing and speaking quickly. "What happened first?"

"Well, we were on our way out, Beth and I," Kira stopped, tears flowed but she choked them back with obvious difficulty. "Well, Beth and I hit the curb in the car, and well, the tires popped. We were calling for a tow truck when these boys came up, and well, they tried to hurt us. They knocked Beth out, and were trying to," Kira paused, a tear formed "well, you know. They were trying to" Kira paused again, her nose ran a little as she teared up, "umm," Kira took a deep breath "rape me when Jackson drove up. He got out of the car so strong and confident and scared the boys off. When he was helping me up, that's when he fell over on me."

John studied her, "So you weren't together?"

Kira looked at John with a curious gaze, "With Jackson?"

"Yeah," John said, "You guys weren't out on a date or nothing?"

"Sir, we came up from Lexington for a concert, we never met Jackson before. He's just the guy that saved us," Kira said with the same quizzical look on her face. Her face changed, a sad expression came over her, "I don't know what we would have done if he hadn't come along."

"What did the police say?" John asked.

"They accused me at first, then Jackson, or something like that," Kira started, "It was so confusing. Then they had me lay on the ground and looked at where the shot may have come from, and then they let me come down here. My dad will be here soon, but I need to stay for Beth. I want to say thank you to Jackson too, but I am sure my dad will be furious. He never wanted me to come here to begin with. He always says stuff like this will happen. I guess he was right."

"Stuff like this?" John asked, wringing his giant hands still.

Kira kept talking, her voice quavering with nervous energy, "Well, yeah, my dad thinks everyone is out to kill us or kill me or make the world a worse place. He spends all his time trying to protect me and never any time just talking to me." Kira stopped, and again her eyes teared, "I'm sorry sir, you don't care about any of this. Jackson is a special man. Tell him thank you and I will leave you alone." She started to leave.

"It's OK," John said. Kira stopped and turned at his words. "I bet Jackson would say the same thing. I spend so much time protecting him from all the things I've seen in life, that I am not being as good a dad as I should be. I am here now thinking about all the things I should've done, all the things I should've said. You are right, Jackson was right. I should've been paying more attention. I'm sorry I accused you of, well, of anything or made you feel bad. I know Jackson would've liked you, it's just that he doesn't talk to me like he used to when he was younger." John looked down at Jackson, "I think I'm just in the way now."

Lindsay walked over to the big man, smiling up at him, "I 'm sure that isn't true. John, it is all going to be ok. The doctors say he'll be fine."

John stood straight, "Kira, right?"

"Yes sir," Kira said softly, her eyes glazed with her now stopped tears.

"Kira, what do you think really happened?" John asked.

Kira looked down at the floor, then she began pacing. "It was so fast," Kira started, "I just don't know." Continuing to pace, the back and forth rhythm helping her focus. "It seemed like it was going to be a good night. We drove, then the turn was wrong, we popped the tires, and we were stuck. We thought we could get help and I called my dad. He was so worried; he's going to be so worried. I was talking to him when the boys drove up. They acted like they were going to help, then Jackson stopped them from hurting me. Beth, well, she wasn't as lucky. I just don't know."

"You said something about posing," John pressed.

"Yeah, they had me pose an officer on the ground, then they had a guy stand over her and when I told them where Jackson was standing, they looked out into a field. They were talking but I honestly don't remember," Kira said with a tear in her eye. "My dad is so right, people are bad. Why did they shoot Jackson? Why did someone do this to Beth? Those boys were just mean."

Walking up next to Kira, Lindsay put her arm around her, "It's OK Kira, it will all be OK."

Kira looked at the girl, "No it won't. Jackson and Beth don't think it'll be ok."

John put his massive hand on Kira's shoulder, "It will be OK. They will get the person who did this, and those boys too."

Kira glanced around the room with unsure eyes. Her face was wet with tears and she looked up again at John. "I believe you." She said quietly. "I should go sit with Beth. Can I visit again?"

"Yeah," John said, "Why don't you stop by a little later. We'll talk about other things."

"OK," Kira agreed. She paused as she reached the door frame and looked at the grey paint on the door, "Thank you sir," she said quietly. "Jackson has a good dad."

John looked through her, lost in the moment, "Jackson maybe deserved a little more."

John paced for a moment wringing his hands together. He walked to the chair next to the bed and sat down while Lindsay checked Jackson's vitals.

"He's a strong boy," Lindsay said.

"I know," John said in a hushed tone, "It'll be OK."

John put his hand on his son's bed and began the wait for him to wake up.

Chapter 5

Sarena Prince arrived at the hospital and sat in the car for a short time. She watched people bustle in and out of the doors like ants looking for food. She considered the potential stories of those people and took pause for herself. She had no love of hospitals as the memories were far too pressed, but she needed to follow up to see if there was anything else, she was missing. She was an expert on ballistics, but she needed to understand the people too. Why the shot was made? What motivated it? What was the approach? Perhaps that would help her understand a bit more and develop the picture.

Her cell phone rang, and she looked down at the crisp display.

Sarena glanced back up at the people walking in and out of the hospital and was envious for a moment of their ignorance of what happens in the world day by day.

Sliding her finger across the screen, Sarena answered the call.

"Yes," she said in a monotone voice.

"Sarena, it is good to talk to you again," the voice returned.

"Thank you, sir," Sarena rolled her eyes slightly in the car.

"I know you are not fond of me or dealing with potential witch hunts, but it was good you called again," the voice said. "And you can call me Tyrel you know; sir is so formal."

Sarena knew Special Agent in Charge Tyrel Tennison was a good man, but he pushed his own agenda strongly and had pressed her line of command to have her report any shootings that were not obvious. She was aware there were quite a few unsolved homicides yearly, but Tyrel seemed to be looking for the proverbial windmill to fight. Many people did not like him, and his constant conspiracy theories were laced with enough truth that he was both well respected and questioned all the time.

"Yes, sir," Sarena repeated.

"OK," Tyrel said and paused for just a moment. "This area has had more than a few instances of unexplained shootings and a few we think were covered up. Your summation that there may be a fit is likely correct. Engage local law enforcement and determine a course of action but keep the situation low profile. We can ill afford excess publicity," Tyrel stated in a very businesslike tone. "Remember, we are trying to find a link, not spook whoever is behind all of this."

"Yes sir, but it is of course possible that this is just a random shooting," Sarena started.

"Sure, I hear that a lot," Tyrel broke in, "but there is something else here and quite frankly, the big picture is a bit over your pay grade."

"Sir," Sarena pressed, "I am well aware of your theories. Over my pay grade or not I was told to report items to you that were suspicious, but never to cover up or deceive any law enforcement group. This is quite irregular."

"I just spoke to your Officer in Charge, and due to the nature of this shooting, you have been assigned to me temporarily. This will allow us to uncover more and maybe get to the bottom of this shooting. I'll be flying into Indianapolis tomorrow to work with you." Tyrel stated.

"I have open cases sir, I can't just step away," Sarena fumed.

"We will reassign as necessary while I'm with you. I'll be setting up downtown and will contact you when I arrive. Don't worry Sarena, this will be a good move and may prove to be a good boost to your career."

"Yes, sir," Sarena said again.

"So where are you now?" Tyrel asked.

"I'm at the hospital, about to go see what the witness saw, and see if the doctors can give me anything on the actual bullet," Sarena stated. "You do know the Indy police are all over this, they're good, they'll get to the bottom of it."

"Don't count on it. I'm betting they are looking all over for a location and can't find one. Hell, it is lucky they had a body this time. This may be our big break," Tyrel said.

"Really? Why?" Sarena asked.

"No one ever lives and for the most part we hear about these second hand. You and several others were told to call me when you found cases like this. We get quite a few but most of them don't pan out. Having someone alive puts a new twist on it all. If I were a betting man, I would say they'll try to clean up their loose ends," Tyrel said, excitement dripping from his voice.

"Who is 'they'?" Sarena asked.

"Don't worry about it, we'll get into it when I am there," Tyrel promised, "and Sarena, be careful. Maybe have someone guard the kid."

"Loose end?" Sarena asked.

"You catch on quick," Tyrel said. "I'll see you tomorrow."

Sarena hung up the phone. She looked at the people walking in and out of the hospital. So many of them. Sarena sighed, got out of the car and locked it, then walked towards the beckoning building.

Chapter 6

The sun rose quickly over the massive pine trees that stretched across the back sky of Jonathon Michael Masterson's Michigan home. The sunrise sparkled and shimmered through the fine needles of the white pines, making the morning seem almost like a firework show as the light bounced off the morning dew. A chickadee sang in the background and another joined with their distinct song echoing across the landscape.

The incredible house was built with money he had made as an assassin, both for the government and for certain private firms that called upon him from time to time. Michael had amassed a fortune, and a change of direction had forced him to retire, or he had forced a change of direction. Either way, all Michael wanted to do was enjoy the rest of his life.

Michael was watching the sunrise from the observation room on the top floor of his home. The home allowed him to watch the sunrise and the sunset easily, the sunrise over the pristine West Michigan countryside, the sunset on the majestic shores of Lake Michigan. Michael's broad shoulders flexed as he enjoyed the sunrise and did pullups from the bar on the ceiling. The observation room was not so much a floor or attic but a room on top of the house, almost like a turret.

The windows of the house were open, and the cool breeze wafted across Michael's skin. The breeze and the beads of sweat were invigorating as he sped up his workout to get the most of it. The sunrise gave him a moment of peace as he considered recent events in his life.

Pulling his body tight, Michael moved until he was hanging parallel with the ceiling and began pulling his body flat to the bar above him. He kept his body rigid and stared at the ceiling as he did another 25 repetitions while his black t-shirt fluttered ever so slightly in the wind. Listening, he heard many birds, but then a creak and light footsteps coming up the stairs to the side of him. He smiled and looked to the stairs where he saw Abby Tarkington's face smiling at him.

Abby and Michael had been together since college. She knew of Michaels past and was more understanding than anyone should be give his situation. All of Michael's need to enjoy his life was intertwined with this woman.

Laughing, Michael asked, "What are you smiling at?"

"You," Abby grinned as she walked up the remaining stairs. "I was wondering if you were superglued to the bar?"

Michael laughed and strained as he finished his workout, then dropped catlike, without a sound to the floor. His bare feet were lithe and powerful on the marble floor. He looked at Abby, her golden hair tied back in a ponytail and smiled again.

Abby put her hand on his shoulder, "Very sweaty," she said with a grin. "I may never get used to how quiet you are falling to the floor." She looked up into his crystal blue eyes, "but I like it."

Michael laughed and turned back to the rising sun.

"Pretty isn't it?" Abby asked, her hand still on Michael's shoulder.

Michael looked at the sunrise for a moment more, then down at her, "Not as pretty as you." He said in a soft tone.

Abby looked up, smiling, then began to giggle, "Pretty corny."

Michael frowned for a second.

Abby saw his frown, "but sweet."

Michael laughed, and she suddenly knew he was kidding, so she punched at him. But he bounced back, then impossibly moved forward and picked her up around the waist. "You really are more beautiful than a sunrise," he laughed as she hit him with short little punches on his chest.

"You're manhandling me," Abby laughed.

"Yep," Michael said and lowered her to the ground.

Abby laughed again then turned and ran down the steps.

As Michael ran behind her, the stairs opened to a magnificent view of Lake Michigan. The house, a near duplicate of his other home in Wyoming, had one distinguishing feature. The upper floor with a room to watch the sunrise and sunset. Michael loved the sunrise, but the West Michigan shoreline gave sunsets that were usually only found on west coast shorelines or the Hawaiian Islands. It was a treat to see both sunrise and sunset here, so Michael had the home built with both options. As there were not real cliffs to build into, the house was on the top of a dune and was open to the beach. Not a defensible as his other homes, but equally as formidable. The sliding glass doors were open, and the breeze blew in from the massive lake, cooling the house even on the most heated days. The lake was rarely over 80 degrees, so the air crossing it was usually cool.

Abby ran out to the deck and gazed out at water that could easily have been an ocean, then stopped. She turned and looked back at Michael.

"It's awesome here," she said.

"Yep," Michael retorted with a grin.

"Whatever made you build here?" Abby asked, "I mean, I love it and all, but you like the mountains."

Michael leaned against the railing and looked out across the lake in front of him. The other side was over 80 miles away, so it could not be seen. "I had been to oceans many times growing up, but we never had come up here. When I came here to visit a man about a job, I saw the lake and well, it was clearly an awesome spectacle."

Abby leaned against the railing as well, Michael's white cotton shirt barely covering her dark blue bathing suit as the wind blew it open.

"Spectacle, yeah, I can see that."

Michael smiled. "I saw the land up for sale, so I bought it a long time ago. And when I had the house in Dubois built, I had this one built as well. I wasn't sure if we would come here, but I wanted it to be an option."

"Why didn't you tell me?" Abby asked.

"It wasn't a worry," Michael said. "I didn't want to mess anything up."

"What?" Abby asked.

"Well, it was just a house. We have each other, I just didn't think it was important," Michael said.

Abby looked at the beach, the waves crashed down driven by the wind. It was beautiful, but she also thought about the houses in Dubois, and Ivel Kentucky, then she thought about Michael. She turned, "You're right," she said, "It isn't important."

Michael put his arm around her, his black t-shirt and the white cotton shirt she was wearing a perfect opposite. He held her as they watched the waves crash against the sandy beach. In the distance, boaters were heading out to try to catch fish in the bigger waves, and they saw several kite surfers already out in the morning surf, greedy for any wind and wave. They were diehard thrill seekers, often flying through the sky for hundreds of feet in strong winds. Abby and Michael held each other as they watched.

Michael kissed Abby's neck and she shivered uncontrollably, he whispered in her ear. "Anywhere with you is home."

Abby smiled.

"Breakfast," Michael asked.

"You know it," Abby replied and they both headed into the house.

As they walked into the house Michael regarded the morning sky. Pinks and reds dotted the horizon making the sky seem almost unreal. "Red sky in morning," Michael thought to himself.

Chapter 7

Kira was sitting in the hallway staring at her phone. It was not long ago that a concert had been the only thing on her mind. Kira had called her friends at the hotel to let them know where she was and was now mindlessly looking through Instagram posts trying to forget the images dancing in her mind. The last few hours had been more than a whirlwind. And she knew her father was going to be upset, angry, scared and stern with her shortly, making sure she was upset, angry and scared.

Looking down the hallway, she saw the guards outside of both Beth's and Jackson's rooms. That moment she saw flashes of Beth laying on the ground, prone and broken and she began to tear up. She pushed the thoughts away as she went back to her phone, hoping a new picture would somehow block the events of only a few hours ago.

Police had been back and forth to the rooms and the desks, but no one had come to Kira again. They seemed more focused on Beth and Jackson, and not so focused on her. Kira liked it that way. She felt as though she could just get her breath. The concert seemed so long ago, and the idea of going out now seemed like it had been such a bad idea. They could have waited, why was she even here at the concert? Would her car be ok? Would Beth be ok? It all ran together, and she felt a little muddled as she stared absentmindedly at her phone screen.

Kira heard footsteps and saw a tall woman walked to Beth's room and then spoke to the officer outside the door. The woman was taller than the officer and dressed in a leather jacket with a white shirt under. Kira thought "cop" immediately. She watched as a nurse went over and lead the woman to Kira.

The woman walked forward and looked down at Kira sitting awkwardly in the hallway.

"Hey," The woman asked said. "Are you Kira?"

"Yeah," Kira responded and began looking at her phone again.

She didn't know why she was a little nervous.

Sarena tried to act calm even though she was a little irritated at being dismissed. "My names Sarena." What are you looking at?"

Kira was guarded, she knew this woman was a cop, but didn't know why she was here. Was she going to be blamed again? Was there something else going on? "Nothing," Kira said in a weak voice.

"Can I ask you a few questions?" Sarena asked in a respectful tone.

"I'm not sure I should be talking until my dad gets here," Kira lied. She knew she was over 18 and could talk any time she wanted, but she had been accused though and she wasn't sure what she should do.

"It's OK Kira," Sarena started. "I know this all is scary. I also know you are over 18 so we can talk if you want, or we don't have to talk. My name is Sarena. I just want to find out what happened to your friend Jackson."

"Why does everyone think we're friends," Kira started, "I mean, I just met the guy and he got shot over top of me, but I had never met him before. Everyone, including his dad, thinks we know each other. What's up with that?"

"Sorry Kira," Sarena said. "I am coming in late to all of this. I am just a person with the FBI that knows a little about weapons, and I would like to try to figure out what happened to Jackson. Do you think you can help me do that?"

Kira looked down at her phone. She thought about the night and how Jackson had tried to help her. The scene played over and over in her mind, and she felt more than a little overwhelmed. Her eyes began to tear up, feeling her control slipping. Coughing a little, she choked back the tears. Looking away, she wiped her face with her hand before she looked up at Sarena. "Sure, why not."

As Kira stood up, Sarena backed up a little, giving her room.

"What do you want to know?" Kira asked. "I told the guy who accused me of shooting Jackson everything."

"I am sorry anyone did that to you," Sarena stated, "I know you didn't shoot Jackson."

Kira eyed Sarena suspiciously, "OK."

"Kira, do you know who the other boys were?" Sarena started. "They said Jackson scared them off."

"No. We blew the tires and they stopped to help us. Well," Kira paused, "not really. They stopped to be jerks." Kira noted with sudden fury.

Anger was better for Sarena. She knew with anger Kira would give out more information. This was a good sign. "I would say jerks would be a nice description for them," Sarena agreed. "Could they have shot Jackson?"

"No," Kira said, "They were scared. They ran off in a hurry in the Jeep and I bet they are home tucked in their rich beds right now."

"Why do you say that?" Sarena asked.

"Well, one boy said that *coach would be upset*. I bet they play football or something," Kira said almost nonchalantly.

"OK," Sarena continued as she took out a small pad and began writing, "So did you hear a shot?"

"No, he just fell over on me," Kira explained. "It was all of a sudden," Kira's eyes started to glaze over a little, "I was just sitting there, reaching up for his hand and he suddenly fell over on me." A tear rolled down Kira's cheek and she wiped it off with the palm of her hand. "I didn't hear anything. It was so quiet."

"OK," Sarena said. "Did you see a flash of light or anything that might give us a starting point?"

"No," Kira said, "There really wasn't anything. One minute he was standing there, the next he was falling over. He seemed like such a nice boy. I spoke to his father and he father obviously thinks he's awesome, but all I saw then was he was trying so hard to make it OK."

Sarena smiled, "Thanks Kira." Sarena looked at the young lady. "Do you think you could come back out there with me later? I know it would be hard, but out to where this happened?"

"My dad is on the way," Kira said, "I'm sure he won't want me talking to you."

"Why not?" Sarena asked.

"My dad is not a real trusting guy," Kira explained. "He tends to be a little overprotective and he's not fond of the police."

"Maybe he'll like me," Sarena smiled.

"Don't get your hopes up," Kira rolled her eyes. "I'm not sure he even likes me. All he did was yell at me when those boys were attacking us. I mean he should have at least acted like he cared."

"Parents do strange things sometimes Kira," Sarena said to the young woman.

"So, is that all?" Kira asked.

"Yes," Sarena handed her a card, "When your dad gets here, call me or have him call me. I know you're 18, but I want him to feel good about this. We just need to go back out and start figuring out what happened."

Kira sat down on the floor of the hallway and stuffed the card into her back pocket as she leaned sideways. "I'll tell him."

Sarena walked back down the hallway to the nurse's station and waited for a moment. She looked at her notes. They really didn't say much more than she already had known, and if the dad was as bad as Kira described, it was going to be a long winding road to nowhere fast.

Sarena looked back at Kira and wondered to herself, "What could she have seen that she doesn't realize?"

Chapter 8

John Sheldon paced the floor. He was restless as Jackson lay on the bed next to the path he took back and forth. John ground his big hands together, then looked down and wondered if there was a growing pile of skin powder from all the wringing he was doing. John stopped, put his big hands in his pockets and continued to walk back and forth.

A million thoughts seemed to plague John's mind. He was full of ideas. Full of hopes, fears, concerns and more. It seemed that he could not keep a straight thought except that Jackson needed to be ok.

For a moment, John's mind wandered as he thought of his past again. He remembered his childhood. The troubles he had seen. Sure, everyone wanted him to play football, but lots of people wanted him to do other things too. If it hadn't been for the Army, he wouldn't have become the man he was today. He remembered being in boot camp. His drill instructor had been tough. He and a few friends had worked hard to stay on his good side. John remembered how he and those chosen few had been sent in because they always fought hard. He had to fight hard. John hoped Jackson had that same drive to fight as hard as he did.

"Dad?" a voice came from the side of him, waking him from his daydream.

John looked down and saw Jackson blinking his eyes.

"Dad, what happened?"

"Jackson," John said as a tear ran down his face, "I'm here boy. You're going to be ok. You're going to be just fine." John reached down and touched his son's shoulder.

"Dad," Jackson repeated, "What happened?"

"Someone shot you son," John explained as Jackson looked around the room, "Someone shot you while you were trying to help someone else."

Jackson moved a little and winced. His father reached down as if to comfort but looked awkward as if he was not sure what to do. "It's OK Jackson. Just take it easy, it might hurt for a while."

"I remember a little," Jackson struggled with the words. "The girls, are they OK?"

"Yeah," John said, "What were you doing out there? You done gone and got yourself shot."

"Dad," Jackson interrupted, his eyes clearer, "We had gone out for a while and had coffee downtown. I was dropping Tyler off at work when I saw three guys beating up a girl. Did you want me to drive by? Would you have driven by?"

John looked down, ashamed, tears flowed, "I'm sorry son, you're right. I'm proud of you. You were so good to put yourself out there. I just don't want to lose you."

"Dad," Jackson smiled weakly, "I'm not going anywhere. How many times have you been shot?"

"It's not the point," John said in a brisk manner. "I may have been, but you don't have to be like me."

"Dad, there is no one in the world like you. I kind of like who you are. Not many of my friends can say that about their parents. But you and I, we're a team," Jackson's voice was getting stronger.

Jackson winced again as the nurse walked in. "It is good to see you moving young man," the white-haired lady said. "My name is Francine. I'll be taking care of you for a little while. How are you feeling Jackson?" she asked as she looked between the small computer in her hand and the machines hooked up to the young man. "Looks like you gave your dad quite a scare," Francine continued.

"Yeah, he worries too much," Jackson said.

"Well, getting shot is not a good thing, I am sure the police will have some questions for you. They've been roaming around here all morning. We didn't expect you to wake up so soon. I hear you saved those little girls," Francine's manner was very matter of fact while being almost musical, "Quite the hero."

Jackson smiled a little and winced, "Not a hero ma'am. Just trying to help is all."

Francine took Jackson's blood pressure with a large cuff as she spoke, "Don't play it down. I am sure the press will be here sometime to talk to you too. There are a lot of people talking about this, you know. Someone getting shot just trying to help."

John said, "No, we don't need any press. The press always throws things out of proportion and makes it look bad."

"Dad," Jackson argued "It won't be a big deal. No one is going to worry about this."

"Jackson," John started as Francine looked at her computer, checking boxes with dutiful precision using her middle finger. "Jackson, the world is a scary place. They will make you a hero or a villain depending on what sells. We should leave it be."

Francine smiled and looked at John, "He's a hero sir, he did a good thing. You should be proud of him."

"I am proud ma'am, but we don't need the press to feel proud," John preached.

There was a light rap at the door as a tall woman walked in, "Excuse me," she said, "My name is Sarena, Sarena Prince. I am with the FBI and I have a few questions. I know you just woke up, but I would like to talk if you can before things go too far. Will that be OK?"

Sarena looked to both Jackson and the giant next to him, then to the nurse in front of her as if asking for some type of approval.

"Ma'am, I'm John, Jackson's father" John said, "Jackson has just woken up. Can he have a little time please? Just a little so he can feel a little better."

"Dad," Jackson said, "It's ok. I can talk for a few."

Sarena looked at the man who dwarfed her and realized she was not used to feeling this small. Turning back to Jackson, who looked beaten and tired, she knew this opportunity had a small window. She looked back to John, "It will only take a few minutes, and I'll stop if he gets too tired."

John began wringing his massive hands together again as he looked at his son, then back to Sarena.

Francine studied Sarena. "Not too long, I'm calling the doctor." Francine put her tablet to her side and walked out of the room.

"It's ok Dad," Jackson said.

"Well," John started, "for a few minutes I suppose."

Sarena studied Jackson as Walter Franks walked into the room.

"Sarena," Franks interrupted, "You were going to start without me?"

"Didn't know you were here," Sarena said, "Jackson just woke up but is pretty tired. I was only going to ask a few questions."

"You do that," Franks said, "but this is our investigation. I just asked for some thoughts, not for you to take over." Franks looked at John and was suddenly aware of his demeanor. "Sorry sir, Walter Franks, I'm with the local police."

Sarena noticed Jackson wince, "Are you ok Jackson?" she asked with obvious concern in her voice.

"Yes ma'am," Jackson said, "I just hurt a bit."

Sarena smiled at him and he gave a little smile back. Sarena laughed, "I bet. I remember the first time I got shot. It hurt for a while, but it gave me a cool scar."

Jackson's smile grew a little more. "A scar, yeah."

Smiling at Jackson, Sarena looked briefly at John, then Franks before returning to the boy. "Can you tell me what happened Jackson?"

"Yes ma'am," Jackson started, "Me and some friends went downtown for an open mic night. My friend Tyler, he likes to write poetry and he was wanting to read it to all of us. Tyler rode with me, and we got to drinking coffee and talking about his poetry. Some of us were laughing and making stuff up and getting up and reading it. Well, I had taken Tyler down to the little place, Pearings. Well it got too late and Tyler had to be at work, so instead of taking him home and back... well I took him to work. He gets off at noon." Jackson turned to his dad, "Dad, I need to pick Tyler up. Or can you?"

"We'll take care of it," Franks said. "What happened next."

"Well, Tyler works down in the warehouse area, and well, I took him to work. I wanted to get home quick because I had to study for an exam. I cut through a different way and saw a Jeep and a car on the side of the road. It was weird because no one was out that late usually. Then I looked over and saw the girl get pushed to the ground. I drove over and got out of the car to scare the boys doing it."

"Did you get a look at them?" Sarena asked.

"Yes ma'am," Jackson continued, stopping to cough lightly with obvious pain crossing his face. "Yes ma'am." He repeated, clearing his throat. "One looked like a ball player I knew, but I don't remember which school."

"Ball?" Sarena asked thinking about something Kira said.

"Football ma'am," Jackson said. "They got up really quick and said something to me, but when I told them I called the police, they got spooked and left the little girl alone. I saw the other girl too and was a bit worried. I went over to help her up, and then I woke up here."

"Jackson," Sarena asked, "did you hear anything when you were helping her up?"

"No ma'am," Jackson said.

"Did you see anything? A light, or a flash, or anything like that?" Sarena pushed.

"I'm not sure ma'am," Jackson said. "I don't remember much after walking over."

Jackson's brow furled, obviously trying to remember. He winced a little from pain as he adjusted himself in the bed, concentrating. "Why can't I remember?"

"Sometimes the mind protect itself," Sarena said. "Don't push."

"Is that it?" Franks asked.

Sarena shot Franks a look that could freeze water. "Sorry Jackson, can we maybe talk again later after you rest?"

Francine walked back into the room. Following behind was a young man in a white coat and draped with a stethoscope around his neck. He held both sides of the stethoscope, making it look like he had a long necklace. His name badge read Tim, but the last name was obscured by the stethoscope.

"I think we're done for now," the doctor said. "This young man has had a long morning and needs some rest."

Sarena looked at the doctor and scanned the room, "I'll come back and visit later Jackson. You rest."

Franks looked at the doctor, "I have a few questions."

"Take a tip from your partner, come back later," the doctor said.

Franks looked down at the doctor's badge, "Well doctor Tim, I just need..."

Franks was suddenly pushed out by Francine, the little nurse. "Not now. The doctor said, get, get, get." She continued to push, winking at Jackson as she passed the bed

Jackson smiled.

"Do I need to go sir?" John asked the doctor as he looked between the computer in the corner and Jackson.

"No, Dads are allowed, so you can stay. Jackson needs some rest." Tim smiled.

John looked down to see his son was fast asleep.

Chapter 9

Ronnie Comer was looking out over the beauty of the Red River Gorge. The area, in eastern Kentucky, was famous for good trails and amazing views. It was one of the better kept secrets in Kentucky even though it wasn't that big of a secret.

Ronnie turned and looked back at the people with him. Next to him was Barbara Stone. Although they acted like a couple Ronnie was never sure what Barbara really felt. They had gotten close, held hands, and hugged a lot, but never more. Ronnie still blushed when Barbara was close to him. Barbara was a goddess, tall, lithe, and sporting long blonde hair that played with the wind. She changed the color occasionally, but Ronnie was mesmerized by her eyes all the time. They sparkled like fresh diamonds in the sun. Ronnie had never known a woman like Barbara.

A moment later Jim and Alex appeared on the top of the hill. They all looked out over the gorge together and it was silent except for the wind for a few minutes. Alex Brown was the commanding officer of their little group. Of normal height and obvious stocky build, Alex was driven and determined always to do the right thing. Ronnie had met Alex when he and Jim came to the army depot. Meeting him had changed his life, given him confidence, and given him status as he was part of an elite team. Ronnie still didn't know why Alex had chosen him. After all, there were far better people at the depot than a boy from the hills. But Alex always told him he was doing well and that he appreciated Ronnie all the time.

Jim Simpson made Ronnie laugh all the time. When Ronnie had met Jim, he thought he was just another aging ex-army veteran who had gained weight and told dumb jokes. But the first day after they met, Jim had shown he was still in tip top shape to go with his razor wit that made everyone giggle.

There was a rattle in the woods and suddenly Rachel Brown busted into the clearing.

"Thanks for waiting guys," Rachel bellowed with sarcasm.

Ronnie had known Rachel since he was stationed at the Bluegrass Army Depot. He thought she was the type of soldier everyone should be. She was tall, six four, kept her hair cut short and worked out more than anyone. She was constantly trying to beat Jim in sparring, and it was entertainment for the entire depot when they were going at it. Jim had not lost really, but he had walked away a few times making Rachel angry. In a fight, Rachel was the teammate to have. Ronnie had seen her lift a grown man a foot in the air and throw him to the ground before.

There was another member of the team, Terry Drake. He was the pilot of one of the planes they flew. Terry was currently off on another mission and the team had been given some time off.

"Whose idea was it to come here," Rachel demanded.

"Shhhhh," all four others said in unison.

"Don't *shhh* me," Rachel said. "I'm part of this team and I can be pissed at walking through the woods if I want to be."

Jim raised an eyebrow at Rachel. "C'mere." Rachel dropped her pack and walked to the edge of the hill. A ravine opened out below. "You see all this?" Jim spread out his hand as he put his other arm around Rachel's shoulder. "All this is at the heart of what we fight for. All of this is why the general did all he did in his career. It is why I joined and so many others. Not to fight or to be Billy Joe Badass, but to protect this great country."

Jim looked out and for a moment Rachel looked out as well. The hills stretched in the distance while the Red River trickled below. The leaves on the trees swayed in the wind and all around them the sounds of animals beckoned with the patient call of nature. Birds flew around them, and the five stood for a moment watching the scene below them.

Rachel backed out of Jim's arm, "Yeah, whatever, we should have done the zip lines."

Alex and Jim started laughing while Ronnie and Barbara just smiled.

"So, we are on top of this hill Ronnie has been talking about and we see all this fun nature stuff. What now?" Rachel asked.

Barbara set out her pack, "Now we have lunch up here."

"That's what I'm talking about," Rachel said as Ronnie spread out a big blanket.

Jim and Alex took off their packs and the group spread out on the blanket. In the middle of the blanket was a large "UK" a logo for the University of Kentucky Wildcats. People in Kentucky usually followed either the Louisville Cardinals or the Kentucky Wildcats. Both were longtime rivals at basketball and one or the other were usually in the Final Four. It was different than many states who had rivalries. If one or the other lost, nearly everyone switched to the winner as it was better for one of them to win than none of them to win. The Wildcats had won many titles and were legend at basketball.

"UK huh," Jim said. "Good choice."

Ronnie grinned, "I always wanted to go there. Maybe when I leave the service, they will let me go and get a degree. We didn't have a lot of money, so I joined the army to serve my country. Someday that will be good for me and my family."

"Ronnie, you are the picture of the American dream," Jim mused.

"There's a scary pic," Rachel started laughing.

"I think it's sweet," Barbara broke in, "I think Ronnie is one of the sweetest men I have ever known." Barbara leaned over to Ronnie and kissed him on the cheek. As always Ronnie turned bright red, almost as red as his tightly cut hair.

"You know you ought to just start dating him Barbie," Rachel laughed. Both Jim and Alex looked at Barbara as she set food out on the blanket, waiting for her response.

"Ronnie is such a good guy," Barbara said, "I just don't want to ruin it, or him. We work well together, and I like him." Ronnie looked up at her listening as well, "I just don't think I am good enough for him."

Ronnie had a strange look on his face. Everyone looked at him and even Barbara stopped.

Jim knew what was coming, "Go ahead Ronnie, say it."

Ronnie looked down at the ground. He seemed to be considering his words then he looked directly into Barbara's eyes, "You are good enough for me," he began, "You make me feel happy all the time when we laugh and tell jokes. You explain the things to me I don't know and are not mean about it. I know I haven't been all the places and done all the things you guys have done, but I am learning. Barbara, it's you that might be too good for a redneck country boy, born in the hills and raised by coal miners. I'm always in awe of you."

It was Barbara who turned red this time, "Ronnie I didn't mean... I mean... I'm sorry. It's just that I like you a lot and I always ruin it."

"Oh my god," Rachel groaned, "Someone get me my violin."

Jim picked up a pinecone and threw it at Rachel. Ducking, she rolled backward and grabbed another pinecone and whipped it at Jim. He caught it in his hand, then set it down again. "Ewww," wiping the pine sap off his fingers.

"Yeah, see, as sappy as that pinecone," Rachel smirked.

"Yeah yeah yeah," Jim rattled, "I know."

Rachel smirked, "Love, who needs it? Give me a staff or an M16 and I'll have more fun."

Jim looked off to the gorge, silent for a moment. The group looked awkward and was just as silent.

"Time to eat," Barbara said, now composed.

The spread before them was more than expected. Sandwiches of different types, fried chicken, rolls, and a variety of sides were literally attacked by the five. Jim opened his bag and pulled out a stack of drinks, beer, soda, and a few odd cans. They threw them to each other playfully. Ronnie opened a Pepsi and it sprayed a little on his face. Barbara wiped it off with her napkin, then again kissed him on the cheek.

"Yum, what's next," Rachel asked. "I mean, we haven't been sent anywhere for a few weeks. That's pretty rare for us."

"Don't knock it," Alex took a drink as he spoke. "We seem to be dropping team members with Melody heading off to Wyoming or wherever."

"She was a temp," Rachel said as she ate, "We are the team."

Barbara said, "Well, with Terry, yeah. We can handle anything thrown at us. Or at least Rachel can."

"Damn straight," Rachel boasted. "I'll handle it all if I have to. Broken ribs heal."

Jim reached over and poked at her ribs, "How are they doing?"

"Doctor said I was fine," Rachel winced only a little, "Well, at least for someone who had a whale jump on them."

The team laughed, and Rachel made a muscle showing off an impressive bicep, "That whale found out who not to mess with."

Alex and Jim laughed, then Jim said, "At least he didn't bash your face in."

The group looked at Alex whose face was still bruised from a recent bout having been nearly black only a short time ago. Alex had taken a beating at the hands of a group paramilitary types in Michigan. Rachel had fought a man many times her size and won, but at the expense of a few bumps and bruises. The team had been in great danger until Abby and Michel had stepped in.

"Thanks," Alex touched his cheek, "it was worse than it looked."

"I hope not," Jim munched on a potato chip, "You looked like you were dead."

The whole group laughed hard.

"I know, I saw a mirror," Alex was still tapping his face. "I didn't know myself at all. It is rough when you look in a mirror and don't see who you were expecting."

Rachel broke in, "So what's next boss? I will not run around the hills of Kentucky looking for places for red boy," Rachel nodded at Ronnie, "to find a way to propose to his girl. We need to find some action."

Ronnie blushed almost in sync with the words flowing from Rachels mouth while Barbara just smiled.

"Seems like action almost always finds us," Alex said. "It's pretty nice to be quiet for a little while. Who knows what's next?"

Rachel shoved another piece of chicken in her mouth and ate heartily.

Jim laughed, "Chew girl."

"I get the job done," Rachel said, finishing yet another piece and putting it on the plate.

Jim looked out over the hills, "It sure is peaceful."

Rachel finished her last piece of chicken and policed all the items and put them in a small bag to their side. "OK, ready for zip lines?"

"Let me finish eating girl," Jim was still munching on potato chips.

"God. Didn't the army teach you how to eat? No time to sit around, present arms and stuff food."

"It may have," Jim said, "but retiring taught me to slow down. You need to learn that as well."

"Why waste time eating when I can do something fun?" Rachel began to pace.

The group laughed and started cleaning up the area as Ronnie folded the blanket. They policed all the trash and items until just five people with packs remained. Looking around Alex was pleased. He surveyed his team, "No trace, good job."

"Zip lines," Rachel said running down the trail as the rest of the team fell in behind her. A few moments later the hill was clear and quiet, and only nature remained.

Chapter 10

Sarena Prince and Walter Franks walked outside the hospital and were immediately surrounded by reporters.

"Can you tell me who was shot?" one asked with a microphone in Franks' face.

"Was it gangs?" another questioned.

"I heard two girls were killed as well?" another exclaimed.

The questions fired quickly at them, and Sarena backed away as Franks moved forward.

"I will make a statement so we can at least set up some ground rules," Franks said. "I am confirming there was a young man shot last night and two girls were hurt. We will not be releasing names as we are in the middle of an investigation. We have no suspects at this time. We have no motives currently. We have just begun looking into this, and your Indianapolis Police force is on it. Please allow the families time to get together and let us do our work. We will have an official briefing later today." Franks scanned the group, "Don't try to go around us or interfere until we have more information available. Thank you for your cooperation."

The group spattered questions out at Sarena and Walter as they walked back into the hospital. A uniformed officer was at the door. Franks looked at him and beckoned, "Make sure these nuts don't get in here."

"Yes sir," the patrolman said.

Walter put his hand on Sarena's elbow and guided her back through the front doors of the hospital, "I guess this isn't going to stay quiet. What is your stance here? I mean are you helping us, or working for the Bureau? What is going on Sarena?"

Sarena lightly pulled free as they moved to the side of the main doors, "I'm doing my job. For both of us. Let's work together, solve this, and be done."

Walter smiled, "Yeah, sure. We can do that. Just don't talk to the press."

"I don't. Someone did though, so you better figure that one out," Sarena glared at him.

"Yeah," Walter said, looking out at the reporters in the parking lot, "I will."

Sarena looked at the group, "I'm going back upstairs to see if I can get anything else."

Walter looked at her, "I will draw the press and put together a more official statement. Let me know what you get." His tone changed, "Look, I know you don't like me much, but I appreciate you doing this."

Sarena turned to him, "Thanks," she said and walked back to the elevators.

Franks watched her go, then turned and sighed before walking back towards the door. He wished he had a cigarette, but he had quit years earlier.

Taking a piece of gum from his pocket, he put it in his mouth and started chewing. Turning back, he saw Sarena get into the elevator. Walter shook his head to himself as the elevator door closed, then walked out the front door through the waiting reporters towards his car.

Chapter 11

Kira knocked tentatively on the door to Jackson's room. She was nervous but had heard from one of the nurses that Jackson had woke and wanted to thank him. When there was no answer, Kira slowly pushed the door forward and saw John walking towards her.

"Come in Kira," John said quietly. "Jackson just fell asleep. It's OK though if you want to sit in here."

"I don't want to be a bother," Kira whispered. "But I heard he was awake."

"I am," Jackson said. "I'm tired, but I can't fall asleep here. Kira, right?"

Kira walked to the bed, "Thank you, Jackson. I know you didn't know me, but you saved me."

Jackson looked at Kira and smiled, "You would have done the same for me."

"I doubt it," Kira said. "I'm a bit of a chicken sometimes."

"I saw the tires on your car. One of you is not a chicken," Jackson was obviously tired as he grinned slightly.

Kira laughed, "Well... OK... but anyway, I wanted to say thanks, and I'm sure Beth will too."

"How is she?" Jackson asked.

"Still out. The doctors think she'll be ok, but she has a huge lump on her head, and hasn't woken up yet." Kira explained.

"Sorry," Jackson said.

Kira moved her hand along the bedrail next to Jackson. "Looks like I was the lucky one."

"What do you mean?" Jackson asked.

"I'm the only one not in a hospital bed," Kira smiled.

Jackson laughed, then grimaced as the laugh hurt. John reached over to help Jackson, but Jackson waved him away, "I'm okay, Dad. Kira, what happened to get you into that mess?"

Kira laughed, "Well, it would be a funny story if it didn't end so poorly."

"Yeah, what happened is right?" came a voice from the door.

"Dad," Kira turned and grabbed her dad in a hug.

Her dad looked at Jackson and around the room. He reached out for John's hand with Kira tucked under his arm. "Zach Calloway."

"John, John Sheldon sir. This is my son Jackson," John said, shaking his hand.

Zach was far smaller, barely taller than Kira and had on jeans and a light red jacket. His messed brown hair was combed slightly with a left part. He looked as though he had not slept in a long time. "I drove here from Lexington as soon as I heard Kira was on her way to the hospital. I was against this whole thing. Girls shouldn't go to concerts alone."

"You were at the concert?" Jackson asked. "I was going to go but was with a friend reading poetry."

None of them saw Sarena standing at the edge of the room, just waiting.

"Well, it was good meeting you, John. And thank you, Jackson, for saving my little girl. I am going to get her car fixed, then get her home," Zach stated.

Sarena entered the room further, "I'm afraid her car is in impound for now. They will be going over it tomorrow I'm sure, trying to pull out anything that might be on it or in it."

"And you are?" Zach asked impatiently.

"Sarena," Sarena noted and handed Zach a card. "Sarena Prince."

"FBI," Zach said, looking around the room, "Why is the FBI in this? I thought this was a local issue."

"It was a local issue and still is a local issue," Sarena replied, "I'm a ballistics expert. There are some things we are trying to get straight here about the shooting."

"Really?" Zach said in a nervous voice, "What does that have to do with Kira or her car?"

"Maybe nothing," Sarena said, "Maybe something. There was a lot to this that was a little strange. Who shoots the person saving someone else? It seems so... disjointed. Were they trying to shoot Kira? Was it a stray bullet? I have a lot of questions and I am just trying to help the local police come up with answers."

"So, this isn't really an FBI case?" Zach asked.

"No, not really, but we are interested," Sarena replied. "I happen to live here and have a special interest. Because of my unique qualifications, I was called in for a consultation and kept going from there."

"So, how do we get her car?" Zach asked.

"Well sir," Sarena started, "I think you will need to wait until tomorrow. I can recommend a few places locally to stay if you would like. I would hate for you to drive all the way home only to come back. We also don't know if Kira may be targeted again, so we want to keep an eye out for her."

Zach frowned, "Well, I guess we'll have to consider that."

"Ma'am," John began, "Is there a problem with Jackson and I?"

"No sir," Sarena said, "We will keep a few officers here. There seems to be a lot of press hanging around, and we want to be certain they aren't bothering you. I know Mister Franks has asked them to respect all of your privacy, but I am not sure if they will." Sarena turned to Zach, "Do you know if Miss Turnbull's parents or anyone are coming for her?"

"No," Zach said, "I didn't talk to them."

Kira broke in, "I did. They will be up later today if they can. They were in Florida. They are flying back to Kentucky and driving here."

"Good," Sarena said, "I'll be talking to her shortly. The doctors said she woke up a short time ago, but they're with her now."

"Beth is awake?" Kira said excitedly.

"Yes," Sarena replied, "Give them some time to check her out, then I am sure she'll want to see you."

Kira was tearing up, "That is so much better. I was worried... well... that she wouldn't wake up." Kira wiped a tear from her eye, "She's been out all day and Jackson woke up so much quicker."

"Head injuries are like that," Sarena said. "So have the two of you talked about anything about last night yet?"

John looked at Sarena, "No, they haven't really. Kira had just walked in and was checking on Jackson and thanking him."

"Can we go over a few things together for a moment?" Sarena asked.

"Not without a lawyer," Zach jumped in.

"A lawyer?" Sarena asked, "No charges are being filed, we just need to figure this out."

"A lawyer," Zach reinforced. "I know how you guys twist things. Kira said she was already accused of shooting Jackson. We won't be taking any chances."

"Of course, that is your right," Sarena began, "So I will assume you have something to hide, and we will be taking you both to the downtown station to go through questioning. I also assume your lawyer will be here within the hour."

"We'll cooperate," Jackson said, "Right Dad?"

Continuing to address Zach, Sarena was direct but nodded at the young man's cooperative nature., "This should be easy. We are trying to find a shooter that could have tried to kill your daughter or this young man. If you want to make it hard, I can."

Zach was red-faced and started pacing. Kira looked up at him, "Dad, it is no big deal."

"OK, OK. What did you want to know?" Zach snapped. "But if it goes towards accusing anyone, I'm done."

Sarena looked directly at Zach, her eyes glared with a fire all their own, "No one is accusing anyone, but you are making it easy to move that way."

Kira stepped between them, "It's ok, we'll cooperate."

"We'll wait for your friend and try to tie it all together. Then we'll see about getting your car and get you on your way, Kira," Sarena said in a much nicer tone.

Zach paced a little.

"Is that OK, sir?" Zach mumbled in response and Sarena repeated the question, "Is that OK?"

"Yes, fine, whatever. Let's just get this over with so we can go home," Zach turned to Kira, "I told you this concert was a mistake. God, what have you gotten us into?"

Kira looked at her Dad with tears in her eyes, "What?" Turning away, she walked past Sarena and into the hall.

Zach looked around the room, all eyes were on him, "What?" Then he followed Kira into the hall.

"He's just upset," John said in a soft tone. "I was scared about Jackson too."

"Maybe," Sarena replied. "We'll talk in a few minutes. I am going to see how Beth is."

Sarena left the room. As she walked out, she saw that Zach and Kira were talking heatedly in the corner. Stopping at the nurse's station, she asked, "How is Miss Turnbull? Can I speak to her for a moment?"

"The doctor is assessing her situation. You can wait for him to speak to you. There is a neurologist on the way as well," a nurse said.

Sarena turned and heard, "Do what you want, I'll be back." She watched Zach walk away and Kira walking, fists clenched, towards her.

"He is such an ass sometimes," she said. "I'm over 18. It is my choice, not his. He's going to get a hotel, or maybe he will just leave me. Right now, I don't care."

Sarena didn't know how to respond for a moment. "OK, we'll get this over as soon as Beth is available."

"It doesn't matter," Kira verified. "She was out before Jackson got there. I told the other guy that already. Franks. They hit her very early. I thought she was dead. She will only remember the boys. And no one is even worried about them or what they did. When are we going to talk about what was done to us?"

Sarena saw that Kira was tearing up, "We will focus on both. I promise this is not just about the shooting."

"You promise?" Kira sobbed, "I don't know you. I don't know any of you."

Kira stomped back into Jackson's room. Sarena considered how she was going to turn this around. Kira's father's arrival had made things less than perfect, and now it was getting even more complicated. All the talk was getting them nowhere closer to the shooter, and Sarena worried nothing was going to turn trust back in her favor.

Sarena waited in the hall. She took a moment and walked the hallway for a few minutes, then returned to Jackson's room.

Kira looked up and glared at her. Jackson was paying attention to Kira, looking weary but alert. John was obviously agitated.

"Look," Sarena said, "I'm sorry." Sarena paced a little, "I am not accusing any of you of anything." Sarena turned and looked at Kira, "Help me find who shot Jackson, and I will find who tried to hurt you and Beth. Give me a chance. Give Franks a chance."

"Franks?" Kira asked.

"He is ok when you get used to him," Sarena said. "It is kinda like a fungus thing."

It was quiet for a moment then Sarena cracked a smile and Kira started laughing. "OK," Kira said, "I'll listen to you and try to help."

Sarena looked at the three of them, "Good, let's look at this for a minute."

Sarena pulled out her phone and opened up Google Maps. As she did, she switched on the overlay that showed the street. The screen was large, and she zoomed in on the area where Jackson was shot. "Isn't technology great?"

She walked to Jackson's bed and realized he was showing some weariness. He was a strong boy, but he had been shot and had surgery in the last 12 hours. She was quiet and patient as she talked to him, "Jackson, can you show me where you were standing?"

"Ma'am," Jackson started, "I can't remember it all, but I remember parking my car here, then walking up. So somewhere here." Jackson pointed to areas of the map on Sarena's phone.

She tapped each area with a small stylus, leaving pins. "We discussed that you did not hear a sound or see a light, but you were facing this way coming from your car."

"Yes ma'am," Jackson said.

"Thank you, Jackson. We are done and you need some sleep," Sarena said in a quiet voice.

Kira was over her shoulder, "I was there, right in front of where he pointed. And that is where he reached down and took my hand to pull me up."

Sarena switched to street-view and looked at the pins she had dropped. It was rough, but the warehouses were the only place the shot could have come from.

Sarena acknowledged John, "I'm sorry this has been so hard. I'm going to go out to the site for a while."

"You think it's probably a sniper of some sort. Flash suppressor and silencer?" John asked.

"I'm not sure," Sarena said. "You were in the military, right?"

"Ranger, ma'am," John said. "They were gonna toss me because of my size, but I worked hard and wanted to serve."

"Yeah, I hear it is tough," Sarena said.

"It wasn't too bad," John recanted, "Well, it was hard. A lot of good men work hard and well, it is not for everyone. Making it is a lot of work and I have a great deal of respect for everyone who went through with me. My team was good, and we worked hard to help each other. There is no better feeling than having a good team behind you while you press forward."

"I know the feeling," Sarena said. "Thank you, John, for your help. Jackson, thank you. Kira, tell your Dad we are done for now."

Sarena left the room, looking at her phone. She had a lot of questions. Heading to Beth's room, she told the officer there she was leaving, then walked to the elevator. As she walked, she studied the street-view of the warehouses. The angle was wrong for the shot to be taken from the field. It had to come from a higher level. But the warehouses and factory were over 1000 yards out, and it would be like finding a needle in a haystack to see anything there.

She studied the map for other areas as the elevator went to the ground floor, then got out and walked towards that main entrance of the hospital. Once outside, several reporters rushed up to her. "No comment," she said, walking to her car with no hesitation. All the while she stared at her phone, trying to see an angle that would be more likely to have been a point of origin.

Sarena looked up and out into the parking lot. Several reporters milled around the area. She laughed to herself that it was like a bad zombie movie.

Sarena's phone rang.

"Hello," she said.

"Report?" came the voice on her phone.

"Well," Sarena sighed, "There are a lot of possibilities. The boy will be ok. The girls as well. But the shot was a precision shot from an unknown vantage. The more I look at it, the less I think it is possible. This may be a wild goose chase, sir."

"Why do you say that?" came the expected question from Tyrel.

"Easy," Sarena stated. "There aren't a lot of people who could make that shot. I only know of a few if it came from where it looks like it came from."

"Funny you should say that," Tyrel said. "One of the companies within line of sight has an ex sniper working there. I was expecting you would check it out and let me know something like this. Tech dug this up faster than you could visit. You may want to check him out."

"I will do that sir," Sarena said, "But what motive, sir?"

"What do you mean?" Tyrel asked.

"Well, think about it, sir. Suddenly in the middle of the night, someone saving someone is shot in a street where there are no witnesses and no cleanup. Why would they shoot him?" Sarena asked.

"Not for you to question," Tyrel stated. "Your job is to find him and bring him in. Let Indy come up with the motive. You need to come up with a shooter. This case may be part of a long open case, and we need to start closing some loose ends on it."

"Yes sir," Sarena said and hung up the phone.

Sarena dialed a number and the name "Franks" came up on her screen.

"Yeah," came the voice.

"Franks," Sarena said.

"Yeah," Franks replied.

"Can you take a minute and meet me at the factory behind the shooting?" Sarena asked.

"Yeah," Franks said.

"God, do you know any other words?" Sarena said in a louder voice.

"Yeah," Franks said with a comical tone in his voice.

"God, you are an asshole," Sarena said. "How long will it take you?"

"About 15 minutes to get there," Franks said, "I was just walking out to get in the car. You got something?"

"Who knows," Sarena said, "but let's play it out. Since it's not my case, I don't wanna push too hard, but I am betting you can."

"Yeah," Franks laughed.

"God, why did I have to work with you?" Sarena stammered.

"You're just lucky that way," Franks said, laughing again.

Sarena growled a little and hung up. Then she dialed another number.

"Hello," came a groggy voice.

"Good morning, Anthony," Sarena said.

"I was up all night, Sis. Are you still working?" Anthony asked.

"I am," Sarena said, "When you wake up, call me. I have a few questions for you."

"Sure," Anthony said. "I'll call you later."

The phone went dead.

Sarena closed the cell window and again looked at the map.

Fateful Friend

Starting the car, she put it in gear and began to drive.

Chapter 12

Franks leaned against his Crown Victoria, waiting at the small factory area. It wasn't really small, but it was not a huge company either. It was mid-day and the warehouse was hustling with people scurrying back and forth to load trucks, wrap pallets, and create new items, whatever those may be. Franks looked at the bright colored sign and wondered what it was that Quality Castings made. He bet it was something industrial, but as far as he knew it could be fishing lures.

Franks was wondering just how long he was going to be waiting when Sarena drove up and parked next to him in the visitor's lot. She sat in the Camaro for a moment looking at her phone and playing with a stylus, before she stepped out and put on a jacket. Franks was always impressed with Sarena, he just didn't like her much anymore. She was a necessary evil and her brother made sure everyone remembered how good she was at her job.

"Been here long?" Sarena asked.

"Not really," Franks admitted. "Was just sitting here wondering what they did here."

"Metal fabrication," Sarena said, "They press forms or plates for other companies and ship them out. They also have a few items they sell. According to their website, they used to be famous for boat downriggers, but I had not heard of them until I looked them up."

"Answers that question," Franks said as they began walking towards the entrance.

"We are looking for a Stephanie Wise," Sarena said. "I called ahead, and she is the head of security here. Not a big operation, about a hundred and fifty employees and some support crew."

"Well," Franks said, "I guess we know who did their homework."

"Yeah," Sarena said, "I really hate to be caught without knowing anything."

"We all know that," Franks muttered.

Sarena stopped and turned facing Franks who almost ran into her, "I know you don't like me, but I am trying to help you here. Let me know what I should be doing, if you want me to do it a little differently. I will, but the sarcasm? Well, I am going to start laughing at you and then you'll be pissed off, so let's dump it."

"Sure," Franks replied in an almost cautious tone.

Sarena turned and finished walking to the glass door of the immense warehouse. It was not a pretty building but upon opening the door they were definitely not in Kansas anymore. The walls of the reception area were done in diamond steel and the floors in black tile with a high ceiling. The ceiling was covered with birds made out of sheet metal. A few steel animals made from sheet metal were placed around the area and plants towered above them, made of sheet metal as well. The walls were decorated with pictures and several cabinets adorned the area that showed off products the company had obviously made.

"Ya don't see that every day," Franks said as he looked up at the panorama above him.

"No," Sarena studied the abstract art, "You are completely right there."

"Miss Prince," a woman's voice came from behind them as they heard shoes clap on the tile. She was tall, about five-ten and thin but solid. Her red hair was pulled back to a tight ponytail and her black pants and black shirt both had logos on them with a big QC.

"Yes," Sarena said, "I take it you are Stephanie." Sarena used her first name to see what response she would get. There was none.

They shook hands and Sarena was impressed by the firm handshake. Franks obviously was as well as his eyes grew a little large as

Stephanie grabbed his hand and obviously was stronger than expected.

"Why don't we step into the conference room," Stephanie directed.

"Thank you," Sarena stated as they walked to a door that was all but invisible in the wall. The steel plate and angular door handle looked almost to be an optical illusion. Stephanie opened the door and a plush conference room waited for them. Lights flipped on automatically as Stephanie led the way in. Stephanie walked to the far side and opened a cherry credenza revealing a small refrigerator. "Water? Coke?"

"Coke please," Franks said.

"Water please," Sarena said.

As Stephanie pulled out three bottles she started speaking, "You know I rarely get visits from the police and this is a first for the FBI, so excuse me if I am a little inquisitive. What can I do for you?"

Sarena took the water and grabbed a coaster from the cherry table. "Well," she started, "We are looking into a shooting near here."

"Oh," Stephanie said, "I heard about that, a young man got shot?"

They both looked over as Franks opened his Coke with a loud hiss. They then continued.

"Yes," Sarena continued, "A young man got shot but the point of origin was less than clear. The trajectory points to this building, and we were wondering if anything strange had happened."

"Besides you being here?" Stephanie smiled as she sat down across from them and opened a coke. "Not really. I am sure your information is in error. We do not allow weapons on site except for a few security people. It is against company policy. There are cameras everywhere, and anything like that would have been caught on camera."

"Can we see that footage for the time in question," Franks asked.

Stephanie looked over at Franks, "I will have to get it cleared. We are an ITAR complaint shop. It will all have to be approved."

Sarena looked at the woman sitting confidently across the table, "How long have you worked here?"

"About five years now," Stephanie said. "got out of the service and was looking for a job and this practically fell into my lap. It is owned by a few men from Kentucky. They are rarely here. They just stop by from time to time to check on it, then go back and do something with horses."

"Service?" Sarena questioned, "How long were you in?"

"I did 3 tours then some desk time and got in 10 years. I liked being in, but it was getting tough and my family was having some issues. Coming home allowed me to help them out and be a little closer." Stephanie said.

"What did you do in the service?" Sarena asked.

"MP," Stephanie said, "Nothing too glamorous. I dragged drunks back to the brig mostly. I'm not a suspect, here am I? I can assure you I am not a shooter of little kids."

"Of course not," Sarena said, "I was just asking. You know the FBI, always curious."

"Sure," Stephanie said, looking at Sarena with a more wary eye, "have you been in the FBI long?"

"Long enough," Sarena answered.

"What do you do for the FBI?" Stephanie asked.

"I am a weapons expert, pretty much all ballistics. I enjoy it and am good at math so I can pretty much run most of the calculations in my head. Makes it easier to find points of view." Sarena said.

"Points of view," Stephanie spun her Coke bottle in her hands. "Not exactly a term I am used to hearing."

"No," Sarena replied, "I usually try to speak so people understand me. You have to forgive me. I'm not used to talking to people who can understand what I do."

"I understand," Stephanie said. "I will put in for recordings for yesterday. Any particular time?"

Franks broke in, "From about 11:00 PM to 3:00 AM."

Stephanie looked at him, "A wide time. I will put in for it, but it may require you to view it here. Would that be ok?"

"I think we can get clearance from DOD if necessary," Sarena said.

"You would be surprised," Stephanie smiled. "We have had a few people say that and some people in Washington pulled the plug right away."

"What do you make here?" Sarena asked.

"Nothing I can talk about," Stephanie looked away as she spoke, "but I will see what I can do about your request."

Sarena knew they were being politely asked to go so she pushed, "So who here would be able to make a shot across the field to the crossing."

"I told you," Stephanie focused on Sarena, "No guns. We have a strict "no weapon" policy on the property anywhere. So, no one."

"Hmm," Sarena pushed harder, "do you check everyone's cars?"

"I don't have to," Stephanie said. "The people who work here know the penalty for breaking the rules."

"I'm sure they do," Sarena said.

"Are there any more questions?" Stephanie asked. "If not, I'm pretty busy today."

"Not from me," Sarena said, "Walt?"

"No, not right now," Franks said. "Thanks for the Coke." Franks stood and took the nearly full Coke bottle.

"Thanks for the water," Sarena said putting it in her leather side bag. "You know, this is an awesome office. I love the metal sculptures in the lobby."

Stephanie was distracted for a moment and said, "It is a beautiful place to work. The group here has done wonders both here and for the city. If you only knew how much they help out behind the scenes you would probably be amazed. The owners are truly very generous, and they always come in and do fun contests. The items out there were all made by employees. The birds won a lucky employee a big fat check as a bonus. It was completely off the cuff, and people only had one day. Everyone who turned one in, got $500. The winner got $5000. It makes the whole place more exciting and more bearable."

"Bearable," Sarena asked.

"Most of these people press buttons and check to make sure robots do the work right. It is not exactly a challenging job unless you are one of the designers."

"Got it," Sarena kept talking. "It is beautiful."

As they walked into the lobby Sarena looked up at the birds and again was struck by their beauty and strangeness.

Stephanie shook their hands and they walked to the door.

Franks and Sarena were outside walking back to their cars before Sarena spoke, "What did you think."

Franks smiled, "I always think they're bad, but she is definitely different."

"I am going to make some calls and see who works here," Sarena said. She scanned the lot. "Look at all the pickups, not one of them has a rifle."

"Pickups do not mean someone is a gun owner," Franks said.

"OK, look at all the pickups with Marine and NRA logos all over them," Sarena said, "Is that better?"

Franks scanned the lot, "You may be right."

"I will check in later," Sarena said, getting in her car. Franks studied the lot for a few more minutes. Scanning the lot one last time, he got in his car and headed for the station.

Chapter 13

The beach was full of the thundering quiet of waves smashing against the shore. Michael and Abby walked hand in hand along the beach, barefoot, each carrying their shoes in the other hand. It was a picture-perfect day. The morning mist had burned off, allowing them both to experience the full splendor of Lake Michigan in the summer.

Michael stopped, looking out across the freshwater ocean. "It's beautiful here."

Abby joined Michael and looked as well, "It is. How long do you want to stay here?"

Michael turned to look at her, "Not having fun?"

"Of course, I'm having fun," Abby replied, "I always have fun with you. There is something on your mind though or you wouldn't have opened with how beautiful it is. Where do you want to go?"

Michael laughed. "No one in the world could know me like you do," he said with a wry smile.

"OK, spill," Abby grinned, running around Michael and tickling his ribs.

"Sure," Michael said, "I was thinking about making a trip back to Ivel."

"Ivel," Abby said, "Really? We blew that house up."

Michael looked at her, "I may have overreacted."

"You?" Abby groaned, "Never."

Michael put his arms around Abby, "Well, it happens sometimes."

Abby giggled, "Yeah, like the time you were getting rid of the skunk with your Barret?"

"Well, that did work," Michael said, "I just didn't expect it to explode like it did."

"It took weeks for the smell to fade from the house," Abby laughed.

"I know," Michael said, "I think Ivel was always safe, there was no real covert operation, just a nutcase coming after me."

"Nutcase?" Abby said, "Is that a technical term?" Abby slipped away from Michael and backed away.

"Yes, it is," Michael said as he grabbed for her. He was fast but she was faster and jumped out of the way.

Michael suddenly looked more serious. The game was on and he was moving in on her, so Abby ran. It was less than 10 steps and Michael had caught up. He paced to her and lightly slapped her butt.

"Ow," she smiled, "That was," she grabbed her butt for a moment and rubbed it, "well," Abby grimaced a little, "I think I deserved it."

Michael bellowed with laughter.

"Yes," he said. "You did."

Abby grabbed him and jumped into his arms, wrapping her legs around him. Her shoes fell to the ground as they kissed there on the beach.

"Ivel?" Abby said, breaking the kiss.

"Just for a while," Michael said.

"I'll go anywhere with you," Abby replied.

"And I with you," Michael said as he kissed her.

The waves continued pounding as they held each other close.

Chapter 14

Sarena was considering options. She drove home on 465 thinking about the day. The world had become a far different place from when she was growing up. Flat tires, rapes, shootings, sure they all happened, but in today's world, it meant news stories, commercials, interviews, arrests, appeals, and a never-ending train of proving beyond the shadow of a doubt. All that with this new world having little or no trust in the police.

Sarena shook her head. The facts were clear, someone was lying. The warehouse was the point of origin and somehow someone was trying to make it disappear. Security had to be in on it, but who else. There had to be more to this and the elusive long-term case, that was open in her department, was part of the key.

Sarena got off on an exit and turned towards downtown. Instead of going home, she headed back to the site.

Sarena picked up her phone and dialed a number.

"Hello," came a voice on the other end of the phone.

"Tyrel," Sarena began, "I am going back to the site for a minute. Something doesn't add up."

"Got an idea?" Tyrel asked.

"A theory," Sarena said. "I will tell you about it later."

"Looking forward to it," Tyrel said, and the phone went quiet.

Sarena did not have a far drive and was soon at the shooting location. The cars were gone and a series of small poles with yellow tape blew in the wind.

Getting out of the car, Sarena went to her trunk and opened it. Inside was a large black rifle bag. Sarena opened it and pulled the large rifle scope off the top of the rifle.

She walked to the tape, stepping over it. Small flags were still on the ground and she walked to each one. She remembered the flag where Jackson had been shot and stooped for a moment to look at the ground. There was not much here, but she thought about the bullet angle. She had read the reports that documented the angle of depression was only slight. She scanned the horizon. The only targets were the warehouses.

Looking through the scope, she swept the area. There was not much to look at except the buildings around her and the warehouse factory in the distance.

Sarena went back to the car and got out some oddly shaped equipment that looked like photography tripods and a pelican case. The case was not small, but not large either. She walked back to the small area and began unfolding the stands until they were in two places. Sarena pulled out her phone and looked up some notes. She adjusted the stands, so they matched Jackson's height. Then she articulated the stand as though it were falling forward. The contraption looked very unstable, but as she worked it back and forth, it became easy to see she had mirrored how Jackson may have been standing when he was shot. The series of tripods was actually a device she created and called a bodipod. It was made to mimic a crime scene shooting and allowed Sarena to review her points of view far more effectively than some other staging gear.

She stopped, walked around the strange stand and then went back to the case and pulled out a pen-sized implement and a series of clamps.

Referencing her phone again, she attached the pen to a portion of the bodipod and clicked through a series of settings until it was aligned properly. She pressed a small button on the pen and lights flashed. The pen was a powerful LASER. A spot appeared on the ground about 20 feet away, but she could not see where the other side hit.

Sarena pulled out the scope again and traced along where it looked like the laser should hit. She saw nothing. A small latch in the center allowed the bodipod to swivel from the center. Sarena loosened it and moved the laser an imperceptible amount. Again, she looked with the scope into the distance. She began doing this one click at a time until she saw the small pen of light on the distant warehouse.

Noting where it was, she saw several vantage points and moved the bodipod one click at a time. Each time, she saw the light move further until it was on top of a small window in the far distance.

Sarena smiled. She made notations of the settings on her bodipod then attached a small box to the side of it. GPS readings were taken, and she looked at her phone. She was relatively sure the shot came from the warehouse that it could not have come from. Stephanie had assured them of no weapons, but the LASER did not lie. She turned off the LASER.

Sarena sat for a moment looking at the warehouse. As she did, she saw a flash of light, looked at her chest, and started to move. She didn't hear the dart that struck her. She thought about struggling as she fell to the ground, eyes wide with disbelief. Moments later she was out cold.

Chapter 15

John sat in Jackson's room, reading a small book, while Jackson slept. Kira was in a chair near him playing with her phone. Kira's father had not returned yet.

The fire alarms went off loudly. It was instantly deafening, and lights flashed. Jackson woke and grimaced as he overcompensated, trying to sit up. John had stood immediately and gone to the door. He opened it to chaos as nurses ran every which way. Patients were being wheeled out of the rooms. Zach walked in the room obviously agitated.

"Kira," he said, "We have to go."

"Dad," Kira protested, "Shouldn't we wait for the nurses?"

"No," Zach snapped. "We have to go now."

Zach grabbed Kira's arm and pulled her to the door as she struggled. Kira twisted and yanked, finally pulling free. "What is wrong Dad?" she screamed.

Zach was even more frantic, "We have to go, now!"

John walked over, "Jackson has to wait for the nurses," he said softly.

"Good," Zach said, his voice quavering, "See Kira, they have to wait. We can go." He tried to be calm, but it was obvious he was still agitated.

"Dad," Kira said, "What is wrong?"

"I told you," Zach said in a more patient tone, "We need to go."

Someone began knocking on the door and Zach jumped. Grabbing Kira again, he pulled her away from the door this time as it opened. A nurse ran in as John watched Zach squirm in the corner, then breath for a moment as the nurse checked Jackson.

Jackson tried to sit up for her, but she scolded him, "No, no, we will roll you out on the gurney. I just need to get your lines in order." Jackson laid back, looking at his dad as the nurse walked back out of the door.

John walked to Zach and put his massive hand on Zach's shoulder. "What is going on here?"

The alarms continued to sound, but then they all heard a scream from down the hall. John heard the quick ping of silenced gunfire and moved to the door like a cat. He closed the door, locked it, then looked around the room. A mid-sized dresser sat to the side of the edge as a decoration. John walked to it in a rapid manner and tried to pick it up, but the dresser was screwed to the wall to keep it from being moved or falling. It did not move.

Zach moved to the window and looked to see how far up they were.

John strained and ripped the dresser from the wall, then picking it up with no apparent effort, put it in front of the swing-in door.

"What's going on?" Kira asked in a frantic tone, her lower lip quivering as she said it.

"I heard gunshots," John said. "I am guessing your father knows why."

Zach looked around the room like a cornered squirrel. He was sweating and tears were flowing on his face. "It's too late."

John walked up to Zach, towering over him. "What is going on?"

"Get away from me," Zach swung at John. John barely moved and grabbed his arm. Zach struggled but John's grip did not falter nor move an inch. "What do you want from me?"

"The truth," John said.

"Daddy?" Kira sobbed. "What is going on?"

John let Zach go.

Zach grabbed his arm, saying in a quiet tone, "It's too late, it doesn't matter now anyway."

"Dad?" Kira pressed.

"I just had to save you," Zach said, "I just had to save you," Looking at the floor, Zach slowly crouched down.

A sound came from the door. The knob was turning and then turned again.

John walked over and moved Jackson's bed to the inside wall.

Jackson tried to get up, "Dad, I can help."

"No," John said, "Stay safe."

Zach was crying in the corner holding on to Kira. John stepped closer to them, "Get over by Jackson," he said in a far more direct tone. Kira stood but her dad did not move. She tried to pull him up, but he just sat on the floor.

"Get up," John said, sounding more imposing.

Zach looked up and was obviously terrified, but he moved forward into the door area just as the lock and door began exploding. The rapid muffled sound of silenced gunfire was deafening. The wood around the lock and then the lock split, falling away. Then the pounding started. John pushed Zach and Kira into the corner near Jackson where they were out of the door's line of sight, just as the door pushed open with the dresser still in front of it.

John was waiting as a man walked in and swung his weapon to bear on him. The Glock 17 and silencer swung fast, but John was faster. He grabbed the weapon tightly, forcing it down. It fired once and ricocheted off the floor. John slammed down hard, and the gun fell from the man's grip.

John looked at the man for only a moment. He was maybe five foot ten, wearing a nurse's gown, coat, and scrubs. His dark hair and unshaven beard were abnormal for the nurses John had seen.

"Who are you?" John demanded in a quiet tone while studying the man.

The man eyed the Glock laying on the floor, "No one."

John eyed him, "You best leave," John said, still in a soft tone.

"You know I can't do that," the man said as he jumped for the weapon.

John was faster and caught the man in the abdomen with a punch that threw him back towards the door. The man, staggered, doubled over, and tried to catch his breath. John walked almost noiselessly to the weapon, picked it up, and turned to the man. "Who are you?" John asked again.

Zach threw himself at John like a berserker. "You are going to mess this up," Zach spat as he punched at John. The Glock clattered to the floor.

John twisted and grabbed Zach as the assailant grabbed the Glock from its place on the ground. John tossed Zach to the side, into the area near the window. He moved towards the man rapidly, picking up a table as he went. The assailant fired at him, but only splintered part of the table as John moved in a manner the belied a man his size.

The assailant backed up.

Zach yelled, "Kill him!"

The assailant fired twice, and Zach fell to the floor. John threw the table at the assailant and knocked the gun from his hand again, this time with an audible crack. The man scrambled, got up grabbing his lifeless hand and rushed from the room.

John walked to Zach, who was bleeding from his mouth. Zach coughed. "I just wanted to keep her safe." As Kira rushed to his side. Zach looked at Kira and closed his eyes as he stopped breathing.

"Noooo," Kira screamed.

Jackson was standing and moved to his dad's side with great effort, IV bag in tow. "Is he ok?"

"No, son," John said. "He is dead."

Kira cried as the police ran into the room. John stood and held his son tightly.

Chapter 16

As the group was getting on the fifth zip line, Jim's phone rang. He had just hooked up to the wire and was standing on the platform about to jump out overlooking the gorge. Reaching into his pocket, he pulled out the phone and looked at the display. A sudden look of concern crossed his face and Alex, who was strapping into the next line asked, "Who is it?"

"It's John," Jim replied.

"Sheldon?" Alex asked.

"Yeah," Jim said, "I haven't talked to him in years." Jim slid the bar on his Galaxy 9 and answered the call. "John, this is Jim. Umm, I am in the middle of something, can I call you back?"

"Sir," the attendant said, "You need to go."

Jim nodded and held on to his phone as he pushed off. "Sir, your phone, you need to put it away."

Jim was listening as he barreled down the line. He saw the end of the zip line coming and said, "Hey John, hold on for a moment." Then slid the phone into his pocket and slowed down to a stop where two men helped him. He quickly got undone from the cable, walking to the side of the platform, he began making his way down.

Reaching into his pocket, Jim spoke into the phone, "Sorry John, you caught me in the air. Go ahead."

It was barely a moment later that Alex joined him. "So is Jackson OK?" Jim asked. Jim nodded to the phone and Alex looked concerned.

"John," Jim said, "Let me talk to Alex. I will take some time off and head up there in the morning. You stay safe."

Jim hung up the phone.

"Well?" Alex asked.

"Well," Jim sighed, "I am not sure what to think. John is at the hospital and Jackson has been shot."

"Little Jackson?" Alex asked.

"Not-so-little Jackson," Jim said, "He has got to be a big boy now."

"So why the call?" Alex asked.

"We both owe John and you know it," Jim said. "He was calling to ask me to come keep an eye on things. They just got jumped in their hospital room, one girl's father and another girl was killed."

"Really?" a voice asked. Rachel had been listening in the background.

Jim turned. "Doesn't concern us all. This is something I will take care of," he said.

"Hey," Ronnie chimed in, "We are a team, I thought. If you need help, we will be there. It wouldn't be right to let you go alone."

"Guys," Jim said, "this is personal, not professional. I just need to go help a friend."

"Who are we going to help?" Barbara asked as she walked up and hung her arm over Ronnie. "Where are we going now?"

"We aren't going anywhere!" Jim said. "I am."

Alex was staring at his phone. The team began walking to the equipment area. "Let me call the general," Alex said. "This looks like something that may get out of hand."

"What do you mean?" Jim asked.

"Well," Alex said, "The headlines alone are pretty out there. 'Black student shot for trying to help,' and 'Racist police coverup,' for starters. But it appears that an FBI agent is missing, and a girl caught in the middle.

At a minimum, we should just follow up. Maybe the general will have some input. He always liked John."

"Dammit, Alex," Jim said, "This is for me to do, not any of you. Don't play games and act like you don't know why either."

Rachel laughed as she began taking her harness off in the equipment area, "I like this," she said, "In-control Jim, out of control."

Alex looked at her with a combination of upset-mom and furious-dad in his eyes.

She raised both hands palms forward in a symbol of mock surrender. "Touchy," Rachel said.

Alex glared at Rachel still, but not as bad, "It is."

Jim was out of his harness. "Let's go guys."

"You won't get there any quicker no matter how fast we leave," Alex said. "I will call Tarkington on the drive."

Jim sighed.

The group walked to the big black SUV and Alex said, "Ronnie, you drive. We need to talk in the back."

"Sir, yes, sir," Ronnie belted off as they reached the car. Rachel climbed into the back row alone, Barbara and Ronnie got in the front, leaving Jim and Alex in the middle row.

"I should drive," Jim said.

"Noooo," Everyone but Alex said in unison.

Jim put his head down for a moment, then smiled and laughed, "It's a fair court," he said.

The group laughed. Ronnie backed up and pulled out of the parking lot.

Chapter 17

Samuel Tarkington sat at his desk, staring at the computer screen, clicking the mouse from time to time. He was used to computers and systems but was stuck in drudgery at the moment. Sarah Collins walked into the room, carrying a few file folders.

"These are the numbers you asked for, sir," Sarah said.

"I hate budget time. It f.." he trailed off. "It really annoys me."

"Yes, sir," Sarah said, "I know what you mean."

Tarkington looked around the room, "Is anyone else here right now?"

"Not that I know of, sir, but you know how they operate," Sarah replied.

"Yeah, I do. And a promise is a promise," Tarkington said, working with his mouse again.

"Will there be anything else?" Sarah asked as the phone rang. She stopped, picked up the phone, and answered, "Operations, General Samuel Tarkington's office."

Sarah nodded for a moment, "Let me put you on speaker, Alex. He is here" she said.

"Thanks, Sarah," Alex said.

"Yeah, I'm here," Tarkington said.

"Sir, do you remember John Sheldon?" Alex asked.

"Of course, I do. I am old, but not senile, you little..." the general answered. "Yes, I remember him."

Alex paused but started a moment later, "Sir, John reached out to Jim for some assistance. It appears on the surface that John is in the

94

middle of a problem in Indianapolis. Request permission for Jim and I to check it out. To just help John out if he needed it?" Alex said in an inquisitive tone.

"What would that big..." the general trailed off again. "Alex, John is a big man, literally, why would he need you?"

"Sir," Alex said, "It appears there is a mess brewing up there. It really doesn't concern us, but we owe John. He was in our squad, and it just makes sense we should be there to help."

The general sat looking at the phone, his face was red.

Sarah spoke up. "Alex, I don't remember John. What is he in the middle of?" she asked.

"There was a shooting. Someone shot his son, now there has been a murder in the hospital there and an FBI agent was shot. John was also attacked in the hospital room, but we have no details. I am just suggesting Jim and I take a run up there to see if we can help John. If not, we would be right back. It is only a three-hour drive," Alex said.

"Let me call you back," Tarkington snapped and hung up the phone.

"Get me that d..." he started, "Get me the director of the FBI I talked to last week."

"Yes, sir," Sarah said and walked out. Sarah was thin and her hair was now long and blonde. She had dyed it recently to be more bleach blond and enjoyed the looks that people gave her. As she walked back to her desk there was bustling going around in the office. She ignored it, picked up her phone and dialed a number.

"Alex," she said, when the phone answered.

"What's with the general?" Alex asked on the phone.

"Nothing," Sarah said, "I am calling the FBI. Do you have any more details?"

"Nothing more than what's on the net," Alex said.

"We'll get back to you soon," Sarah said.

"Are you sure nothing's wrong?" Alex asked.

"I'll tell you later," Sarah said.

"OK," Alex said and hung up.

Sarah logged on to her computer and pulled up a number. She dialed it and waited.

"Director Vance?" Sarah said. "This is Sarah from General Tarkington's office. Do you have time for a brief call?"

"Yes, ma'am," Vance said, "and howdy, Sarah." The south Texas accent was palpable. "What does the general want today? I mean we haven't talked in what, a few weeks?"

"Has it been that long?" Sarah said in a shy voice. "I would really rather the General talk to you. He is much more articulate than me." Sarah replied.

"I am sure that's not true but put him on. I have a few minutes," Vance replied.

"Hold on, sir," Sarah said hitting a button as she got up and walked back into Tarkington's office.

"Sam," Sarah said as she opened the door, "Mister Vance is on the line."

Tarkington hit a button and motioned Sarah in. She came forward, shut the door and sat down in the chair opposite Tarkington.

"Vance, it's me," Tarkington said.

"So I hear. What can I do fer ya?" Vance said in a tone so smooth it could have been in a John Wayne movie.

"There is some trouble in Indianapolis, and an agent missing I hear," Tarkington said.

"Yeah," Vance replied, "that would be my bad news for the day. This on or off the record."

Tarkington smiled to himself, "Consider it off."

"Well," Vance began, "we were never there in an official capacity. One of my supervisors decided he would use one of our ballistics experts in the area to go on a personal witch hunt. It pretty much appears that the witch found them first. I'm sending him in tomorrow to start it over and start taking the city apart to find his agent. We don't have much, but she was good. She may have figured something out before she disappeared."

"Where was that?" Tarkington asked.

Vance sighed, "They assume at the crime scene. She had a rig set up, but it was damaged. She was good at her work, but I have others," Vance paused. "So why would you care?"

"One of my squad's old members is in the middle of this," Tarkington started. "The team has asked if they can go up and poke around."

"Send them," Vance said, "More eyes are better. Maybe they can give me some insight into the supervisor who got us involved. I'm sending him to run the investigation and will send more when I can."

"Thanks," Tarkington said.

"Hey Sam," Vance quickly stated, "I heard about your run-in with the corner office, are you ok?"

"I'm fine," Tarkington replied.

"Well, if it means anything, Sam, it was a good call," Vance said. "You let me know if y'all need anything."

"I will," Sam said and hung up the phone.

"You heard the man," he said to Sarah. "Send them up."

"Alex and Jim?" Sarah asked.

"H..." Tarkington started, "umm, heck no. Send the whole team. Let's get this solved and maybe I can get some people off my back."

"Yes, sir," Sarah began to turn but hesitated. "Sir?"

"What is it, Collins?" Sam asked.

"Sir, if it means anything, I think you are doing well," Sarah said.

The general grumbled and waved Sarah out of the office, "Let me know if they need anything."

Sarah walked out to her office, closing the door behind her.

Chapter 18

John, Jackson, and Kira were in a new hospital room. A guard was posted at the door and checked every ID for every person coming or going into the room. Kira had been offered a second room or an escort back home for her, but she decided to stay. Her father was her only family in the area, and he was now dead. Kira was truly alone.

Beth's family had arrived and no matter how many times Kira said she was sorry, they looked at her with sorrow. Kira understood. After all, their daughter was dead. The gunman had finished Kira before coming to their room. This had given John an advantage. Kira's friends had left and gone home, leaving her alone at the hotel. Not one of the girls who went to the concert even visited. Kira found that "crying" was a state she was in far more often now.

Kira began crying again as the realization of the day replayed in her mind.

John walked over to her, "Are you ok?"

Kira looked up, tears filling her eyes.

"No dad, she is not OK," Jackson said.

It had only been one day, but Jackson was feeling much better. Since the bullet had been a "lucky" hit, meaning it did not hit any major organs or bones, he was doing well. The fact that he was an athlete and in good shape helped even more.

"I know son," John said, "but I wanted to ask."

"Don't mind him, Kira. He is a tried and true overprotective dad," Jackson explained.

Kira smiled a small smile through the tears. "It's ok Jackson, he cares more than my dad ever did."

"Yesterday was a rough day, Kira," John said, "Maybe we should get you a room somewhere so you can sleep."

"I feel safe here with you," Kira replied. "I really don't want to go anywhere else at the moment." Kira teared up again, "John, thanks for saving me."

"He does that," Jackson laughed trying to lighten the mood.

Walter Franks walked into the room, "Hey guys. We are going to move you one more time to a bigger room."

"Is it true Sarena is..." Kira trailed off.

"Missing? Yeah," Franks said looking at the window for a moment. "Her brothers are a mess and frantic looking for leads. She is the golden child, the one who was more than just a cop, she was that person everyone wanted to be."

"Sorry, sir," John said.

"Won't matter now," Franks said. "Some hotshot government team is coming up to help. I am sure this is not going to be fun. I have been asked to request you stay for at least a while, Kira. You as well, John. Kira, we will get you a room here and you will have someone assigned to you at all times."

"I think I would rather stay with John and Jackson," Kira said. "Is that ok?"

Franks looked a little confused, "I mean... umm... yeah, it is ok with me, but is it ok with them?"

John smiled his patient smile, "Sure it is. She can stay wherever you put us."

"We got your luggage from the hotel, Kira. Reporters were milling around, and we didn't want the hotel to be tempted," Franks said. "I will have them bring it up. We will get two adjoining rooms until we can move

Jackson somewhere without doctors."

"I am sure we will get moved soon," John said.

"You mean the team coming, don't you?" Franks replied.

"Yes, sir," John said. "I am sure we will be taken care of well."

"I hope so," Franks said, "I don't know anything about this group. No press information, not much of anything and an FBI agent, Tyrel, will be meeting them here."

"We will cooperate, sir," John said quietly.

Jackson piped in, "Yeah, we will. Dad has..."

John quickly jumped in, "...been involved with shootings before in the service. It won't be an issue. Thank you, Officer Franks."

Jackson looked perplexed but was quiet. Franks spoke, "Well, we'll be back up soon. There will be a guard outside, let them know if you need anything."

"Thank you, sir," John said as Franks left the room and closed the door behind him.

"Dad," Jackson said, "you said you knew these guys coming, right?"

"These guys don't need to know that," John said. "We don't know who is good or who is bad."

Jackson looked, "You think this guy might be in on it?"

"I don't know, son," John replied. "I just don't want to take any chances with you," John started then turned to Kira, "or you either. I have seen way too much and know anyone can sometimes be a problem."

"But the police?" Kira asked.

"In other countries, the police are the first ones who go bad," John said. "I mean, Jim and I had a run-in once with a few cops and if it had not been us, well, we would have been dead."

"Don't get him started," Jackson said. "He can tell army stories all night. You would think his friend Jim is Superman."

John looked at Jackson with a stern glare, "Don't you try to give Jim any problems, he is a good man."

"No," Jackson said, "he is a good Superman."

Chapter 19

The trip from Richmond, Kentucky to Indianapolis was uneventful. The scenery was something that anyone in the Midwest was used to from time to time. A series of long drives through country and small cities, then an outlet mall, then another series of small towns. Each area had a unique appeal, and the interstate begged for cars to exit and become a part of a local economy.

The team led by Alex Brown was only four this time as Barbara and Terry were to standby in Lexington instead of being in the midst of this rather normal investigation. The group was far more accustomed to dealing with terrorists, ex-military problems, militants, and a series of people that are quite a challenge. Alex had decided a full team would probably stir up more issues than it would solve. The two pilots were the logical choice to stay behind.

Jim and Alex rode in the front of the big Suburban while Ronnie and Rachel took the back seat. Ronnie sat almost carefully in jeans and a blue t-shirt, occasionally looking out the window at the passing cars. Rachel, on the other hand, wore tight workout pants and a red tank top, showing her well-defined arms. Her short cut hair seemed to make her look imposing as she watched out the window on the other side of the car.

Occasionally, the group would pass a car with children in it and Rachel would stick out her tongue at the kids as the waved to her.

Jim looked back at Rachel each time he heard her make sounds, sticking her tongue out, and he snickered. His Ray Ban sunglasses hid his eyes, but it was obvious he was enjoying himself, watching Rachel be amusing.

"Still don't know why we didn't just fly," Jim said.

"Yeah," Rachel interrupted as they passed another car. "It would have been quicker."

"No," Alex said, "by the time we filed, took off, landed, taxied, got cars and got moving it would be about the same. It is not a big deal. This is just over 3 hours. We can deal."

"By the time we get there, Rachel will have terrorized every child in the area. Or made them giggle themselves to death," Jim laughed.

Ronnie jumped in. "I am not sure I understand what we are doing, going up here and all. Sir, this isn't a military thing."

Rachel looked at Ronnie, "We are going to have some fun and try to be normal. Doesn't that sound fun, Ronnie?"

"Not really," Ronnie said and winced, ready for a punch in the arm. This time it did not come.

Since the team was created, Ronnie and Rachel had fallen into a pattern of acting more like brother and sister than teammates. Rachel, once overly regimented, had softened a little and was protective but tough on the younger Ronnie. This led to a few funny interactions. But when the chips were down, the two were completely professional.

Alex considered the team for a minute and was happy it had turned out so well. The group, on their own, could have been considered a series of misfits. In reality, every time they went out their skills became more refined, and each of them had unique skills that made the team better. Alex knew that the playful banter was to deal with the sometimes complex and difficult situations they had been placed in by their jobs. Recently, each had proven their worth in a bare knuckle free for all with a group of doomsday preppers. Each of them was more than competent.

"Are we there yet?" Jim giggled.

"Yeah, are we there yet?" Rachel echoed.

"You guys are being mean to Alex," Ronnie said. "He is driving, and you should treat him with respect."

This time the punch on the arm did come, and Ronnie pulled to the side. The punch was light and playful, and Ronnie could not help but laugh. "Stop it, Rachel!" he said but his smiled showed through.

Jim spoke up an approximation of an older woman voice and said, "Don't make Nana come back there, you two."

Rachel started laughing, "Nana nana nana nana ..."

Jim and Rachel both said it at once, "Batman."

"You guys need to stop," Alex said. "Has anyone looked over the files?"

Ronnie began talking in a more serious tone, "Sir, there is not much. The police files were not complete. This FBI girl, Sarena Prince, she had some things in her files, but it wasn't finished either. I read all the stuff about the people and the crime scene. It is not much. There was a mention of a security woman, Stephanie, at a warehouse, but that is not complete either. The papers are talking about it like it is a hate crime now. The internet says that the boy was shot because he was black and the girls were white, but that doesn't make much sense either, sir."

"Thank you, Ronnie," Alex said.

Jim started, "Tarkington got us into this so we can look around, but how are we going to play it, Alex?"

Alex frowned, "I wish we had Melody here," he said. "We are not really that type of group."

"True," Jim jumped in, "but we know a little about shootings and snipers."

Alex sighed, "Unfortunately. Maybe we should have brought Terry," Alex continued, "he is the sniper among us."

"Well, he could fly us back," Jim laughed.

Ronnie broke in, "Sir, I think we should talk to the people again, and then look at the scene. The warehouse seems to be where the shot came from but the stuff in the reports says the cameras didn't see it."

Alex nodded, "OK, we will get settled and go over things in order. Do we know where the girl and John and Jackson are?"

"Still at the hospital," Ronnie said.

"Good," Alex replied, "We will stop by the scene then head to the hospital."

"Nice plan," Jim said.

As the car passed by 465, Alex wondered what John and Jim's past was going to get them into.

Chapter 20

Michael walked downstairs to the massive gym under his home. The house was located on the shores of Lake Michigan, so he had it built above the waterline. Even though it was carefully constructed, Michael had the contractors seal the basement completely so it would not flood and more likely float in the event of extremely high water. The basement's lowest point was still 20 feet about the lake's normal level and there were hundreds of feet of sand in front of the house to protect it from the waves.

As he turned on the light switch and the high ceilings lit up bright white. The glowing LEDs would not burn out and each area of the room looked perfectly clean.

Walking to the weights on the far side of the wall, Michael lifted three weights in sequence. First, a hundred-pound weight, then a forty-pound weight, and finally a three-pound weight. There was a click in the wall, and he pulled the wall towards him, opening into another large room.

The lights in the room came on upon Michael's entry. The room was bright white, with a line of cabinets on the left side of the room with sealed doors and drawers filling the cabinet spaces. On the far side, a large desk was coming alive with 6 computer monitors over a computer. The computer was churning and came up to a login prompt after just a few moments.

Michael went to the cabinets and opened a large lower drawer. Inside were a series of bags and he picked out a small backpack. Closing that drawer, he moved to a thin drawer in the center. As he opened it, a FN P-90 rifle and a FN-57 pistol became visible. Michael took out the FN-57 and pulled back the slide on the weapon.

The FN-57 was a 21-shot pistol that used the NATO 5.7x28 ammunition. The standard ammunition was very high velocity and allowed the weapon to be used in a variety of situations, and with the custom ammunition, could shoot through a variety of light armor. Michael checked over the weapon. Opening a small shelf to the side, he set the weapon and the backpack on it.

He then opened another drawer that was filled with magazines for the FN-57. Taking two magazines, Michael placed them in the bag, then took a third and set it on the shelf. Michael closed the magazine drawer and the weapon drawer, leaving the FN P-90. Then he opened another drawer and pulled out a silicone gun cloth. With patience, he worked over the FN-57 and made sure it was clean and well oiled.

Closing the drawer but not the shelf, Michael then opened another drawer that was full of holsters. Michael picked out a shoulder holster that would allow him to be flexible, put the weapon in the holster, then put the holster into the black backpack.

"Packing for Kentucky?" Abby asked from the door.

Michael left the backpack back on the shelf and walked to Abby. "Do you have any idea how much I love you?"

Abby smiled. She was far smaller than Michael, but the fit was perfect. Michael reached down and his lips brushed hers ever so lightly. She put her hands on Michael's face, pulling him closer and kissed him with a hunger that surprised them both. Michael wrapped his arms around her and with no noticeable effort lifted her off the ground as they kissed with urgent passion. With slow deliberate tenderness, Michael set Abby down, and his lips brushed hers again.

"Not half as much as I love you," Abby said. "How are we getting to Ivel?"

Ivel, Kentucky was the site of a house Michael had partially destroyed when he thought he had been located by enemies. He had actually been located by the United States Government and the reason for destroying the house was not necessary. An exact duplicate of the vault-like room, he was in right then, was still intact with many weapons in Ivel.

"I am thinking that it may be a fun drive," Michael said. "In a few months, this house will be covered with snow and ice. I was thinking we could go to Kentucky and work, or maybe Dubois later. We may catch a transport along the way with the car, but for now, let's have some fun."

"I am game," Abby said.

Michael smiled, "Well, we can take our time, see some lighthouses, stop by the golden dome of Notre Dame, maybe see the giant bull in Kokomo, Indiana or the museums in Indianapolis. The point is, we are in no hurry."

"I know," Abby said, hugging Michael around his muscular chest. "It will be fun if it is with you."

"We have an appointment with a contractor in Ivel on Friday," Michael said, "That gives us five days to get 400 miles."

"Wow," Abby said, "We should take the DB-9, it will let us get there when we want."

Michael laughed again, "You just love driving it."

"Who said I wanted to drive?" Abby winked.

Walking back to the cabinets, Michael picked up the pack, and met Abby back at the door. They walked out together. Michael closed the door until he heard a latch, then dropped the weights back in place. He pulled a little and as far as anyone could see the wall was solid.

"Michael," Abby questioned, "have you heard anything from Alex or my dad?"

"Nope," Michael said.

"How about Alan or Melody?" Abby continued.

"Nope," Michael said.

"Is that all you can say?" Abby smirked.

"Nope," Michael laughed.

Abby was energized and chased Michael across the room. The clean mats were soft on their bare feet as they crossed the floor. At the last minute, Abby turned and tried to flip Michael. She stopped and attempted a Judo throw that seemed to have worked as Michael rolled over her shoulder. At the last second, Michael hooked under her stomach, and he rolled to the ground, pulling her over his shoulder. Abby was vaulted into the air, but Michael had control. As she came towards the ground, he slowed her, and she barely felt her body land on the mat.

Michael looked down into her crystal blue eyes. He smiled, and she giggled back. Michael lowered his head to hers and began kissing her again. Soon there was a pile of clothes next to them, and a passion few could understand.

Chapter 21

It was near noon when the team arrived in the warehouse district. The four stepped out of the car and were met by a lone patrol officer as they stretched and surveyed the area.

"I'm sorry," the officer said in a rather stern tone. "This area is off-limits."

"Thank you, officer," Alex said as he pulled out his identification. "We are here under FBI guidance and orders."

The officer was obviously on edge from Alex moving for his ID and reviewed him with a suspicious gaze. He reached out and took Alex's military ID. Looking it over, the officer eyed Alex suspiciously. "You are with the army. This is not an army matter."

Alex tried to look calm and disarming. "We were asked to consult on this case because of a special situation."

"Why would the army be interested in a case like this?" the officer pressed.

"You know," Rachel chimed in loudly, "that's a good question. I was wondering that as well."

The officer reached for his weapon, and Rachel looked directly at him, her bright eyes sparkling a little. "Don't get all antsy on us, Officer," she looked at his nameplate, "Moody?"

Dan Moody looked at the strange woman in a peculiar manner, as she started laughing, "This is highly irregular. I will need to call it in."

A black Crown Victoria pulled up to the area. Moody looked at the car with a little bit of obvious relief as Walter Franks stepped out.

"I suppose you are the group from Kentucky," Franks said. "The FBI guy show up yet? Tennison?"

Alex walked to Franks and put out his hand, "Yes sir, we are from Kentucky. No sir, no FBI yet. We were just about to review the area."

"Not sure why the army has any interest in this case," Franks pointed out. "We will get them and find Sarena Prince."

"We aren't here to take over the case," Alex said in a crisp tone. "We are here to try to help. We understand there have been a few challenges."

"I doubt it. You haven't been here long enough to understand," Franks said. "It is obvious that someone in the factory over there is not telling the truth." Franks nodded towards the distance.

"Would be quite a shot," Alex said as he gazed out towards the area Franks was looking.

"About 2500 yards depending on where they shot from. So yes, it would be quite a shot," Franks agreed. "We will be interviewing every person there. The head of security has been informed, and all personnel records for anyone with military experience have been pulled."

"Why military?" Jim asked.

"2500 yards? That is one hell of a shot," Franks said. "You are welcome to look around, but we will take lead."

Alex looked at the distant warehouse factory. "Sure," he replied, "we will help in any way we can."

"Knock yourself out," Franks said, "I think you're wasting your time, but do it all over, check out the site, investigate. Your time, why should I care." Franks turned to Officer Moody, "Let them look around. Keep everyone else out."

"Yes, sir," Moodynodded.

Ronnie had been quiet but looked at Franks and with his soft-spoken manner said, "Thank you, sir, we will be respectful."

Franks studied the young redheaded man. "I am sure you will." He turned and went to his car.

Rachel smiled at Ronnie and slapped him on the back of the head, playfully, "Suck up."

Alex and Jim looked over notes that had been forwarded to them and walked the small area. They looked to each side then towards the warehouse in line with the shot again. From the angle they were at, there was nothing close enough to have taken the shot except that building. Alex pulled out a monocular and looked over the area. There were other points of view, but they were excessively long, far beyond a shot range for any normal sniper or shooter.

Jim whispered to Alex as Ronnie and Rachel set up a camera in the center of the roped area. "Maybe we don't need to be here. Let's just go take care of John and Jackson and move on. We don't need to butt in, do we?"

Ronnie and Rachel walked away from the camera as the tripod it was on did a small series of clicks and began a slow, steady sweep of the entire 360-degree area.

"No," Alex said, "Maybe not, but this smells bad. You know that this smells bad. There is way too much going on here for it just to be that simple. A shot from the only obvious source. Why then? Why any of this?"

"Why take a cop?" Jim asked. "That's what you mean, right?"

"I am more worried why someone would try to clean it up," Alex clarified. "I am sure Franks and his group are as well. Why would anyone try to kill the witnesses and the officer who was likely going to work it out? You read her file. She is a genius on ballistics. Why take her unless there is something to hide?"

"Alex," Jim said, "we aren't cops. They are. Let's let them do their job and move on."

"We were given permission by the FBI and by Tarkington," Alex said.

"I know, and it's John, but we are not experts, no Melody here. We get the job done, but we don't have all the training the Indy police do," Jim stated. "I mean, I am good with anything."

"Doesn't sound like you here, Jim," Alex stated.

"What do you mean?" Jim said.

"You are usually all in, in everything," Alex said in a dry tone.

"Maybe," Jim said, "but maybe we have gone a little overboard from time to time. You could have been killed up in Michigan, and you act like nothing is wrong. Lisa was killed, and for what? Revenge? No, not really, she was killed because she got in the way."

"It's our job," Alex pointed out.

"Yeah," Jim relented, "maybe it was our job, but crap like this is why I got out in the first place. Do we really want to go down this path? What if it is Ronnie next," he looked around then back at Alex, "or Rachel?"

Alex looked at Jim and considered this unique outburst. "Jim, it was our job and is our job. We have lost people."

Jim broke in, "We shouldn't lose them on our soil. Alex, I will follow you. You know I didn't come back willingly, but I will follow. But I don't think this is something we should be in the middle of if someone else can do it better."

"Point taken," Alex said. "We see all we need to see. Remember you pressed for this."

Jim smiled, "I know, I owe John, but something about this feels wrong. You really need your buddy here in the middle of it all. He would know more than any of us."

"My buddy?" Alex asked.

"Michael," Jim noted. "He is the sniper that scares little recruits."

Alex looked around. He seemed to be pondering a few thoughts.

"I wasn't serious," Jim said. "It was a joke."

Behind them, the camera stopped. Ronnie and Rachel walked back to it and began taking it apart, putting each piece in the slick pelican cases.

Rachel looked at Jim and Alex and said, "We're done here."

Alex stared off in the distance, wondering about Jim's words and the strange eddies in their life that put them all back together.

Chapter 22

John was pacing. Time was not going the way he expected. The room was adequate and better than what they had before, but John still knew the rule he had learned in the service: *if someone wants you dead, they will find a way.*

Jackson was feeling a little better. Though the after-surgery pain had set in, the doctors had given him several medications to control it. Kira sat close to him with her phone plugged into the wall near her. The new room offered a better way for them to get cleaned up and be more comfortable. Kira had showered and changed into clean jeans, a pink tank top and a white dress shirt covering it.

"My aunt is on her way," Kira said. "The family is pretty torn up about dad."

"How about you?" John asked. "How are you feeling?"

"I will be fine," Kira replied. "I suppose it will hit me harder later, but for now, I am ok."

John sat down next to Jackson, "How about you, Jackson?"

"I am fine, dad," Jackson said. "You ask me that every five minutes. I am fine."

Kira giggled, "Yes, you are."

Both John and Jackson looked at her.

"Sorry," Kira said, "Force of habit. I joke when I am nervous."

Jackson laughed, "Yeah, but if you say stuff like that, Dad will think you are trying to steal me."

Kira looked at Jackson, "Oh, who would I be stealing you from?"

Jackson looked away, "No one," he said, "I am good."

"That's what she said," Kira laughed.

John looked at the young lady again, and as he did, he found a little bit more respect for her as she had faced a lot in the last two days, more than a lot of people face in a lifetime. He smiled. "Cute," John stood back up and walked to the door. "Very cute."

"Dad," Jackson said, "You've checked the door a hundred times. Nobody else is coming for us."

"I will check it a hundred and one times if I want. I will keep the two of you safe no matter what," John said as he opened the door, glanced out and saw the officer in the hall, and then closed the door.

"Dad," Jackson said and looked down. Kira turned to him.

"Yeah," John asked.

"Dad," Jackson said, "I know I kinda never thought much about your stories, I mean, they are stories, right? I mean, but I never, well, Dad, what I'm trying to say is thanks for saving Kira and I."

Kira looked up at John, "Yeah, thanks."

John looked down at his hands as he rubbed them together, "I just did it. It was what I had to do."

"But Dad," Jackson said, "I have never seen you move so fast in your life. It was like watching a movie with Tom Cruise in it, only bigger."

John rubbed his hands together and looked at them as Jackson spoke. "I just did what I had to do," John said quietly. "There is nothing good about it. It is just who I am."

Jackson looked at his dad in a quizzical manner. His head cocked to the side.

There was a knock at the door. John looked up, his huge arms flexing for a potential confrontation.

The door swung open, and a nurse walked in, leading Alex Brown, Jim Simpson, Rachel Brown and Ronnie Comer. The officer outside stood behind them and said, "Don't worry, they check out."

John rushed forward and gave Jim a bear hug, smiling, moved back for a moment and shook Alex's hand, then nodded to both Rachel and Ronnie. "Thank you so much for coming."

Jim shook his head a little, "I owe you, man, but I'm not sure what we can do here."

John looked down at Jim, "You came, that's a start. I don't know who to trust. People died, Jim. People died."

Jim looked over to the bed, "Oh my god, is that Jackson?"

John spun and looked at his boy, "Yes, sir, that's my boy."

"It has been, what, six years?" Jim said. "He was a bit smaller back then. Remember me, Jackson?" He asked with a smile.

"Dad talks about you still," Jackson said.

"All bad, I assume," Jim laughed.

Closing the door behind them, the nurse walked to Jackson and began checking vitals to enter into a tablet.

Alex looked around the room as Rachel and Ronnie stood almost uncomfortably.

John looked at Alex, "Alex, you know I respect you, and Jim and I, we have been through more than anyone could understand." Ronnie and Rachel leaned in close, and Jim moved over as well. The room was spacious, but slightly crowded now. "Alex, I want my boy safe. I mean, who would come after him like this? Who would shoot him in the first place?"

Alex looked at his old teammate and sighed, "John, we will get you safe, but I'm not sure what we can do."

The nurse finished, "Do you need anything else?"

The group stopped and listened. "No, ma'am," Jackson said. "It only hurts when I laugh or move."

The nurse looked at Jackson before turning to Kira, "Stop telling jokes," then she looked back at Jackson, "Stop moving. It will get better."

Jim turned to Jackson, "I remember the first time I got shot. The medic said that to me, and I punched him in the face."

Jackson started laughing and then grimaced with pain.

The nurse turned to Jim, "Are you going to be a problem?"

Jim looked over the nurse. She was probably 50 with grey hair in a tight bun. The white nurse uniform was crisp and nearly flawless. Her thin frame was evident under the tight uniform. He smiled, "I can always be a problem, or so my ex-wife says."

The nurse laughed a little, "I bet you can." She walked back toward the door and said to Jackson, "Hit the call button if you need anything."

"What about me?" Jim said.

"A few cold showers would be good," the nurse said as she walked out the door.

Jackson laughed again then Kira giggled as Jackson grimaced. "It's not funny, Kira."

John rubbed his hands together more, obviously agitated, "Alex, I know you. You can do anything. Just keep my boy safe."

Jim watched John rub his hands together with a grim solemnness. "Still can't sleep?"

"I was doing good," John said, "Just me and my son, until all this. They came here and tried to kill us, Jackson and this little girl, and they killed the little girl's friend." The tension in John's voice was thick, and he was sweating lightly. "I mean, why would they kill her?"

Jim looked at Alex, "We can set up in John's house or somewhere else, and we can poke around. I know I said it is not our job, I know I am being wishy-washy, but god, Alex, it's John."

Alex turned to Rachel, "Go find out when Jackson could be moved, Find a doctor, a nurse, or someone."

"On it," Rachel said and left the room.

"Ronnie."

Ronnie was focused on Alex.

"Go to security here. See if we can pull a tape, get footage, or find out who this was. Police probably already have. If they have, find them. Let's see if we can find out what we're up against."

Alex looked at John, "We asked Tarkington and he has us hooked up with the FBI. I was going to bow out, but we can stay for a few days."

John wrung his hands and looked at the floor. "Thank you, Alex."

"Jim, why don't you take John down and get some coffee. I will stay here with the kids," Alex said.

"No, sir, I should keep Jackson safe," John said.

Jim looked at his old friend, "Let's go, and you can wash your hands before you rub all the skin off."

John looked down at his hands and stopped, shoving them in his pocket. "Sorry, sir," John said.

Jim put his hand on John's massive shoulder, and they walked to the door. "Keep them safe," John said to Alex as they reached the door.

"I will," Alex replied, and Jim and John left the room.

Alex looked down at the floor for a moment and considered how many men had come back this way. John was one of his best, he could heft an M60 for days as though it were a paperweight, but he cared. Alex sighed then looked up at Kira and Jackson.

"Is my dad ok?" Jackson asked, "I have never seen him this worried. He is always concerned and pushing me, but he seems so tense. I mean, you should have seen him when that guy came after us, but now he seems almost sad."

Alex considered the two of them, "You should ask your dad about it. Not my place to say."

Jackson looked at Alex, "You are the Alex Brown Dad talks about. You made my Dad leave the service."

"Not exactly," Alex said.

Kira was looking at both of them. "Not exactly?" she echoed "That is what my dad says," Kira looked at the ceiling for a second, "said to me when he was lying to me. *Not exactly* seems to be equal to *I am gonna tell a lie*."

Alex sighed, "John needed to be home with you, Jackson. It was a good thing, right?"

Jackson eyed Alex suspiciously, "I suppose."

Alex sat down on the opposite side of the bed from Kira, keeping himself between them and the door. "Kids, we're not policemen or detectives, but we are used to things that get pretty complicated. Is there anything you might know that the police are not aware of or anything you remembered that could get us closer to finding who shot you? You don't have to talk to any of us, not even me, but it would be nice if you did. We deal with some pretty off-the-wall stuff, and we can help."

Jackson shook his head, and Kira did as well. It was Kira who spoke, "We were talking to the lady, Sarena, and she didn't need anything else from us. I don't think there is anything else we have missed. I had my back to whoever shot. Jackson just fell forward. I never heard anything. There really wasn't too much to it."

Alex smiled and tried to be casual, "Can you walk me through everything one more time, please?"

Kira started. She even put in more detail as she remembered why she was going out with Beth, and where they had intended to go. It seems to her like the last few days were years long. They were so stupid to go out alone so late at night. They should never have been out there. Kira should have been paying attention to her driving. They should have called for help right away. The list was long. Now Kira had seen her father die, her friend had died as well, and her whole world was upside down. She realized all of this in the fraction of a moment and felt her tears start to flow.

"Are you ok?" Alex asked quietly.

Kira wiped the tears from her face, "It all seems so long ago, but it was not long, not long at all. I just don't know why any of this is happening, and it all seems like my fault," she replied.

Alex reached out to Kira and took her hand, "None of this is your fault."

Jackson put his hand on Kira's shoulder.

"How could it not be?" Kira replied. "I had no business going out. I was trying to be an adult, and I had no idea what being an adult was like. My entire world changed because of what? A stupid run to get something dumb after a dumb concert?" Kira stopped for a second, wiping tears away again. "What has my life been but me trying to make me happy?

God, I have been so stupid. Now my actions have devastated a bunch of people, and Jackson got shot, and my dad is dead. None of this would have happened if I had just stayed home and not been trying to do for me."

"It's ok, Kira. We all find our center from somewhere. So, let me ask again, did anyone know where you were going?" Alex asked.

"No," Kira said, "It was pretty much spur of the moment. We didn't have any real idea of where to go."

"And the boys? Did you know them?" Alex asked.

"No, I think we have established I am not from around here," Kira replied, drying her tears.

"Do you remember anything about them that would be of use?" Alex asked with a soft, almost melodic tone.

"Well, the one boy's name was Jimmy, and they were worried about their coach," Kira said. "But I am not sure anything else will help."

"Did the police do a sketch artist or a computer artist?" Alex asked.

"No," Kira said, "nothing like that."

"Do you think you could remember any of them? It has been a few days. Normally they do it right away," Alex said.

"I think so," Kira said, "I am pretty sure I will remember them forever."

"I am sorry, Kira," Alex said, "I am sure this is hard."

Kira looked at Alex and started to tear up, "I miss my Dad."

"I know," Alex said. "Do you have someone coming?"

"My aunt," Kira replied. "She lives in Atlanta but was in Lexington this week with my dad. She is driving this way now. She is from Lexington so I am not sure how this will work out."

"OK," Alex said, "I am sure it will all be ok."

Alex walked to the door and considered the next move. He wondered for a moment why they were there, then he thought of John and his debt to John. They all had a debt to John, and it would be paid.

John and Jim returned with small cups of coffee.

Jim walked over, "We should get them somewhere safe," he whispered.

"Where's that?" Alex said.

"Not here," Jim replied. "This is a tactical nightmare. If the boy can laugh and move around, we could get him to a hotel or a motel, or a house, or... hell, to the airport. As long as they are here, they are targets. The security here in the hospital is good, but they got in once, they will be able to do it again."

"Probably," Alex started. "Where would you suggest?"

"No *"probably"*," Jim said. "They tried to kill them. They are cleaning witnesses. This is something bigger than a random shot. Sure, we can stay involved, but not if we have to babysit as well. Get them in the clear. Then we can be free to look around or do whatever. Maybe we can get them to a big chain hotel unseen and disappear. I am sure they have eyes all over us right now."

Alex walked to the door again, looked out, and saw nothing. Alex closed the door.

"Have Ronnie get us a hotel with cash," Alex thought for a moment, working strategies in his head, "something normal and something close. I don't want to move Jackson too far." Alex stopped again considering options, "Get a suite if they have it. Something big enough we can defend but not be on top of each other."

"On it," Jim said, taking out his phone as he went in the hall.

"John," Alex said. John walked over. "We are gonna try to obtain some neutral ground. You good with that."

"Yes, sir," John said as he took a sip from the small cup. "But will Jackson be ok."

"We will make sure if it," Alex said. "If I need to, I will get him a nurse."

John looked down at the cup and realized he could not wring his hands together. "Thank you, sir, I appreciate it."

"I owe you, John. We are good," Alex said as he put his arm on John's giant shoulder. "I owe you."

Chapter 23

Jokes ran rampant in the Aston Martin DB9 as Michael and Abby drove south on US 31. The drive from the North Muskegon, Michigan area to Ivel, Kentucky was almost 600 miles and would take nearly 9 hours if the two were driving without stops. Instead, they intended to stop in several cities along the way, breaking the trip into at least two, but likely three days. They had discussed flying but decided there was no airport close. They had discussed going straight through, but there was no hurry. In the end, Abby had pulled out a long list of places in between that were interesting or something she had not seen. Michael had laughed at her ingenious way of killing time without killing themselves. After all, he had a list too.

Their first stop was in Holland, Michigan. It was not a far distance from Muskegon, but they wandered out and saw the Holland lighthouse, watching the waves creep up to the beach and recede back into the massive lake. Abby and Michael spent twenty minutes in silence, just watching the waves before Abby reached over, kissed Michael on the neck and announced she was ready to go.

"I guess that means I am ready too," Michael said in a playful voice. He stood up effortlessly and smiled at Abby.

"Now you are beginning to understand the rules," Abby retorted as she bolted to the car. In a few quick steps, Michael caught her then with very little effort spun her around and pulled her close.

"Do you know how much I love you?" Michael said.

"A lot," Abby laughed then they kissed for several moments.

A quick drive from the lighthouse brought them to a giant windmill and home of the tulip festival. Holland's tulip festival was an amazing display of color and frivolity. It was not the season now, but there were flowers at the small park, and the preserve around the area was well kept and the trip relaxing.

The drive continued with both Abby and Michael laughing as they passed into Indiana and the GPS bade them a formal welcome. The roads changed and were a little better, but not much. The sound in the car was only slightly modified as the vehicle was a testament to automotive engineering. The acoustics quieted nearly everything from outside.

About an hour later, they suddenly made an unscheduled stop at the Grissom Airforce Base museum. It was very noticeable off the road, and a quick right put them in the middle of a bed of history. Planes from many eras were parked and stood as silent sentinels over the area. Their deadly wares now disabled, but the power they represented quite intact. The museum was small and outdoor, but the weather was perfect, and the company even more so.

While they were looking at the A-10 Warthog, an older gentleman walked up. "Did you have any questions, son?"

Abby looked at the man in his pressed shirt and pants, wearing a "Vietnam Veteran" cap. "We are just looking around. Michael wanted to stop here and see the planes, so we just stopped."

"They don't make them like this anymore," the man started. "Used to be that a pilot flew the plane, now it is all computers and do-dads that make it more of a plane flying the pilot."

Michael laughed, "Computers have a way of doing that."

"Name's Carson," the man said as he put out his hand. "Pleased to meet you."

"Michael," Michael said, "And this is Abby."

"Pleased to meet you both. Was watching you walk, how you hold yourself. Were you in the service?" Carson asked.

Michael pondered for only a moment and said, "I never went through boot or was formally in the service."

"Spook, huh?" Carson laughed.

Michael laughed with him. "No such thing."

"That's what a spook would say," Carson laughed.

A small group of young men and women walked into the park, laughing and running around each other. They walked to the planes and began whooping and yelling as children sometimes do.

"Excuse me," the older gentleman stated. He walked to the small group and was talking as he had to Abby and Michael. Michael put his arm around Abby as they walked to the next plane.

"Jay would be in heaven here," Michael said with a smile. "I would be willing to bet he has flown about everything that is still in the air. We have talked about it before. He loves to be in the air."

"I am sure," Abby said. "We should try to see Jay and Janet when we can. They're always there for us when we need them."

There was a commotion, and they turned back. The small group of young adults was laughing at the older veteran as they surrounded him from three sides. The three girls sat back and laughed, as a fourth boy spray-painted on the plaque of the T2-C jet.

The three young men yelled at the Carson, "We will do as we want. We pay taxes, so this is ours."

"Yeah, who cares about his stuff," another boy yelled.

"Stop!" the man said.

"Or what?" the bigger of the three asked as he walked up to the veteran.

Michael stepped that direction, and Abby followed with him. "They are kids, Michael," she reminded in a quiet voice.

The veteran didn't waver nor back down. "You may be younger than me, but don't think that gives you any advantage."

The boy's eyes were full of fire as he pushed even closer. "You think?"

The veteran was probably 70, but it was obvious he was still in shape. Michael saw his arms flex and tense, ready for action. His fists circled and uncurled as he prepared for the worst. "It is time for you to go," the man said.

"Lookie here," one of the boys said, "another hero." He pointed toward Michael walking in their direction.

"None of your business, boy," the bigger boy said. "Walk away."

Michael nodded to Carson, "You ok?"

"I'm fine," Carson replied. "I guess I found the vandals I have been cleaning up after."

"I guess you did," Michael smiled.

"You don't need to worry," Carson said, "I got this."

"You ain't got nothin', old man," the bigger boy said and pushed Carson.

Michael smiled for a moment as the boy noticed Carson didn't give up much, and he had pressed against solid muscle. The boy reached back to swing, and the world went in slow motion. Carson stepped back as the boy swung, and Michael pulled two 6-inch Kunai throwing knives from his belt. The knives were woven into the belt and would have been unnoticeable except for the small rings. As Carson blocked the boy's punch, Michael threw the first blade toward the boy holding the spray can. The knife spun quickly and found its mark, piercing the spray-paint can and causing a massive rush of paint in the air, all over the boy holding it. The second knife was already in the air, flying towards the foot of the boy facing him. The blade went deep. Michael had placed it perfectly between the big toe and second toe of his shoe and embedded the knife into the ground. The boy tripped and fell forward, looking at his foot in amazement.

The girls all huddled together in shocked silence. The control they thought the boys had dissolved and the fun they were having was now gone. The other boy looked at the knife and stepped back away from the whole scene.

Michael moved forward to intercept, but as the boy swung at Carson, Carson blocked the punch and landed a solid gut punch. The boy to double over in pain, dropping to his knees and gasping for breath.

Carson surveyed the scene and saw one boy covered with paint, one trying to extract a knife from his shoe, the third shivering, while the fourth still tried to gasp for breath.

"Yep," Carson said. "I was right." His eyes glinted a little at Michael.

Abby walked up to Carson, "You ok?

Carson laughed, "Haven't had this much fun in a while."

Michael walked up to the boy effectively pinned to the ground by his shoe. The boy was frantic and was trying to pull the knife from his shoe. As Michael approached the boy glanced up with more than a little concern. Michael reached down and the boy closed his eyes expecting the worst. Michael pulled the blade from the ground and his shoe with no noticeable effort. Free, the boy opened his eyes still eying Michael. Michael smiled as he examined the blade and said to himself, "Awww, no blood."

He slid the blade back into his belt. The second blade lay on the ground still embedded in the spray can. The boy next to it, trying to get paint out of his eyes. Michael reached into his pocket and pulled out a small cloth. He put his foot on the can and pulled the blade from it. It had worked itself loose as the paint rushed out. Using the cloth, he mindlessly cleaned the blade as he walked back to Carson.

Carson pulled out his cell phone and hit a number. He explained on the phone that there was some trouble there and what had happened. He hung up and looked at Michael. "Thanks, I think."

"You think?" Michael asked.

"Haven't met many spooks," Carson said.

"Still haven't," Michael said.

"Guess not," Carson said. "I had this. You didn't have to do anything."

"I know you did," Michael replied. "Was just trying to help."

"Thank you for your service," Abby said and gave Carson a short hug.

The boys stood as MPs came to the area, and Michael and Abby walked back to the car. Michael turned and nodded to Carson. The veteran smiled, waved, and busied himself with the MPs, lining up the small group of young men and women. The DB9 backed up and shot out of the parking lot and onto the interstate.

A short drive later, they came to Kokomo, Indiana and stopped to see Big Ben, one of the world's largest bulls. Michael was not impressed, but Abby laughed as they wandered through the small park with the giant stuffed bull in the center.

"Well, this was not so thrilling," Michael said.

"Get in the spirit of it," Abby said.

Michael smiled a large fake smile and said, "What a load of bull!"

"That's it," Abby lapped his shoulder. "Work the thoughts behind it!"

Michael rolled his eyes as they walked back to the car. Abby poked him in the ribs a few times.

Their stop for the night was Indianapolis, Indiana, where race cars made the world go a little crazy each year. The hotel was unassuming as Michael would have wanted it. It was a chain hotel, but he paid in cash, so there were minimal questions. Abby and Michael went up to a room with a beautiful view of the interstate. Michael laughed at the irony.

"There was a time I would not have been caught dead in a hotel like this," he said.

"I know," Abby replied, "but it is only for one night. Tomorrow we will be on the road having fun and back in Kentucky for a little while."

Abby smiled and ran then jumped on Michael. He caught her easily in the air.

"Tough guy, huh," Abby snickered.

"Nope," Michael said back, holding her in the air inches from the ground.

"Yeah," Abby said, "I got your number."

"Yes, you do," Michael smiled.

"Well, I am gonna dial it right now," Abby said.

"Umm, that is pretty corny," Michael laughed.

Abby started giggling, grabbed Michael's head, and pulled him close.

Michael pulled Abby close, but she was still suspended over the ground. As she pressed against his body, Abby wrapped her legs around

Michael and whispered in his ear. "I love you, Michael."

Michael kissed her. It started as a slow, loving kiss, their lips barely touching. Rapidly, it progressed to feverish passion. Abby held Michael's head as the two kissed, and their tongues fought for domination. In the end, it was a tie.

Michael carried her to the king-sized bed. "I love you too," Michael said as he lowered her to the bed. "I love our life."

"That's pretty corny," Abby said with a wry smile, "but I love our life too."

Michael kissed Abby again as he took his shirt off. Moments later, they were naked on the bed.

Chapter 24

It turned out that the hardest part of getting out of a hospital is the paperwork. The hospital didn't seem as concerned about Jackson's leaving as they were about getting the liability forms signed and making sure someone was going to pay for the visit. John had already filed all the paperwork with them, but since they were leaving early, there were more and more forms ensuring that no one would want to leave unless they were told to leave. They were advised the surgery was still a major concern, but that Jackson's vitals were good. That could mean everything was fine, but it also could mean there could be an issue at any time. Every manner of doubletalk was used.

In the end, John simply said, "I would like to take my boy home," and finally, things started moving.

As the group waited, Kira's aunt arrived in the room. Jenny Calloway was a young woman of 40. She contrasted with Kira considerably as she was tall, well-built and had long flowing red hair. Her green eyes seemed to dance as they looked at you, and her pleasant smile was calming in a mysterious sort of way. When she arrived, she walked to John immediately. "What is my niece doing here with you?"

Alex introduced himself immediately. "You must be Kira's aunt. My name is Alex. Alex Brown," Alex took out his ID and showed it to the woman. "We have been making sure Kira has been safe after all that has happened."

"All that has happened?" Jenny started, "My brother died, my niece nearly raped, and a bunch of goons hanging around in a room is safe."

"Aunt Jenny," Kira started.

"Aunt Jenny nothing," Jenny continued. "Why in the world aren't there police here? And why is Kira still in this hospital? She could be better off somewhere else."

Alex was soothing, "Ma'am, there has been a lot happening. The police are involved and should have been right outside the door. A full investigation is running, but we were equipped to keep Kira safe."

"The army is necessary?" Jenny said, "There is something wrong with that picture. I doubt you can offer any more protection than the police here in Indy. I used to live here; they are-."

Alex cut her off. "- are very busy right now. Look, Miss..." Alex paused.

"Jenny," Jenny replied. "Jenny Calloway."

"OK, Jenny, the police are on this. But John is a friend, and we wanted to make certain he and his son were well protected. You are right. The Indianapolis police are amazing, but we offered to help keep John and Jackson safe, and it made sense for Kira to be with us too. That way we had all the people in question in one area. Let us know what you want to do, and we will help. If you don't want us involved, well, that is fine as well. We are just here to keep everyone safe."

"That didn't do my brother-." Jenny began.

Alex jumped in again, "That was before we got here. To be fair, John saved Kira, but your brother, well, we had no involvement in that, and the outcome was not good."

Jenny looked at the ground, "Yes, I know."

"So, where do we go from here?" Alex asked.

Jenny looked around. Jim quickly brought her a chair, and she sat down. "I just," she started, "Well, I don't know." Jenny's gruff beginning was replaced with a high level of unsureness. "I had all of this planned, but my brother," A tear welled up in her eyes, "Kira," a single tear fell down her cheek, "everything seems to be crushing down on me."

Alex knelt on the floor. "I understand Jenny," he said, "but we need to move now. Someone has tried to attack Kira here once. They may try again. Do you want to take her home, or should you come with us?"

"That's doesn't seem normal," Jenny pointed out.

"Nothing about this is normal," Jim finally opened his mouth and spoke.

It was John who spoke next. "Ma'am," the massive man said, "Ma'am, these are my friends. I know that doesn't mean much to you, but I have known them for a long time. If Alex says he will keep you safe, you can be assured he will keep you safe. So, Miss Kira is in good hands with him. So are you if you come along."

Jenny looked up at John's dark brown eyes. "I don't know," she said.

"Yes, you do, ma'am," John said softly. "You want Miss Kira to be safe. She is safest with us right now. So are you. Ma'am, you can go when all this is over, or when you want, but aren't you most sure that Miss Kira should be safe?"

"Well," Jenny started, "Yes, I am sure we need to be safe," she paused, "but how do I know?"

"We never know," John said. "We just try to do the best job we can as parents and hope we make good choices."

"What do I need to do?" Jenny asked.

"Nothing," Alex replied. "Nearly everything is complete, and Kira is not a patient, so we can just go. I just need to confirm our arrangements and get us picked up."

"I have a car," Jenny said.

"Good," Alex replied. "At least one of us will ride with you."

"Jenny," John said, "it is going to be all right. I know it is. I will make sure of it."

The group busied themselves with making arrangements. John was able to find a wheelchair for Jackson, and the doctors came in one last time. They had started trying to move at 6:00 AM, it was now 8:00 AM.

"You know, I normally would not let a patient go this quickly," the doctor started, "but you seem to be doing much better, Jackson. Do you know where you are going?"

"No, Doc," Jim said. "We probably will head up to Anderson while Jackson recuperates, and this gets figured out."

"Is there anything you need from me?" the doctor offered. "If you tell me where you are staying, I could come up and check on Jackson on my way home."

Jim smiled, "Maybe the new Holiday Inn up there. I heard it is nice."

"Does Jackson still need the IV?" Alex asked.

"No, in spite of the surgery, he was lucky. No lifting. We don't want it to start bleeding again," the doctor replied.

"Sounds good," the doctor said as he left the room. "I'll get the papers together and have the nurse remove the IV."

When the doctor was gone, Alex looked at Jim. "I said *maybe,* Alex," Jim replied.

They both laughed.

Alex picked up his phone and dialed, "Ronnie, we will come down to the lobby, are you there?"

There was a pause before Alex continued.

"Have Rachel look around while we are coming down. We have one with a car, Jim will be riding with Kira and her aunt. I will ride with all of you and Jackson."

Alex hung up the phone.

"Jim, take Jenny and go get her car. Run it up front next to Ronnie. We will all leave together. We will wait five, then come down with Kira and Jackson. You and Rachel can ride with Kira and Jenny. John and I will ride with Jackson and Ronnie." Alex said. "Keep your eyes open and let Rachel know what is going on."

"I always keep my eyes open, or else I would fall on my face," Jim laughed.

"Smartass," Alex said.

Jenny looked nervous, "Don't worry Jenny, Jim will take good care of you." Alex said. The two left the room with Jenny looking in her expensive purse for the keys to her vehicle.

A nurse came in and removed Jackson's IV, putting a bandage on it. She then began removing all of Jackson's monitors. She stopped and checked over the machines. She did not speak to anyone and quickly hurried about her business.

Alex looked at John, "Nothing like a good bedside manner."

John laughed.

"John let's get Jackson in the wheelchair," Alex continued.

Jackson was a big man, well, a big young man. He weighed well over 200 pounds, but John helped him put on clothes while Kira pretended to cover her eyes. John then lifted Jackson with no apparent effort, placing him lightly in the wheelchair.

Kira got behind the chair and held the handles.

John looked at her, "I will push."

Kira looked at him, "I think you would be better with Alex, watching us."

"She's right, John, Kira can help him. You and I will take front and back. Let's not make it look weird, though. Just one happy family," Alex said.

"Police are still out front," John said.

"I will take care of that," Alex stated.

Alex left the room. He was gone for several minutes and returned with a few sheets of paper.

"What's that?" John asked.

"Just some papers to make us look official," Alex said.

John picked up a stack of papers in a folder and handed them to Alex. "If you want to look official, at least get it right, sir."

Kira and Jackson laughed.

Alex looked at the stack of papers, "Really?"

"Yes, really," John said.

Alex took the papers and opened the door. "It's been five, let's go," Alex said and walked out the door, looking both ways.

The hall was a bustle of activity. People came and went constantly, and the officer outside the door walked to him. Alex wondered why Jenny hadn't seen him.

"Sir, I spoke to the sergeant on duty. He said to cooperate. Should I walk with you?" the officer asked.

"Thank you," Alex said, "but just wait here. It will keep the room looking occupied. Give us twenty minutes and then take off as you see fit."

"Yes, sir," the officer said.

Alex looked back, "OK, John, here we go."

Alex took the lead. Kira and Jackson came down the center as John walked less than a step behind but to the side of the wheelchair. It was a pretty easy walk to the elevator. They were not stopped or questioned along the way. The doctor walked past them, and it seemed he did not even notice. Still, Alex watched him out of the corner of his eye until he was out of sight."

The unlikely quartet reached the elevator together and waited for a moment.

"So far so good," Alex smiled at John.

John smiled his big smile then laughed.

"What's so funny," Kira asked.

"It is something we used to say when we were out," John paused, "together."

"What's the joke?" Jackson questioned.

The elevator opened. The group got in, Alex pressed "L", and they waited for the doors to close. No one else got on.

"It is from a movie," Alex quoted. "It goes, "Reminds me of that fella back home who fell off a ten-story building. As he was falling, people on each floor kept hearing him say, 'So far, so good.'" So, we used to say, 'so far, so good' when we weren't sure about what would happen next."

"Sounds more like you knew you were going to lose," Kira smirked.

"Well, we never did," Alex said, "and we laughed all the way. John and Jim used to go at it like little girls all the time."

John smiled, "We did not."

The door opened to the first floor. "Hard part is out of the way. Let's go," Alex said, and they began walking.

The elevator opened into a long white hallway with pictures conveniently placed all along the hall. Closed oak doors were spaced about 30 feet apart on their way to the lobby. The hall was nearly 15 feet wide, giving plenty of space for people to walk.

"Nice place for an ambush," Alex muttered.

John walked straight, a few steps behind Kira and Jackson.

A door opened to the right, and Alex spun to see who was coming. A young woman in a lab coat wandered by them mindlessly, not even acknowledging they were there.

"See Dad, no issues," Jackson said as he was rolled forward.

Alex looked back at John. They both sighed for a second and continued.

The lobby was less than 75 feet away when a small group of guys turned down the hall. They were mindlessly talking and laughing. John and Alex watched them as they approached. Alex counted three men in early 20s. As they walked past, the lead man nodded to Alex and they kept walking. John turned and watched them walk beyond them into the distance and go through the doors.

Two female nurses walked towards them in candy stripe outfits. They held clipboards to their chests as they walked and talked. Alex continued forward as the women paid them no mind. A few moments later, the two groups began to pass, and Alex leapt on the first girl. Kira stopped, and John looked on.

Alex struggled for a moment then looked at Kira and John. "Get Jackson to the car."

Kira looked at him. "What are you doing?"

The clipboard Alex had been wresting came free and fell to the ground. A Walther PPK with a silencer fell to the ground and bounced. Kira looked on, dumbstruck. She started pushing Jackson towards the door, picking up speed as she went. John grabbed the other woman's clipboard and pulled it away from her revealing another silenced PPK. John grabbed the weapon and with a practiced move removed the slide in seconds. He then threw both pieces in different directions where than bounced with metallic noises.

A spring shot loose from the barrel and lay near Alex.

"You know, you could have just pointed it at them and saved us some trouble," Alex yelled.

"Sorry, boss," John said. "I didn't think of that."

The woman struggling with Alex kicked upwards, hitting Alex in the groin. He doubled over. Reaching for the other PPK, the woman kicked it away from him then ran for it. Alex grabbed her by the leg, and she kicked him in the side as she fell. They both struggled on the ground.

John had grabbed the other woman by the wrist, and she flailed like a fish being pulled out of the water. She kicked at John, trying to bite him. One of her kicks caught John in the side with a glancing blow. Amazingly, he just lifted her off the ground with a full, outstretched arm. She grabbed at her straining wrist, trying to keep it from breaking under her weight then switched and tried to grab John's wrist.

Alex was struggling on the floor. The woman laughed.

"What the matter, Alex, don't want to hit a woman?" she laughed maniacally as she pulled closer and closer to the pistol.

A cowboy boot kicked the pistol away just as the woman reached it. The woman looked up at Rachel standing over her. Rachel grabbed the woman by her jacket. "You don't get to play the woman card on me. I have no problem fighting back."

Rachel picked the girl up as she struggled and kicked at her. Rachel merely smiled, then hit the woman with a haymaker punch that put her out cold.

The second woman looked on as Alex picked up the pistol. "Rachel, bring her with us."

John dropped the woman. Rachel grabbed her with great force and drug her along. There was some struggling for a second until Rachel grabbed her hair. "I can carry you little girl, but I would rather not and you would end up with a big headache."

The woman's struggles subsided. As they entered the lobby the police rushed in. Alex saw Franks walking in with several officers.

"Down the hall," Alex said.

"And her," Franks asked.

"She is going with us," Alex said.

"No can do Alex," Franks replied. "Police matter."

Alex considered for a moment, then nodded at Rachel who pushed the woman into Franks.

"All yours," Alex said.

An officer ran back, "Hall is empty."

Franks looked at him, "She was there a few seconds ago."

"Sure she was," Franks said as he put cuffs on the girl with him. "Where you headed?"

"Out," Alex said.

"Makes sense," Franks replied. "Keep in touch."

The group walked out to the cars waiting. Ronnie was driving the Suburban while Jim stood outside of a Range Rover behind them. Kira and Rachel got in the Range Rover as John helped Jackson in the back seat of the suburban and took a seat next to him. Alex and Ronnie were in front. They closed the doors and the two cars left the lot at a normal rate of speed.

Chapter 25

Walter Franks had a problem. It was called a lack of answers and too many questions. Officers were getting nervous and there was the matter of Sarena Prince. Her family was tied to many people in law enforcement. They wouldn't let everything stand for long.

Franks paced back and forth as he waited in the interrogation room. The room was small, non-descript and had a single table in the center. The wooden chairs were harsh and unyielding, making people squirm just by sitting in them. Which was why Franks was pacing, he really did not want to sit until he had to sit.

The woman being processed had no name and was not talking. Her fingerprints were not in the database, which wasn't unusual, but the scans took longer than normal, which was unusual. Franks paced some more and looked at the phone on the wall. Why did they still put phones on anything? It was not like anyone used them anymore.

Franks pulled out his cell phone and looked at the time. Processing and booking had become far more efficient. There was no reason it should have taken this long.

An officer walked into the room heading to Franks.

"Yates, right?" Franks asked.

"Yes, sir," Yates replied. "We have a problem, sir."

"What is it?" Franks asked.

"Your prisoner is dead," Yates replied as his eyes darter around. "We put her in holding, alone. When we went back to get her, she was dead."

"Dead?" Franks asked in a low tone. "How?"

"That's a problem too, sir," Yates stated. "She is just dead. No gunshot, wound, no nothing, just dead."

Franks slammed his hand down on the table, "What else can go wrong?"

"I'm not sure, sir," Yates said.

Franks looked up at him, "Really? It was rhetorical."

"Oh," Yates said.

"Let me know when they know cause of death," Franks stated as he searched his phone for a number.

Yates left the room and the door clicked shut. Before Franks could dial the phone rang.

"Brown here," came the voice.

"Alex, your prisoner is dead," Franks said.

"Expected as much," Alex replied. "Had James Bond written all over her."

"How's that?" Franks asked.

"Walther PPK with a silencer? Might as well be in a Bond film," Alex replied. "Anything else?"

"Where are you?" Franks asked.

"In the ether, visiting the ether bunny." Alex laughed.

"Now look, smartass," Franks began. "It's not even a good joke."

"Nice talking to you, Franks," Alex said, and the phone hung up.

Chapter 26

Sarah Collins picked up the phone.

"General Tarkington's office, how many I assist you?" she said in a pleasant voice.

"Good morning, Sarah. This is Alex, is the General in?" Alex asked.

"Of course, Alex. How are things going?" Sarah asked.

"They are going, Sarah. Is he in a good mood?" Alex asked.

"I am not sure what to call it," Sarah said. "This imposition on his language has been quite a challenge for him. He has been quite worked up about it. I would never say he is in a bad mood now, but he is definitely different. At least, he is trying to keep a good attitude."

"I think he always had a positive attitude as long as it is his point of view," Alex said.

"I am sure you should tell him that," Sarah laughed.

"I am sure I'll pass on that conversation," Alex laughed back.

"I take it you didn't call to discuss this with me and need to speak to him?" Sarah asked.

"Yeah, we have a situation as always," Alex said.

"Hold on, I'll get him," Sarah said, and the line went dark. The pause was not long.

"Tarkington," the General said in a near monotone.

"General, it's Alex," Alex said.

"No" there was an short pause. "I am aware of that obvious statement, Alex, did you require something?"

"No, sir," Alex said, "I just wanted to get you up to date. John and his son are with us now. We are on the way to a secure off-site location. We have had another attempt on us, and we have been driving around trying to lose a tail for a while."

"Your point?" Sam Tarkington asked.

"Well, sir," Alex stated, "this reads bigger than what we were thinking. I mean, I expected to help John, but there have been multiple murders and multiple attempts on John's boy, Jackson. I think we are in the middle of something a lot bigger than I expected."

"You think huh?" Tarkington asked. "There is a contact at the FBI, Tennison."

"He was supposed to meet us already. He hasn't even contacted us." Alex said.

"Find him," Tarkington said. "He knows something I'm sure. Don't get killed. I would be annoyed at that."

"Didn't know you cared, sir," Alex laughed.

"I don't," Tarkington said, and the line went dead.

"What's the story?" John asked.

"First, we get you safe. Then we need to have a visit with the FBI," Alex said.

"Do you want me to go with you?" John asked.

"No, I want you to take care of your son and Kira. Let us handle the tough stuff, you've earned this," Alex said.

"OK," John said, "but if you need me, I'll be there."

"I know John, but this time we are here to help you." Alex looked at John who was not scared, but obviously relieved.

Alex's phone rang. "Yeah?" Alex hung up. "We think we have lost the tail; we are heading to the hotel."

Ronnie had found a nice chain hotel with a parking structure and mall nearby. Ronnie was learning that the best way to not be found is to leave no trace. This was a lesson they had run into several times. They pulled into the mall parking lot and got out of the vehicles next to a church bus. John helped Jackson get to the front seat of the bus. Jim drove and soon they were a block away at the hotel. The bus pulled up to the door, and everyone but Jim and Rachel got out.

As John helped Jackson into the hotel, Alex and Ronnie watched the door then followed them in with Kira and Jenny close.

The room was a top floor executive suite, and after a short elevator ride, they walked into a well-furnished two-bedroom suite with a large board room. John helped Jackson into the second bedroom, and Alex came followed. Jackson's wound was seeping, but he said it did not hurt and he was ok. John checked the wound, cleaned it, then rebandaged it. The new bandage was cleaner than the original.

As they got Jackson settled, the door opened, and Jim and Rachel walked in. They looked to the side of the boardroom and living room and found two single cots.

Alex looked at Jenny and Kira. "You two take the other bedroom. The rest of us will sleep out here. John and Jackson will be in the smaller bedroom.

"Sir, I got the cots for you and I, sir," Ronnie said in his respectful voice.

"I have Rachel and Jim on either side of this room. You said defensible and I thought they would be able to cover from each side if things got bad sir. I also checked; this hotel has aluminum wall inserts. If we have to, we can go through a wall to the next room on either side." Ronnie handed the keys to Jim and Rachel.

"Sir, I figured you and I could take shifts watching the room sir." Ronnie continued. "I didn't know about Kira's aunt so they will have to share."

Alex smiled but it was Rachel who said, "Good job, little guy. You continue to surprise me. Already places for Kira and Jenny. Very nice, very nice."

Alex looked at Ronnie. "Good job Ronnie. We will have four shifts at night. Jim and Rachel can keep an eye on things from their rooms."

"Umm, sir, I also got this Reolink camera. It runs on battery and I have the computers for all of us set up to watch it. I put it in the hall under the hotels camera so it looks like it should be there."

"Wow," Rachel said again. "Way to overdo!"

"Good job, Ronnie," Alex said again.

"Thank you, sir," Ronnie said, and they began to spread out. The room configuration made it easy for the group to meet and still maintain control of the area. Ronnie had not only set up cameras in the hall, but on the lot and the main lobby giving them access to a lot of tactical information if they needed it.

"Sir, there is one more thing," Ronnie said looking down.

"What is it Ronnie?" Alex asked.

Ronnie went to the computer and played the video stream. It showed a man and woman entering last night as the time code ran at 11:00 PM.

Jim looked over, "So what?"

Ronnie made an adjustment and blew the picture up.

It was Michael Masterson and Abby Tarkington.

Chapter 27

Michael and Abby woke to the sounds of the traffic and talking in the hall. They lay naked in the king-sized bed, Abby's leg draped over Michael's legs while she held his shoulder and curled on the pillow loosely pulled onto him. Michael's muscular arms wrapped around Abby and he stared at the ceiling.

"I don't miss this," Michael said in an absent-minded drone.

"Miss what, Michael?" Abby asked. "Me?"

Michael's arm flexed and brought her over to him, intending to kiss her.

Abby stopped him, "Morning breath."

Michael held her tight. "I don't care." He kissed her slowly, and she yielded.

Michael eased up. "I don't miss the hotels, the city, the bustle and talking everywhere.

Abby looked at him and smiled, "I know, I don't miss it either. Well... much."

"Much?" Michael looked amused.

"Well, Michigan was a turn up if you ask me. I don't want for anything with you, but sometimes it is nice to see people, nice to go shopping. In Ivel, we had, well, not much. Dubois, well, not much, and Michigan we have some stores within an hour, but not many. What I mean is, we have each other, but sometimes it is nice to get a new pair of underwear." Abby laughed.

Michael laughed, "OK, underwear is now a deciding factor in choosing a home?"

Abby hit him on the chest and said, "You know what I mean silly."

"I do. I do know what you mean," Michael replied. "There is a lot I was not thinking of when I got the houses. I should have talked to you about them, but I didn't want to bother you with details. I had them all built as we graduated college, we were together, but I didn't put every detail out there, just never seemed necessary."

"I know Michael, but I am a big girl. I can kick some ass too so I think I can handle some decisions in our life," Abby said.

Michael kissed her again. "I will talk more to you, but to be fair, I did all this a long time ago."

"I know, Michael," Abby said. This time she kissed him and moved from his lips slowly to his neck, then worked her way down to his chest, nibbling along the way. Abby's long hair draped over Michael and he was lost in the moment.

There was a loud knock at the door.

"Umm, housekeeping," a voice came.

"Housekeeping?" Abby asked.

Michael was up with underwear on and a FN 5.7 pistol in his hand.

"We have late checkout. 1:00," Michael whispered.

Michael walked to the door and slid as close to the wall as he could while Abby put on a shirt and shorts. He slid the locking bar back from the door and opened it slightly. The door swung open a little further and a hand appeared. Michael grabbed the arm with his right hand and pulled it forward while aiming with his left hand. The intruder fell to the ground and turned over.

"Jim?" Abby asked.

Michael didn't waver the pistol. It was aimed squarely one inch above Jim's nose.

"Should I have said room service?" Jim asked. "You know if you fire that thing it will probably take out the people below us. And the ones below them too."

"They don't have room service here," Michael said in monotone. "And concrete center floors provide minimal chance for penetration."

"I know, it sucks," Jim said as he began to stand. "The room service that is."

"What are you doing here, Jim?" Michael asked as his weapon tracked Jim's eyes.

"Well, it is a funny story," Jim said. "We apparently picked the same hotel to be on the low down with as you did. This has nothing to do with you, but we thought it would be good to let you know we were here in case we crossed paths."

"We will be leaving shortly," Michael said.

"Leaving? You are a tree now?" Jim laughed.

"Always the jokester," Michael said as Abby walked to him.

"Jim's a friend, Michael," Abby said. "We know him."

"The odds of this chance meeting are," Michael began.

"Astronomical is what Ronnie said," Jim finished.

Michael squinted his eyes at Jim, then let the pistol drop to his side. "Who is here?"

Jim looked at Michael and relaxed a little. "You know, I really didn't want to see how good a shot you are in close quarters again." Jim lowered his head for a moment then looked at the two. Michael was only in black underwear holding his black 5.7 in his hand loosely. His muscles were well defined, and he seemed to signify pure power. Jim had sparred with him before and been quite impressed.

Abby on the other hand was much shorter that Michael but was beautiful beyond compare. She wore a dark red tee shirt and he supposed shorts but the shirt all but covered them. Her long flowing blonde hair was slightly mussed but still she looked amazing. Even though she looked small, Jim knew she could stand her ground almost anywhere and with nearly anyone.

"Ronnie, Rachel, and Alex are with me. This was supposed to be easy, but it has been a bit of a shit show so far," Jim said.

Michael smiled, then started to laugh. "Housekeeping, really?"

Jim shrugged, "Look, Alex was going to pass, and I thought it would be good to let you know we were here. In case we run into each other."

"OK, you have let us know," Michael said. "Thank you."

"Umm, could you put some clothes on? You are giving me a fat complex," Jim said.

Abby laughed. "Oh Jim, you are cute, and we know it." Abby jumped over the edge of the bed and grabbed an overnight bag. She pulled out a few things and scurried to the bathroom. "I'm gonna get dressed."

Michael raised an eyebrow. "You do that." Michael looked at Jim. "Why so bad?"

Jim sat down on a small desk chair. "Well, it seems nothing is as it seems. We got a call from a friend from way back, his son had been shot. It was an impossible shot, but it happened. Then the hospital was attacked twice, and a lead FBI agent came up missing trying to determine the point of origin."

"Who was the agent," Michael asked.

"Her name was Sarena Prince," Jim stated.

"I know of her," Michael began, "She is quite an expert on ballistics. I read some of her papers on long range trajectories. They were good but lacked practical experience. She tried to debunk one of the shots I made, saying it was impossible until the camera footage was sent to her anonymously."

"Is there anything you aren't good at?" Jim asked as Michael put on a black t-shirt.

"I'm sure there are lots of things I am not good at, I just work every day to reduce the list," Michael said. "For example, I am not good at music, well, at all, but I will learn."

Jim heard the shower come on. He snickered to himself that he was in a room with a master assassin and his girlfriend was naked a few feet away.

"Anyway," Michael continued, "If they sent her on the case there is something difficult to determine."

"We expect this other agent, Tennison, is going to be pushing harder now," Jim stated.

"Tyrel?" Michael asked.

"Yeah, know him too? Play pinochle together?" Jim quipped.

"Not exactly," Michael said. "Any way we can sit down for a few and discuss this with Alex?"

Jim eyes Michael, "Umm, why?"

"Remember when we talked about how I got started? Remember I worked with a group?" Michael asked.

"Yeah, I remember, you said it when Lisa and I visited you once," Jim replied with a soft edge in his voice.

"Well, Tennison is poking into things that group did, there may be a connection," Michael said.

"That's just great. You coming after us now?" Jim asked.

"No, not really," Michael said, "I have not had contact with them in some time. They were a little upset at me when I killed one of their members years ago. He had contracted me to kill his wife. Gave me a story about how she was cheating, involved in drug trafficking and abusing their children. After doing some recon I found it was him that was cheating, involved in drug trafficking and abused her and the children and was just trying to skip a messy divorce, so I killed him."

"And saved her a messy divorce," Jim laughed.

"I suppose so," Michael said. "Anyway, if they are involved you may be outgunned."

"Swell," Jim said.

"Swell?" Michael asked. "Now there's a word you don't hear every day."

"Sorry, habit," Jim sighed.

"I will go talk to Alex, we are in room 442, just down the hall," Jim said.

"I'll get dressed. Abby and I will walk down," Michael said.

Jim stood, "Thanks for all the bad news," he laughed.

"Don't mention it," Michael said as he opened the door, FN 5.7 still in hand, and looked up and down the hall. "I'll call you first."

Michael closed and locked the door and considered his past. He had worked with these people a lot. He had also worked in the past with the group they were discussing. It would be an interesting crossing of swords.

He heard the shower still running and opened the bathroom door. Steam billowed out.

"Michael is that you?" Abby asked.

In a high voice he said, "No, it's the boogie man," and laughed a little.

"Well get in here and boogie with me, boogie man," Abby said.

Michael took off his clothes and got in the shower with Abby.

Chapter 28

Tyrel Tennison was angry. Not only had he misplaced a good agent, no one knew where his witnesses were. And no one knew anything about the two, yes two, attacks on the hospital.

He had never been more certain that this time he would uncover something new about the group killing people around the country. Other analysts saw them as unrelated events, but the trend was simple, where justice was somewhat misguided, this group seemed to dispense its own type of justice.

Tyrel had been following them for some time. It was a pet passion to think there was a group of untouchable ninja gunmen out there who killed for what they thought was the greater good. This time it appeared they missed. Everything fit the MO except the target. Why shoot a young black man? Why try to clean it up? It didn't make sense.

Tyrel arrived at the small café where detective Franks had suggested they meet.

Walking in, he looked around and saw nothing, so he walked to the counter and ordered a small black coffee.

Minutes later, Franks walked in. He had done a review of Franks and walked to him.

"Want coffee?" Tyrel asked.

"Sure," Franks replied.

Tyrel turned and said, "Make it two."

They sat down near the door. "Where is my witness?" Tyrel asked.

"With Tarkington's group," Franks replied.

"Where are they?" Tyrel asked.

"No idea," Franks said. "You were supposed to meet them, right?"

"Yeah. Plane was delayed," Tyrel said.

"Well, they have the kid, his father and the girl," Franks said.

"What new happened?" Tyrel asked.

"As they were leaving the hospital, they were attacked again. It was tense, but they got out. We got one arrest out of it, she wasn't talking and expired in the holding pen before I could talk to her," Franks said.

"Must have been embarrassing losing a potential informant," Tyrel said. "Any idea where Tarkington's crew is?"

The barista brought over their coffee. Franks grabbed sugar from the table and shook the packets, then tore two open and poured them in his cup. Tyrel just sipped his cup.

"Not a clue," Franks replied. "But they are probably in town. Your turn."

"My turn?" Tyrel asked.

"What the hell is going on?" Franks questioned. "And why here, why now?"

"I would say neither of us knows any more than the other." Tyrel said.

"What about all these cases you talk about?" Franks asked.

"A series of unfortunate events. Strange occurrences. People let out of jail that suddenly die. Corrupt officials that go missing and are found shot. Long distance kills from seemingly nowhere. It all adds up to nothing, but it is a difficult nothing to swallow if you consider the numbers. There are hundreds of these. Dozens happen per year. In the end, it is hard to guess the how, but the why keeps coming back to vengeance or justice or something similar." Tyrel recanted.

"Any leads?" Franks asked.

"None I can give you for now, but who knows, this may be the break to point them out. It will be hard to say," Tyrel said. "There is not a distinct pattern except that there is no pattern. It seems like dozens of, if not more, different people killing. No money trail we can find, no communication."

"Are you sure it is there?" Franks asked.

"Yeah, I am sure," Tyrel replied. "My commanders are not always as excited about it, but I am sure."

"What do you need from me?" Franks asked.

"I need to talk to Tarkington's group," Tyrel said. "I need to talk to them sooner rather than later."

"I will see what I can do," Franks said. "I don't have a number, but I am sure they will turn up looking for answers as well."

"Sorry about Sarena," Tyrel said.

"Tell her brother," Franks replied. "I liked the girl, but she didn't much like me. She may still turn up. We are scouring the area."

"Where are her files?" Tyrel asked.

"In the car," Franks said, "I have a USB drive copy."

"OK, I will head out to the site. You still have someone there?" Tyrel asked.

"Yeah," Franks replied, "I will call and let them know you are coming."

Tyrel stood, "Let's solve this and both be heroes."

"Yeah, and find Sarena," Franks said.

"That would keep my butt out of the fire and keep a good agent on the force," Tyrel agreed.

Chapter 29

The phone rang in the room. Alex picked it up.

"Hello," Alex said.

"OK," he replied the voice. "We are all here."

Moments later, there was a knock at the door. Jim opened the door and Michael and Abby stepped in.

"Cleaned up really good there," Jim said.

Michael smiled at him. Abby was wearing a white pant outfit with a white blouse, while Michael was dressed all in black. The Under-Armor t-shirt fit tight and Michael looked like a Ninja bodybuilder in the outfit.

"Michael," Alex started, "It was quite a surprise to see you on the cameras. I am glad it was just random."

"What do you mean?" Michael asked in an irritated voice.

"Well, we are here investigating a nearly impossible sniper shot, and well," Alex began.

"I am retired," Michael stated. "If I wasn't, you would have never known what happened."

Abby stepped between them, "Boys, we are friends, remember." She looked into Michael's crystal blue eyes, "Remember?" Michael shrugged. Abby turned to Alex, "Alex, you should be ashamed of yourself for even thinking that."

Alex looked down for a moment.

"Who has saved your life several times now?" Abby asked.

"Yep," Alex said. "I'm sorry Michael, it is just the shot seems impossible, we have FBI missing, people after us, and then you were here. I made a mistake, I am sorry."

Michael looked around the room, "We should have gotten this room Abby."

Abby laughed, "Sure we should have."

"I said I was sorry," Alex repeated.

Michael turned to Alex, his blue eyes seeming bluer, "I heard you. Not sure if you have the message yet, I retired. I think I may have helped you a few times as well."

John walked into the room and Kira and Jenny from the other side.

"Jenny, John, Kira, this is Michael and Abby," Alex said.

Michael nodded, but Abby walked to Kira, "Hi Kira," shook her hand, then Jenny's, before heading to John. John's massive hand dwarfed Abby's but she smiled. "Wow, that's one big hand."

Alex put out his hand beckoning towards the large boardroom table. Ronnie was sitting at the table with Rachel and Jim. Alex sat down next to them. The table had room for 10 and Michael sat across from Jim at the end of the table.

"Jim says you may have an idea of what is going on?" Alex asked.

"I have not confirmed anything. I wanted to talk to you first," Michael began. "There is a possibility this is part of a large group that is multi-national."

"What do you mean?" Ronnie asked.

Michael looked at Ronnie, "Well, I used to do jobs for a group that started in Kentucky. A few big horse farms were having issues with people getting away with things they shouldn't get away with. They all put together some money and built a shell company. It has a name that that changes occasionally, but the name they used initially was Vengeance

Incorporated. Their mission statement was simply "Thou shalt not get away with it". I read the news clips after Jim left the room and got access to Indy's Police files."

"How did you..." Alex began, "Never mind."

Michael continued, "As I was saying, I looked it over, and this would not be a normal job for them. Jackson was a good kid and in no trouble, and Kira was as well. Based on Kira's story though, her dad may have been involved and tried to get a favor. If so, they are out of bounds for their normal mode. You may think it terrible, but everyone I killed for them was a murderer, a rapist, or worse."

Jenny jumped in, "Why are we talking to this man, he is a killer by his own admission."

Alex looked at her with a stern expression and she was quiet, "Sorry Michael, they should probably be in the other room."

Michael continued, "No issue, she has all the right in the world to accuse me, but Vengeance Incorporated made the world safer for people like her when the law didn't work."

"You really believe that," Rachel said.

"I do," Michael replied, "I may seem cold and heartless, because at times I can be, but the first hit I did for them was a child molester serial killer. When I took him, he had a child wrapped up in a rug in his trunk ready to kill again. Ask him how it felt to be saved. He would be old enough for you to talk to now. Ask him how it feels to be alive. Ask his parents if they would rather I would have skipped that job."

The room was quiet.

"Anyway," Michael went on, "there is a huge network and a lot of it is ex-servicemen, veterans who have been set aside. Some mercs, and some citizens with special skills. It is all very organized."

"So why do you think it is them," Alex asked.

"Jim said you are talking to Tyrel Tennison. He is obsessed with the group. You can bet if he is involved, he thinks it has something to do with them," Michael replied.

"So how do we find out, and how do we stop these attempts on Jackson and Kira?" Jim asked.

"If you want, I can make a few calls. No promises," Michael said.

Alex looked at John, "John, you ok with that?"

"I just want Jackson to be safe," John said. "If you trust this man, so do I."

Alex looked at Michael, then to Abby, "Thank you, please make the calls."

"No promises," Michael said.

"Understood," Alex said as Michael stood up. "And Michael, I am sorry I made a bad assumption."

"Come to think of it," Michael said, "I probably would have made the same assumption."

Abby and Michael left the room.

"Do you trust him?" Jenny asked.

Alex put his head in his hands, "Ma'am, if it was Michael, he is right, we would all have been dead already."

Chapter 30

Back in the room, Michael opened his bag and pulled out a small black leather case. Opening it revealed four small cell phones lined in a row. All of them seemed exactly the same and were obviously new. Michael took the first phone out and dialed a number. He waited for a few moments.

"Mainstream Travel," came a voice.

"God I could use a cruise, maybe for two," Michael said.

"Mikey?" came the voice. "Haven't heard from you in quite a while, since that ex-girlfriend thing."

"I'm trying to retire," Michael said.

"You retired when you took out a client, even if he was a bad person," the voice replied.

"I wish you would tell everyone knocking on my door that," Michael stated.

"I'm sure you didn't call for a job," the voice said. "What do you need?"

"Answers. But I think I need to talk to the CEO," Michael said.

"The CEO would probably love to talk to you, but I am not certain if I can get him," the voice replied.

"It's important," Michael said.

"It always is," the voice stated. "Can you give me a topic for discussion to pass along?"

"Indy," Michael said.

There was a pause. "Please repeat that?"

"Indy," Michael said again.

"Hold on," the line went quiet. Then there were a few clicks.

"Michael, how good to hear from you," the voice came.

"How is it being the CEO?" Michael asked.

"Dreadful," the CEO replied, "I am up to my neck in paperwork. I never get to shoot anymore."

"I would think that would drive you crazy. You need the practice," Michael said.

There was echoing laughter on the phone. "Still shooting that 1903A at the ranges?"

"Not often, I do from time to time though," Michael said.

"So... what about Indy, Michael? You piqued my curiosity?" the CEO asked.

"Well, are you involved?" Michael asked.

"Heavens what a question," the CEO stated. "Involved in what exactly?"

"I'm pretty sure you know what," Michael said. "I am in Indy right now and have been asked a question I cannot answer. Given what I know, I certainly hope you aren't involved as it would not fit the company I had associations with."

"Of that I am sure," the CEO replied.

"But certain things point to an association that makes me," Michael measured his pause, "uncomfortable."

"Hypothetically, Michael, do you see yourself becoming involved in this unfortunate incident in Indy?" the CEO asked.

"Hypothetically, I've not decided," Michael replied.

"Until your unfortunate customer service incident, you were the best customer service employee that we have ever had the pleasure of contracting," the CEO stated. "If there was involvement in the customer service incident in Indianapolis, it was not on the behalf of the board or of me, and as you know, we are the only ones who can authorize any customer service actions. It has come to my attention that certain individuals may be involved from the customer service department but are acting outside the guidelines of the corporation. With that in mind, I can say no, we are not involved but also must say yes, we are at risk."

"That's about what I expected," Michael said.

"The additional cleanups on multiple aisles are also not authorized by the corporation, and as such we cannot admit culpability in any said acts," the CEO continued. "We are currently trying to resolve the situation with some difficulty. It seems the shift in question has many supporters and they have stopped any elimination of further support in an unacceptable fashion."

"I expected that as well," Michael said. "This hasn't happened before."

"As you know, we hold our standards quite high, and as such this has been avoided," the CEO said. "The customer service offering in that area appears to have defined their own sub-corporation and we have been told to, hmm," the CEO seemed to look for the words, "'bite it' concerning our standards and morals."

"I bet that was frustrating," Michael said.

"More so than your mistake," the CEO stated. "At least when you presented your evidence, we knew we had made a mistake authorizing the service expenditure, but we still had to terminate your involvement in the corporation."

"I was well aware of my decision," Michael replied.

"So, I digress. I briefly spoke to the board, and they are quite terse at the moment. If you would be willing to terminate the customer service department in Indy, we would be pleased to give you 5 times your normal bonus plus expenses," the CEO said.

"Let me think about it," Michael replied.

"Michael," the CEO said, "as you know I am quite fond of you. I enjoyed our little shooting matches even though I lost. Be aware, if you interfere without my knowledge it could be a detriment to you."

Michael smiled. "I understand. You also understand the obvious counterstatement."

"Why do you think we leave you alone?" the CEO replied. "Your customer service skill is without compare. I dare say, you would have made the board rich had we not already been rich."

"I will be in touch today," Michael said. He paused a moment. "You should also know, Tarkington's group is involved, I have no control over them."

"I understand, Michael. I know you have the proper confidentiality and honor in place as well. I am sure you will handle the situation with your friends as needed," the CEO said. "I look forward to hearing from you soon."

"You will," Michael said, and the line went blank.

Michael turned off the phone, pulled the chip from it and broke it in half. He then pulled another chip from a small compartment in the folder, put it in the phone and placed the phone back in the case, zipped it, and put it away.

Abby was listening. She walked to him and sat down on his lap, "So?"

"So, it was and wasn't them," Michael said.

"What do we do?" Abby asked.

"Well, they were willing to pay me 2.5 million to clean it up," Michael said. "You could build a store next to a house for that."

Abby poked Michael in the chest, "Sure I could, but I shouldn't. I like our privacy as well."

"I'm torn, I can let Alex and Jim handle this and we can leave, but the CEO took my call, and that is something quite new." Michael pondered.

"Maybe you should take care of it," Abby said. "From what you've told me, and that is not a lot, this group might be tough for Alex and Jim and their group."

"Who knows, the CEO said the group went rogue," Michael said. "We need to talk to Alex."

"Let's go," Abby said.

"Eager, aren't we?" Michael laughed.

"Get your butt in gear," Abby said.

Michael turned around and bounced up and down, "This butt?"

Abby slapped his butt hard. "Yes, that one."

Michael laughed. Opening the door, he checked the hallway and walked towards the group's rooms.

Chapter 31

Tyrel was at the initial shooting site, reviewing notes left by Sarena.

"Where are you?" he muttered to himself, wondering why anyone would have taken an agent investigating a crime scene.

There appeared to be only one obvious point of origin, and they had ruled it out. He looked in the distance at the warehouse. "That would have been one heck of a shot," he said to himself.

He looked at the drawings Sarena had made. The trajectory was doable for maybe 20 people in North America. The alternatives Sarena had in scribbled notes were a helicopter, a cherry picker in a lot, a UFO and a falling bullet from Neptune. "Yes, Sarena, I miss you," Tyrel again spoke to himself.

Tyrel started pacing the site. He was looking for an answer that just wasn't there. Maybe there was something in the warehouse feeds. Maybe there was something else. It had to be the warehouse.

He flipped through the notes again. It was time to visit Stephanie at Quality Castings.

Tyrel got into the rental car and nodded to the officer guarding the site. Tyrel put on a Bluetooth headset and dialed Franks.

"I think the site is done," Tyrel said as Franks answered.

"What?" Franks asked.

"There is no need to keep the site all buttoned up anymore," Tyrel repeated. "We have everything we can get out of it."

"Really?" Franks asked, "What makes you so sure?"

"Did you read her report?" Tyrel asked. "She is sure it came from the Quality Castings, and that means they may be involved with her disappearance as well."

"Really?" Franks said.

"I think you like that word," Tyrel said, "My mom would have made me stop using a word like that if I said it too much."

"Really?" Franks laughed.

"Yeah, Really," Tyrel said. "I am heading to Quality Castings now to talk to Stephanie Wise and see if she has the footage we requested. I don't see it anywhere."

"Never got it," Franks said.

"Curious," Tyrel replied. "Anyway, it is only a few minutes away."

"Stephanie is not too cooperative," Franks said. "Sarena asked questions and she hid behind ITAR."

"I saw that in the notes, but I am having issues finding contracts in their name. We will see," Tyrel said.

"Want backup?" Franks asked.

"No, I want my witnesses. Have you found them?" Tyrel quipped.

"Not yet," Franks replied. "Waiting for the call from Alex or his group."

"Keep me posted," Tyrel said, "If something happens to me, or you don't hear from me, send in the clowns."

"Nice," Franks said.

"Hey, it is a joke." Tyrel laughed and hung up the phone.

Moments later, Tyrel's phone rang, "Tennison." He spoke into the headset.

"Tyrel Tennison?" the voice asked.

"Yes," Tyrel replied.

"This is Alex Brown," Alex stated, "We were expecting you at the crime scene yesterday."

"Plane delays," Tyrel said. "You have my witnesses," Tyrel said dryly.

"I do," Alex stated. "They are safe."

"I can get them safer," Tyrel replied.

"I doubt it," Alex said, "but we need to meet."

"Where," Tyrel asked.

"Shoot Point Blank," Alex said, "Range off 31."

"When," Tyrel asked.

"2 hours," Alex said.

"Don't trust me?" Tyrel asked.

"It's been a long day Tyrel, I don't know who to trust," Alex said. "We'll see how it goes."

"Understood," Tyrel replied, "You just need to understand this is my investigation, not yours."

"Got it," Alex said. "You need to understand that Jackson and Kira will be safe no matter whose investigation it is."

"Got it," Tyrel replied.

"I am headed to Quality Castings," Tyrel noted. "If I am late, it could be bad."

"You won't be late," Alex said.

"Why is that?" Tyrel asked.

"If you are late, I won't be there," Alex said, and the line went blank.

Chapter 32

The group sat around the hotel boardroom table. Abby and Michael had come in and sat down at the head of one side.

"Is it them?" Alex asked.

"Yes and no," Michael stated. "You have to understand I will be impartial here. I also will not help you with anything to bring down the group. I am considering helping solve the issue here in Indy."

"You would side with these criminals?" Rachel asked.

"I will side independently," Michael replied. "You are as much a criminal as they are sometimes."

"Whoa, Whoa, Whoa!" Jim exclaimed. "Let's not get all our panties in a bunch." Jim was standing now. "Michael and Abby are not obligated to help us, at all."

Alex looked at Jim, "You giving the orders now?"

"No," Jim replied, "but this can get out of hand really quick."

"You're right," Alex said. "Michael, what can you do and what can you not do?"

"I can help you get the people behind Jackson's shooting, and the subsequent attacks," Michael said, "I won't help you go any further."

"If we capture some of them, and they help, you won't interfere," Alex said.

"I will not, but it is likely you will not capture anyone," Michael stated in a dry tone.

"Why is that?" Rachel asked.

"They will choose to die before saying anything, even if they are out of the main group," Michael replied.

"What's next?" Rachel asked.

"First, I meet with Tyrel at the range," Alex said. "Then we go to whatever Michael gives us and finish this thing."

"Mind if I tag along?" Michael asked.

Alex looked at Michael, "Sure, we leave in 30."

Jenny spoke up, "We need some things if we are staying for any length of time. I have 2 outfits, but Kira has nothing clean, and the hotel that packed her did not pick up her toothbrush. We need at least a change of clothes and well, a few other things."

"What other things?" Alex asked.

"Girl things," Jenny smirked.

Alex looked at the table, "Can you make a list? Someone will get it for you."

Rachel laughed, "I guess Ronnie can go shopping for girl stuff?"

"No," Alex said, "I was thinking you would."

"Me, shopping?" Rachel repeated. "Not it."

Jim laughed, "So we are down to playing *not it*?"

"I would rather be in a straight-up fight then shop any more than I have to," Rachel replied.

Abby spoke up, "Make the list, I will do it. If anyone wants to come, they can."

Alex looked at Michael, "That ok?"

"Ask her. It's her choice, not mine," Michael said.

Abby looked at Alex, "It is fine," she looked at Kira's aunt Jenny,

"Jenny, right? You can go with me."

"But Kira," Jenny started.

Alex replied, "Ronnie, John, Jim, and Rachel will stay at the hotel with Jackson and Kira. Michael and I will go to the range. Abby and Jenny will get whatever we need."

"Cheetos," Jim said.

"Cheetos?" Rachel asked. "Cheetos make your hands orange."

"OK, what do you want miss snack king?" Jim chided.

"How about pretzels?" Rachel asked.

"Pretzels and Cheetos," Jim said.

"How about we get some snacks and call it a day?" Alex said, trying to take back control.

"Good idea," Jim said. "We also have no food, and pizza will only go so far. I may starve."

"Make me a list," Abby said, "I will take care of it."

"Michael, I am not sure how Tyrel will take you being there. I mean, he may not know you, but I don't know him." Alex said in a low voice.

"It is a gun range, I will fit right in until we can talk to him," Michael said.

"I suppose so," Alex replied. "We will play it how it goes. Tyrel really wants the whole group."

"I know," Michael said, "but he may settle for this one since it is personal."

"You may be right," Alex replied.

John went in with Jackson and checked on him, "Dad, I feel ok."

"You need to rest," John said. "Maybe miss Kira will come play a game with you."

"Maybe you could get my PS4 or my X-Box," Jackson smiled.

"No, I can't do that," John replied.

"How about my phone?" Jackson continued.

"No son," John said, "not until we are sure you will be safe. Everything can be tracked, and I don't want anyone showing up looking for you or Kira."

"OK, so what can we play?" Jackson asked.

"Chess, of course," John said.

"Oh joy," Jackson said. "Do we even have a chess set?"

"No, but I can get one," John replied. "You rest, I will get something."

John went back into the main room and walked up to Abby, "Can you get some games or something for Jackson and Kira to do please, ma'am?" John reached into his pocket and pulled out money, "I have some money that will help."

"John, right?" Abby said in a low voice, "I will take care of it, put your money away."

"Thank you, Abby," John said and walked back into the room with Jackson.

Alex looked at Michael, "We should go so there is no question on anything," Alex stated, "You need something to shoot?"

"Which range?" Michael asked.

"Shoot Point Blank," Alex replied.

"They have rentals," Michael said. "I have a weapon on me, but I would rather leave it in reserve."

Alex shook his head, "OK, let's head." The door opened. "We are out of here," Alex said to everyone. "Thank you, Abby, for having a shopping adventure."

"Thank you, Alex," Abby giggled then rushed to Michael. She stood on her tiptoes and kissed him, "Thanks for being you, Michael." She said. "Have you decided?"

"We don't need the money, but we might need a favor someday," Michael replied.

"I trust whatever you do," Abby said. "I will be back here as soon as I get a few things."

"Our room or here," Michael asked.

"I will just hang out here for a while," Abby said. "Should be fun."

"I will see you soon then," Michael said, then he reached down and kissed her again.

"143," Michael said.

"I love you too," Abby replied, as Michael left with Alex.

Chapter 33

Tyrel had been waiting for nearly 20 minutes when Stephanie Wise came into the lobby.

"Detective Tennison?" Stephanie asked. Stephanie was dressed in a black pantsuit that fit her like a glove, her tall frame was definitely in good shape and Tennison was impressed with her. Her long red ponytail hung behind her and was a crisp as her clothing.

"Agent Tennison," Tyrel replied. "You met with another agent, Sarena Prince."

"Yes. About the unfortunate shooting near here," Stephanie said. "I was not expecting anyone today and I don't have that long. How can I help you?"

"I hate to correct you Miss Wise, but you have as long as I need you. A boy was shot here, several people have been killed, and an agent and a friend of mine has disappeared while investigating the shootings. Unless you want this plant shut down and fifty agents climbing up your ass you will give me all the time I need."

Stephanie was very cool, "Of course, Agent Tennison. I did not mean to belittle the situation, but as I explained to your agent, we have nothing to hide."

"Where are the videos from that day?" Tennison asked.

"They were given to miss Prince," Stephanie replied.

"No, they were not," Tyrel stated.

"I will request them again, but I assure you they were delivered," Stephanie replied.

"How many people work here?" Tyrel asked.

"Enough," Stephanie replied, "As I told your agent, we are bound by ITAR and take it very seriously. I can't tell you much without clearance."

"I have clearance," Tennison said.

"I checked when you called, it delayed me walking out, you have clearance, but not as high as you would need to be here," Stephanie replied in a casual tone. "I am sure you will state as Miss Prince did that you can get clearance, but not many can get the level necessary to be here and we do have to follow the rules."

"We will see," Tennison said. "Anything else you can tell me?"

"Not really," Stephanie said, "As I said we had a shift running but there was nothing to see."

"I will expect the footage by 5 today," Tennison stated.

"I am sure it will take longer," Stephanie said.

"Then I am sure you will need some new IT guys," Tyrel jumped back at her. "Don't test me."

"I assure you I am doing no such thing, Mister Tennison," Stephanie said.

"How about we go watch the video now?" Tennison stated.

"As I am sure you are aware, we must vet our guests very carefully," Stephanie began, "The United States Government has given us a lot of responsibility to make things for them. I know it is frustrating, but you cannot go into the secure areas without proper clearance, and you just don't have that clearance. If you would like I can talk to your supervisor or contact our liaison with the government, and you can speak to them."

"Best idea I have heard all day," Tennison snapped. "Who is your government contact."

Stephanie smiled, her makeup was perfectly applied, and she was quite stunning. She reached into her pocket and pulled out a card, "I took the liberty of writing down his information. Please feel free to call or have your supervisor call."

Tennison looked at the card, it was in perfect handwriting and had a General's name on it, "I will take care of it, you will be seeing me soon."

"I hate to be crass, but I doubt that Mister Tennison," her smile was knowingly wicked. "I think you are fishing for something that certainly isn't here, and I think if you push too hard you will be squashed like the ant you are. Your supervisors are not too impressed with you. Chasing fairy tales and being a rebel only gets people so far. I think you will find things are not as in your favor as you would like."

Tyrel was furious, his dark skin was red with anger, "How about I arrest you right now?"

Stephanie laughed, "Go ahead, that will end your career pretty quickly. What charge do you have? 'I told him the truth and he got mad at me.' Maybe we can get you charged with the shooting for being so out of touch with your emotions." Stephanie made a pouty face, "Now don't go away mad, but it is time for you to go away." Stephanie snapped her fingers and the two guards at the desk walked to her in seconds. "Show Agent Tyrel Tennison the door."

Tyrel walked to the door, the guards walking behind and to either side of him. Stephanie looked at him as he exited and did a half finger wave, then walked into the secure area of the plant.

Tyrel walked to his car as the guards stood like sentinels at the door. He took a deep breath. He wasn't sure how accurate this woman was, but she definitely was sure of herself.

Tyrel got in his car and left, heading to meet Alex.

Chapter 34

Abby and Jenny walked to the parking garage with only the click click click of their heels echoing. It was quiet except for that sound that echoed. Abby had on jeans and a dark blue blouse with 3-inch heels, this was for shopping today. Jenny still had on her Jeans and red blouse from earlier in the day. The two looked as though they could be shopping or clubbing.

As the two walked up to the sleek black car Abby took the fob from her pocket and clicked. The doors unlocked and the two got into the car. Jenny was looking around but put her seatbelt on and was silent.

Abby took the DB-9 out of the parking garage and on the short trip to the mall. It was not far and Jenny was very quiet on the drive.

Abby tried to talk to her, but in the end, there wasn't much to say.

"Where do you live?" Abby asked.

"Atlanta, but maybe Lexington now," Jenny replied.

"Did you go to school in Lexington?" Abby asked.

"No," Jenny replied.

The questions were short and wide ranging, but Jenny's answers were equally short and non-descript. After several minutes of this back and forth Abby finally asked Jenny, "Is there something wrong with me?"

"What do you mean?" Jenny replied.

"Well, I am trying to be cordial and make conversation, and you are shutting me down like you don't want to be here," Abby said in a nonchalant voice. "If I did something wrong, I can just take you back to the hotel and do this alone."

Jenny's eyes began to water, "This is a little terrifying to me." She began, "You are the wife of a killer."

"Girlfriend," Abby smiled.

"What?" Jenny was crying more now. "You're not even married? Why would you stay knowing he is a killer?"

Abby looked at Jenny, "I get it," she said, "This is a lot to take in. Michael is who he is, and his morality is quite different from a lot of people."

"Different," Jenny said, "He talks about death like it is an everyday occurrence. I heard the others talking and they didn't come out and say it, but they are all afraid of him, or at least have concerns about him."

"I could see that," Abby said as she drove through the mall parking lot and came close to the door of a target. Abby pulled the DB9 into the first space above a handicapped slot and put the car in park. "The whole situation is a bit much. I understand that too. Your brother just died, your niece has had two attempts on her life, and the world you know is upside down. I understand it all. To Michael, and really to everyone in that room, death is just about an everyday occurrence. You sound like a college friend of mine, who just didn't see the bigger picture."

"Bigger picture?" Jenny asked.

"Yeah," Abby said as she turned off the car and turned to look at Jenny. "Every day is a gift. The world is not as warm and fuzzy as everyone thinks, and we have to grab onto every day and squeeze the life we have out of it. A lot of people go through life just living on the surface, but a few do a lot more. Sure, Michael can be scary. You should see him shoot or do one of the hundred and one things he is good at, but he is also the most loving person I have ever known and would do so much for so many." Abby looked out the window to the cars ahead of her, people walked in and out of the large Target. "Look at them all," Abby continued. "With all you have gone through and whatever is lying in store for you tonight, tomorrow, and the day after. Do you want one of them helping you, or someone like Michael?"

Jenny had a quizzical look on her face. A tear formed in her eyes as she stared at all the people walking back and forth in front of her. After a moment, she dried her face.

Abby turned and looked at Jenny, "My father is probably one of the scariest people in the world. Somewhere in the middle of my life I lost respect for him, but Michael has shown me a new respect at least for who he is. Most would see him as a good guy, but both Michael and I know what the government does is just as scary as anything else. We just accept it."

People buzzed around in front of them as Abby and Jenny looked on.

"I understand," Abby continued. "you have a choice now. You can be afraid of me, afraid of Michael, afraid of this whole situation, or you can step up and start seeing the world as more than you knew before. You can take care of your niece and show her a world where she doesn't need to be afraid."

Jenny looked out the window and took a deep breath. "I'll try."

Abby laughed and made her face squenched together, "Do or do not, there is no try." She said in a funny Yoda type voice.

Jenny laughed.

"We good?" Abby asked.

"Yeah," Jenny said, "but my eyes will be puffy now."

"We're in a mall," Abby said. "We can fix that."

Jenny laughed again. She stopped and looked at Abby, "I feel so selfish. My world is about to change because I'll have custody of Kira. I was so tied up in me, I didn't stop to consider how the rest of the world was handling all of this. Thanks Abby."

"Good deal," Abby said, opened the door, and got out of the car.

Jenny got out as well and they began to walk in. "By the way, awesome car."

"Michael got it for me," Abby said, "I saw it in Paris and he just surprised me with it. I didn't drive it for a while. We live, well… we live away from most people. I love my little black car, and boy is it awesome inside."

"Abby," Jenny smiled, "Thank you."

"For what?" Abby said as they walked into Target.

"For opening my eyes a little," Jenny said, "I just have one question."

"What's that?" Abby asked.

"Should I be scared of you?" Jenny asked.

"Maybe of these shoes, what was I thinking wearing these to shop," Abby smiled.

Chapter 35

The Shoot Point Blank Range was a marvel of modern gun ownership. The gun store area was brightly lit and crisp as a store should be, full of everything anyone shooting could want. The range was well maintained and well lit, something many ranges were not so good at.

Alex and Michael walked into the range and were greeted by several helpful associates. Michael immediately walked to the range desk and asked for a lane for 2 hours.

"We don't know how long we will be here," Alex said in a low voice.

"Exactly," Michael said, "So I will enjoy myself until Tennison arrives and you introduce me if you decide it is right."

The range officer had Michael fill out a variety of forms and Michael handed him an Indiana license and concealed carry permit and asked if he could try multiple weapons at once. Both IDs read "JM Masters".

"Is that real?" Alex asked in a quiet voice again.

"As real as most of the credentials I carry," Michael said in a whisper. "Is yours real?"

"Of course, it is," Alex whispered.

"Well, I would rather not give out my address to most people." Michael whispered, "Yes, this is a house I spent 2 years creating fronts for and I am going to put it on your piece of paper so you can send me mail showing I like weapons? Seems a little strange to me."

Alex looked down at his driver's license and military ID and wondered about what had just been said to him. He was giving away personal information to a business on a piece of paper and trusting them to take care of it. He laughed, "I see your point." Alex took the forms and filled them out with an uneasy feeling for the first time.

Michael's forms were approved, and Michael handed four one hundred-dollar bills to the clerk. The clerk looked at Michael and said, "Umm, what would you like?"

"OK," Michael said, taking back the money and putting it in his pocket. "Can I have the Dan Wesson Valor Commander to rent as well as an FN 5.7 and 4 boxes of ammo for each."

"Umm, that is a lot of ammo," the range clerk said.

"It will be a start," Michael said. "What are you renting, Alex?"

"I don't know," Alex said. "What do you suggest?"

"Try the Glock 17 Gen5," Michael said, "It is meat and potatoes, but it will be worth it to practice."

"OK," Alex said, turning to the clerk, "I will take the Gen 5 and one box of shells."

"Give him 4 boxes, I will pay for it all," Michael said as the clerk rang it all up.

"One or two lanes," the range clerk asked.

"Two of course," Michael said.

Michael paid the bill. They put on "eyes and ears" and went into the range.

The rangemaster came over and explained range rules. He was very cordial and probably an ex-police or military officer. Michael listened intently and when the rangemaster completed Michael asked, "Is there a speed rule?"

"No rapid fire or bump stocks. You must be in control of your weapon," the rangemaster stated.

"Got it," Michael said.

The two of them were put on two lanes next to each other, and Alex looked at Michael, "I will wait for Tennison."

Michael smiled and said simply, "Fine."

Alex exited the room and watched Michael from the windows while turning and scanning people entering and exiting the establishment.

Michael loaded the FN 5.7 first. Alex was never a fan of the FN 5.7 but had seen Michael work this weapon in ways he actually envied. Michael's passion showed every time Alex had seen him fire.

Michael laid the weapon on the bench and lined up the target. The target was a simple bullseye with a series of concentric circles in black and tan. The center had an X in it.

Michael ran the target out to the length of the range, 25 yards. He shot a single shot, then shot the rest of the magazine in one second intervals. Leaving the target at 25 yards Michael reloaded the magazine of the 5.7 and shot 21 more times at one second intervals. The range officer was watching Michael closely as Alex noticed most others were not shooting as methodically nor as rapidly. Michael repeated the process 2 more times for a total of 84 shots. Then he turned to the rangemaster and must have asked for a new target.

The range officer brought a new target to Michael and must have been a bit surprised. The target looked as though it had been hand-drawn. Alex could see the holes with the light behind them. There was a single hole in the center, then a perfect circle of holes around the first ring, and a perfect circle around the second ring. Alex was both impressed and terrified at the same time with Michael's efficiency. Michael took the target off, crumpled it up and threw it in the trash. The rangemaster had seen the target and was noticeably dumbfounded at the action.

Alex laughed and looked back to the door to see a man entering in a crisp black suit with mirrored sunglasses. Alex walked towards the man and recognized him as Tyrel Tennison from pictures Ronnie had found. Tyrel was dark skinned, about 5'11 and was well kept. His shaven head glistened in the LED lights of the gun store.

"Tyrel," Alex said as he walked to him.

"Alex," Tyrel said, "you look just like your file, but maybe a little more worn."

"Thanks," Alex said, "and you look a little shinier."

They both laughed. The last picture in the database was of Tyrel with short trimmed hair, he had obviously shaven his head in the recent past.

"So, where are my witnesses?" Tyrel asked.

"Witness, just the girl and the victim. They are safe," Alex said with a serious tone.

"Safe doesn't cut it," Tyrel began, "Don't test me today, I already had a run in with a super bitch at Quality Castings."

Alex looked around, "How about we talk over by the range for a few?"

Tyrel looked around at all the people milling around the business and understood why Alex had chosen it. The building was large, and most people were keeping to themselves. The constant shooting from the range, though muffled, made it obvious if someone was trying to listen in. Most impressively, Tyrel noticed everyone on the staff was armed. Any sort of siege by anyone would be met with a pretty even force if not an overwhelming one. Tyrel knew a lot of the people who worked at gun ranges and stores were ex-military or ex police force, so this had to be one of the safer places he had ever met. The only issue Tyrel saw was the salespeople milling about looking for customers. Fortunately, they were quite occupied at the time.

Alex whispered, "Tyrel, I really don't know you. I do know the witness has had two attempts on her life so far, as well as the victim, so excuse me for being cautious."

"What is your involvement again?" Tyrel asked.

"The father of the victim served in my unit years ago," Alex answered.

"That does not make it a military issue. In fact, I am about tired of people pushing me around, thinking they can get one over on me," Tyrel fumed.

Alex was calm. "I am not trying to get one over on you," he paused. "We can get there or talk with the witness but everything that has been recorded is about all you are going to get."

Tyrel was turning darker by the moment, "I think that is for me to decide," he whispered loudly. "Who do you think you are?"

Alex continued to stay calm, "I am someone who is looking at an FBI agent who is here alone. It is not something I see often. FBI, ATF, CIA, are all brothers. They count on each other and work in teams. Where is everyone Tyrel?"

Tyrel looked out the range window. It was obvious he was struggling for control. "Alex, I see your point." He stopped, watched the shooting going on behind the window, then looked back at Alex. "How about I just get a team in here and arrest you?"

Alex looked out into the range as well. "That what you want to do?"

They both watched the range in silence for a few minutes, then Alex saw Michael bringing back yet another target. This one had a line going horizontally and vertically with one shot in the dead center. The range master was walking over with a new target and Michael crushed the target up and threw it in the trash. Alex chuckled a little as the range officer pulled the target out of the trash, looked at it, and shook his head.

"What's so funny?" Tyrel asked.

"Just watching this guy shoot," Alex said. "Look, Tyrel, we are willing to help you. We are willing to help you find what happened to Sarena and Jackson's shooter. Do you blame us for being a little cautious right now?"

Tyrel watched Michael this time as he pulled out the 45 and loaded the magazine.

"It is my case, not yours. Worst case it is Indianapolis PDs case, not yours," Tyrel stated.

"I agree," Alex said.

"So how can I see my witness?" Tyrel was trying to be nice.

"How about I suggest a solution we both win at and the witness isn't put in further danger?" Alex said.

Tyrel rolled his eyes, "What?"

"How about I help you find a group here in town that is running out of control and may be responsible for this whole mess," Alex said tentatively.

"Really?" Tyrel said. "What makes you think there is a group?"

"I have an ace in the hole," Alex said. "Someone who may be aware of more information than we have."

Tyrel raised an eyebrow, "I'm listening."

"We will help you solve what we can, you get the arrests or the credit," Alex said.

"In exchange for?" Tyrel said.

"Nothing," Alex stated. "We work together. I can be sure John's son is safe, and Kira is as safe."

"So, you want to keep them in your custody," Tyrel stated.

"They are not in custody," Alex smiled. "They are our guests."

"Who is this inside person?" Tyrel asked.

"He is not inside anymore, but has working knowledge of the operation," Alex said. "Interested?"

They both watched the range, and Alex watched Michael bring back another target. This one simply was missing the center. It was not ragged or ripped, there was just a perfect series of circles cut and the center was gone.

"Damn," Tyrel said.

"Yeah, I know," Alex said as he watched Michael once again look at the center of the target, then crumple the target and throw it away.

"I wanna quote that old movie and ask if he sleeps with that thing," Tyrel said.

"I happen to know he sleeps with a beautiful blonde," Alex said. "He is our link to solving these murders and attacks."

Michael looked at Alex, and Alex nodded. Michael packed up the pistols, then picked up the pistol on Alex's unused lane and walked towards the door. He nodded at the range master as he left who nodded back and then watched him leave. Michael then walked through the two-door system designed to muffle the sound. Now in the larger retail area Michael walked to the range desk with purpose, but not in any hurry. Once there he carefully laid out the weapons, asked for a bag for the leftover ammo, and took his time going over to Alex and Tyrel.

"You didn't get to shoot," Michael said to Alex.

"Yeah, it happens," Alex said with a wry smile.

"It's why you guys can't hit the broad side of a barn," Michael laughed. "It is a lot like the TV shows. You guys shoot 10 bullets for what can be done with one."

Tyrel was anxious with Alex's statement. "How do you fit into all of this?" Tyrel asked.

Michael looked around, no one was close to them. "I don't," he smiled.

Tyrel looked at Alex. "But you said…"

"I said he is our link, I did not say he was involved," Alex stated.

"What do you know?" Tyrel asked.

"Well, I know there is an issue here in Indianapolis, and I know it is with a small group of radical people. More importantly I need to know what you want out of this?" Michael asked.

"I want justice," Tyrel said.

"Justice is an interesting goal. What does it mean to you?" Michael asked.

Tyrel was impatient again. "Justice is always doing what is right. I want the people who conspired against this boy, and I want them punished for what they did. I want the group behind it all, and I want them punished too."

"Big targets," Michael said. "Want to know who Santa Claus is as well?"

"Who do you think you are?" Tyrel fumed.

"I asked what you wanted. You are the one getting mad. Why?" Michael asked.

Tyrel looked at the floor, then at Michael with fire in his eyes, "It isn't right they get away with murder."

"Anyone who kills someone should be punished?" Michael replied.

"They should face the law," Tyrel said.

"OK," Michael said, "Hey Alex, you need to face the law. I think I do as well, maybe, and Tyrel, you?"

"There are exceptions," Tyrel said. "You know what I mean."

"Enough," Alex said, "Do you want help or not? We can walk right out of here now and you can go chase your windmill."

Michael was quiet and waited. Alex was stoic and looked at Tyrel in a pointed fashion.

After a few moments, Tyrel looked down, "OK, what's the deal? How can this work? Who is this guy?"

Alex looked at Michael, "He is nobody, but he has some connections that may help us get our targets here in Indianapolis. That is what you want, right?"

Tyrel studies Michael and Alex, "I want the organization."

"That is not on the table," Alex said. "We can help you get the local group, but we do not have intel on the organization."

"What's the catch?" Tyrel asked. "What do you want out of it?"

Michael spoke, "Satisfaction, involvement, and a solution that works for justice."

Tyrel looked at Michael again. "And your definition of justice is?"

"All threats are eliminated," Michael replied. "Either through the law, or elimination of resistance."

"Sounds ominous," Tyrel said.

"Not really, just straight forward," Michael said. "I am not a politician. I get things done. If you want politics, work with Tarkington."

"I have heard of his politics. They are pretty cut and dried as well," Tyrel said.

Alex cut in. "Say the word, we do this, we walk when the job is done, you get the credit for the solution, whatever it may be."

"And to clean up the mess?" Tyrel asked.

"If there is one," Alex said, "Yes."

"What do you get out of this," Tyrel asked.

"I keep a few people safe," Alex said.

"That's it?" Tyrel asked.

"Sometimes that is enough," Alex said.

"OK," Tyrel said, "I agree, so what do you know? Where do we start?"

"Give us two hours," Alex said, "We will set a place and time and solve this."

"Two hours?" Tyrel said. "OK, I will be waiting."

They turned and saw the rangemaster had put up one of Michaels targets on the wall, it was one where he had run the rings and made concentric circles.

"Looks like you're famous now," Tyrel said.

"Just a name," Michael smiled.

Michael and Alex left the building. Tyrel followed them out and watched them intently. Alex got into the Suburban and headed out, expecting Tyrel to be in pursuit, but it did not come. They drove out and got onto 465. No one followed.

"Seems easy," Alex said.

"Nothing is ever as it seems," Michael replied. "This guy is a loose cannon. There is something we don't know."

"I think so too," Alex said. "I can call Tarkington and have him look into it."

"It will be buried," Michael stated. "I will ask around."

"So, what's our next step?" Alex asked.

"I will make a call and make myself involved," Michael said in a dry voice. "It will solve some issues for me, but it will make some in the future."

"Make some issues? You are solving a problem," Alex stated.

"True, but there will be people who will question my motives. It would have been better if Abby and I would have kept driving," Michael said.

"You can," Alex said, "this is not your fight."

"When I made a call earlier, it became my fight one way or another," Michael replied.

"Why is that?" Alex asked.

"By calling in, I involved myself. The leadership of the group will be looking for me to resolve the issue alone," Michael said. "I have to admit, I may have made a mistake calling in."

"So what? You leave us out to dry?" Alex said.

"You are outsiders to this group. If they knew I said anything it would not be good for either of us," Michael stated. "I will need to deal with this when we get back to the hotel."

The rest of the drive was quiet.

When Michael and Alex arrived back at the parking garage they checked the vehicle. No bugs or tracking devices were apparent, but they were cautious and parked it on a lower level so if there were something new it would be more difficult for it to be detected. They then walked to the bus and drove it across to the hotel.

As the bus parked. Michael looked at Alex. "I hate to do this, but I will need to take the lead."

Alex looked at the young man. Michael was quite a bit younger than Alex, but Michael had the benefit of a clear mind in most cases. Alex had seen the capabilities Michael possessed up close and personal. Still he was wary. "Why?"

"Well, it is actually pretty easy. This will need to go down one way, or we will all be inconvenienced in some way," Michael said.

"What way is that?" Alex asked.

"I won't know until I talk to the CEO, and find out his terms," Michael stated. "I will let him know I am involving you, and he won't be happy, but he will set a series of criteria to keep them safe."

"Criteria," Alex said, "like what?"

Michael looked at Alex in the eyes, his blue eyes sparkled, "Like who will live, and who will die."

"Just like that?" Alex asked.

"You know I can't kill anyone like that," Alex said.

"No, but I can, and I will," Michael stated.

"You think Tyrel will..." Alex started.

"Tyrel will get his arrests, but no one will know anything," Michael said.

"Oh crap, Michael! We are the good guys," Alex said.

"No, you are the good guys. I am," Michael looked at Alex with his piercing blue eyes, "something else."

Alex looked at Michael again, "How am I gonna work this out with the team."

"You don't need to, you won't tell anyone," Michael said. "I will just do what is necessary and you will get credit."

"You mean Tyrel will get credit," Alex said.

"Yes, Tyrel will get credit, and he won't be able to get above this group." Michael replied. "Did you think this was going to be a gimme? There is very little in life that is free," Michael continued. "This is definitely not one of those things."

Alex paced for a moment.

"Maybe it would be best if we bowed out," Alex said.

"I think you need to consider carefully," Michael stated.

"Consider that someone innocent will die?" Alex asked in an incredulous voice.

"No, that someone guilty will die," Michael said.

"That's not for us to decide," Alex said.

"Sometimes it is," Michael replied. "Do you think your friend would hesitate if Jackson was threatened? What are the rules of most concealed carry licenses? That you must feel threatened or there is a risk to your life or someone else's. There is a risk right now Alex, it is a risk to your life, and to the other people you had in that room. If you don't think there is a risk, ask Jackson if he saw it coming? Ask Jackson if he felt safe before he was shot. There is a flaw in the system, and sometimes you have to protect your own."

Alex looked at Michael. He was trying, "I am not sure I can believe in that."

"You sure believed in it when you came after me at my house in Ivel," Michael continued. "I saw your little group coming up the hill, standard cover formation. You weren't there to talk, you weren't collecting for the march of dimes. You were there to capture or kill me and loaded to kill me. When you climbed that hill, were you loaded with mercy bullets, or was your M16 ready to fire full 223 shells at me? You believed I was a danger to your country. Sure, you were working under orders, but is that what it has to be, an order for it to be real? Does that take away the pain, knowing it was not you who decided? Well, in this case it is me, I decided for you when I looked into this mess. You can either help me, or I will do it myself, and you can explain it to Tyrel."

Alex look at the man before him. "I don't like it, but I will fight with you. It seems I have little choice."

Michael was serious, "Alex, if you try to go against me and it puts Abby in any danger…"

"I know, or I can guess. You will put one of those pretty patterns on my head," Alex broke in.

"Something like that," Michael said. He looked around, "The DB9 isn't back, they must still be out."

"I suppose someone wanted to shop," Alex said.

"That is an understatement," Michael laughed. "Abby has been dying to shop for months. We actually had a discussion about it on the way down. We will be lucky if we can get her out ever."

Alex chuckled for a moment, Michael shook his head and the two walked the rest of the way to the hotel door in silence.

Chapter 36

Abby and Jenny filled the little car full of bags from a variety of stores. The trunk was stuffed with clothes, snacks and more. Abby smiled, "Anything else we need?"

Jenny laughed, "I haven't had that much fun in a while. We don't need anything else I don't think.

"Nice car," came a voice from behind them.

Abby turned to see the three young men walking their way. "Aston Martin isn't it?" another boy asked.

Abby sighed and fixed her ponytail tight. Jenny looked scared. "Get in the car, Jenny," Abby said. "Lock the doors." She pressed a button on her phone and tossed it to her. Tell him what is happening, tell him I have it handled."

"Aww, we just wanna party. Maybe you two can take us for a ride. I mean, hot and hotter is good for us, and we share well," the boy said.

"I don't share well," Abby said.

"I'm not sure we care," the third boy stated.

Abby smiled and pulled a small set of finger gloves from her back pocket. As the boys advanced, she pulled them tight. Then she started moving forward towards them. "Boys, you don't wanna do this. It isn't gonna work out the way you think."

"Sure, little lady," the apparent leader said. "We are just scared to death of you."

Abby leaned back on her heel, swiveling on the point of the heel at the top piece. "Ok, I was nice at least, I was feeling nice today, I warned you," Abby smiled.

The first boy ran at Abby in one quick sprint. Abby pivoted on her heel quickly and swung her leg high striking the boy across the face with her left foot. The top piece of the heel gouged his cheek deeply, and it immediately began bleeding. The boy fell back from the force and grabbed his face and blood flowed from the wound.

The other two boys looked at her. "Jimmy, maybe this isn't such a good idea," one boy said.

"Yeah, Jimmy, the little lady is gonna kick your ass if you keep going," Abby smiled.

"Jimmy, maybe we should leave," the boy pleaded as his friend got up, shirt and face covered with blood.

"Stop using my name, dumbass," Jimmy said as he moved forward.

"It's ok to be scared, Jimmy," Abby said, "It's going to hurt a little."

Abby glanced and saw Jenny talking in the car. She seemed frenzied as she watched Abby but nodded a little as she spoke.

Jimmy ran at her. "Bitch," he said as he dove, but Abby sidestepped and kicked into his knee. He fell to the ground grabbing his knee, rolling back and forth.

"Get her," Jimmy yelled, but the other two boys looked on, unsure.

"C'mon boys," she looked into their eyes, her blue eyes glinting with an inner fire. "I won't bite." Abby moved forward towards them as Jimmy started to get up and fell over when he tried to put weight on his leg.

The two boys looked at each other, "Ma'am, we're sorry. We'll just get our friend and leave."

Jimmy screamed, "You idiots, she is one girl. Stop being pussies and get her."

The two boys looked at each other again, then started circling, but each was wary. They looked at Jimmy then at her, "Jimmy, this is bad, I don't wanna."

"Do it," Jimmy said. "Do it now!"

Abby was smiling now. "Let's do it, boys." Each of the three boys was much bigger than Abby. They looked as though they played a sport and acted like Jimmy was a leader, but he was not. Abby walked forward, purposefully clicking her heels in the parking area of the mall. Several people came out and saw the ruckus and went back into the mall area. A security guard came out and watched from a distance, only to walk back in and call someone on his cell phone.

Abby saw a church van pull up between the mall and them. *The churchgoers were about to get a show*, she thought to herself.

But when the door opened wide, Michael stepped out of the door and looked at her, smiling. He walked over, and as he got closer, Jimmy noticed him.

"This is none of your concern, man. You better leave or get hurt."

Alex walked around the other side of the van and walked towards the DB9. "You guys ok?"

The two circling boys stopped and started to back away from the scene. Michael looked at them and shook his head.

They looked at each other and kept slowly backing up. Pulling a knife from his belt, Michael threw it where it embedded in the asphalt a few inches from their feet. Michael shook his head again.

"This was getting fun," Abby said. "Jimmy and his pals were wanting to play, and they lost the stomach for it."

Michael walked to Abby, "It's ok. I will play with you."

He hugged her, "I knew you would be alright, but we decided to come visit." The two boys saw Michael as distracted, his side to them. They started to back up again.

"Do I have to impale your foot to get you to stop moving?" Michael asked.

The boys stopped.

"Did you say "Jimmy"?" Alex asked as Jenny got out of the car.

"It's what the boys called him," Abby said.

Alex was dumbfounded, "Kira's attacker was named Jimmy. Three boys in a group," he paused, "we could not be that lucky."

Michael walked to Jimmy and grabbed his shirt. The boy was at least 200 pounds, but Michael lifted him from the ground as though he were paper. "Take a picture of him, send it over."

Jimmy grabbed at his hands, "Let me go. My dad will sue."

Michael laughed, "For what, protecting myself and my girlfriend from 3 thugs?"

Alex snapped a picture and sent it forward, then dialed the phone. "Jim, ask Kira if she knows this guy."

"Which guy?" Jim replied on the phone.

"Sent you a picture," Alex said.

There was a pause on the phone. "Umm, she says that is the guy that jumped her. Where did you pick him up?"

"He just tried to jump Abby and Jenny," Alex said.

"He tried to jump Abby?" Jim laughed. "How'd that go?"

"Will talk about it in a bit," Alex said. "Will need to call Franks and Tyrel and get them over here. I am sure the police are on the way."

Michael reached into a side pocket on his pants and pulled out a zip-tie. He zipped Jimmy's hands together and set him on the ground.

Pulling two more, he walked to the other two boys, leaned down and pulled his knife from the ground. He slid it back into his belt and said to the boys, "Turn around." They both did so, and Michael zip-tied their hands together.

Alex hung up the phone and walked over. "Franks is on his way, so is Tyrel. Take the bus back, and I will deal with this."

Michael laughed. "Wasn't your mess, but OK."

"Oh, and do you carry zip ties everywhere?" Alex said. "I don't miss those things and you seem to always have them."

"They have lots of uses, and I like to be prepared," Michael said. He looked at Abby, "Let's head back, Alex is going to take care of this."

Alex walked over to the three boys. They all sat on the ground, their hands zip-tied behind them, "Boys," he began, "here's what is going to happen..."

Michael drove the bus and Abby followed as Alex heard sirens approaching. He waited for the coming barrage of questions.

Chapter 37

Michael had just gotten to the top floor when Abby had called. He had not had time to call back and accept the task Vengeance Incorporated laid before him. There were not many choices, but not many defined targets either. Michael knew he would have to play this out and do what he could to keep Abby safe, and the others as well if he could.

As Abby followed him to the hotel, he wondered about the next few hours and how they would go. He was used to the work from Vengeance Incorporated being very swift, and decisive. His delay would have been noticed and perhaps questioned if he was still active in the group, but his long absence played to his advantage. His work for the government was not quick. In fact, it was slow and tedious in many ways with excessive hours of patient listening instead of action.

The Van and DB9 parked in the hotel parking lot and Jenny and Abby got out of the Db9 nearly in unison. Abby stood outside of the front door and slowly peeled off her gloves. She folded them and put them in a pocket. Jenny, on the other hand, was not so calm. She got out of the car, shaking.

"Wow," she said, "that was intense. I mean you didn't even worry."

Abby looked over at her as she opened the trunk, "They were kids, it was no worry."

Jenny was a little too excited. "Kids that could have hurt you," she started. "I mean, where did you learn to do all that?"

Michael walked over to help. "Maybe from her father," he suggested.

"More likely from him," she poked Michael in the stomach as he took several of the bags. "We work out every day and spar at least weekly, sometimes daily."

"Where do you find the time?" Jenny asked.

"We have lots of time," Abby said.

"But you work?" Jenny asked.

Michael looked at Jenny, "I am retired." He grabbed the last of the bags. "Anything else?"

"Nope," Abby said, "I think that is it." She closed the trunk and locked the doors.

Jenny carried nothing but was still shaking from the ordeal. Abby had two bags, and Michael carried at least 20 bags looped on his hands as they walked to the hotel door. "I have been transformed into a pack mule," he laughed.

The hotel was quiet as they entered and walked to the elevator. Once it came and they were inside, Jenny continued, "Retired, how can you be retired, you are what... 30?"

"Sound investment decisions and a strong work ethic," Michael said.

Jenny stared at the elevator door, "I doubt I will ever retire," she said in a somber voice. "Now with Kira, I will be keeping an eye on her, but she is an adult now. I will help her through college, and well, I struggle sometimes."

Abby looked at her, "I am sure there will be opportunities for you with Kira."

Michael looked at the woman, "Jenny, we are an amalgam of what we need to be to survive. I chose a little tougher path so I could do more. Some choose a path to allow them to live. Some choose less. It is still usually a choice."

"I think I get it," Jenny said. "Still, this seems like something out of a book or movie, not real life."

"I think you would be surprised about real life and all the things it really is," Abby said. "Real life is not very real. Most people live there, secure that they know what happens on a day by day basis is real, and secure in knowing they are safe."

Michael nodded, "Reality is quite different. Every day is a gift, and every day offers us a new possibility, a new potential adventure, or a chance to be more and do more. We just have to choose to live."

Jenny smiled as the doors opened to their floor. "It is weird," she said as she walked out of the elevator, "I was scared when those boys came at us, but when I saw Abby move, I felt safe. I guess it is a little strange, but I wasn't afraid anymore."

"There really isn't anything to be afraid of," Abby said, "except being afraid."

"Sounds so easy, and I suppose it is easy for you," Jenny chuffed. "Not all of us can do the Hiya stuff and cut someone's face with their high heels."

"Maybe, maybe not," Abby said, "but we choose to live in fear or live out of fear. It is pretty simple, really."

They reached the door to the suite where Jenny was staying. Abby knocked. A moment later, the door cracked open, then opened fully. Jim stood holding the door.

"About time," Jim said. "Snacks are in order."

Ronnie walked over to the door as it closed behind Jenny, Abby and Michael. "Miss Abby are you ok?" he asked.

Michael looked at her as Abby answered, "I am fine. I think I scuffed my shoe on the big one's face, but I will be ok."

Rachel guffawed from the side, "I can't believe the dumb kids would try to take you. But then again, you look little. Maybe they thought they were gonna get one over on you."

Abby laughed a little, "I am sure Alex will have them dancing with the feds."

"Yeah," Rachel quipped, "I can't believe it was the same three idiots that grabbed Kira. I mean, do these people not ever learn?"

Jim was grabbing a bag of kettle chips from the table. "Sure Rachel, lots of people need to take a beating over and over before they learn."

Rachel grabbed an orange from the table and threw it at Jim, who caught it with one hand while he was eating chips. "See what I mean? No temper control. Always a way to lose."

Kira came out of the bedroom and walked to the big table, now covered with bags, "What did you get?"

"There are clothes in there for you," Jenny said. "Should be ok until we get you home. We got a few decks of cards and some games too."

"I mean, I'm hungry," Kira said as she rummaged through the bags. She found a box of chocolate Pop-Tarts and literally ripped it open.

"Pop-Tarts," Jim said, "I want one."

"Are you guys a bunch of kids?" Jenny asked.

"Only when we're hungry," Jim replied.

"He's always a kid," Rachel said, pointing at Jim. She then looked at Ronnie and pointed at him, "He may never hit puberty."

"Ma'am," Ronnie said, "they are really good at what we do, but as you can see, they like to have fun a lot."

Rachel looked at Ronnie with a glare that would have turned most people to ice, "Yes, we do, thank you."

Jim laughed, "Hey, I'm happy. I got my Pop-Tart." Jim unwrapped the foil on the pop-tart and began eating."

"Yeah, that's why you have that belly," Rachel laughed. Rachel looked up at Michael and Abby, who had separated the bags and kept one. "So, when are we going to see some action? Babysitting is not exactly my line of work."

"Not my call," Michael said, "I suppose it will be up to Alex and who is going to do what with your team."

"What about you?" Jenny asked.

"I am not part of this group," Michael said. "I do things my way."

The room was solemn for a moment. Abby turned and opened the door. "We will talk later," she said in a cheerful voice.

"Sure," Rachel said as she peeled an orange, "We will see you later."

Michael and Abby left the room.

"What was that all about?" Jenny asked.

Jim chewed the second pop-tart in the bag, "What?"

"What the story with the two of them?" Jenny asked.

"Aunt Jenny," Kira asked, "I'm going to check on Jackson."

"Sure, honey," Jenny replied then looked at Jim, "Is he a good guy or a bad guy? What about her? Is she a good guy or a bad guy? I just saw her beat up three young men like she did it every day."

"I doubt she fights every day," Jim said.

Rachel laughed, "Maybe she takes Thursdays off."

"You people think this is funny?" Jenny asked. "I have a niece to protect, and I don't know what is going on. Abby seems nice and in control then turns into a whirlwind, putting her heels through people's faces."

"She hit him in the face with those spikes?" Rachel asked. "I have so got to get a pair of those."

"Not me," Jim said. "Would cramp."

"You people are nuts," Jenny said, "Abby said the world is not what I think it is, and you people, you try to make it right."

Jim stopped, and his face turned serious. "Jenny, I can't believe I am going to say this to a woman but calm down."

"But I," her eyes teared up.

"Michael and Abby are ok. I spent some time with them when I was supposed to be protecting them. Turns out, they are just as good at this as any of us, maybe better." Jim began.

Ronnie piped in, "Michael, I think, is a little better you said."

Jim glanced at Ronnie but continued, "Jenny, we all do this every day. We deal with it with a little humor and me, well, I deal with too much food. Mostly steak, I really like steak."

"Red meat will kill you," Rachel said.

"It hasn't killed me, ma'am," John said. John had been silent, watching the whole back and forth and stepped forward.

"Ma'am," John started, "this is mostly my fault, but it is a good thing."

"What do you mean?" Jenny said, drying her eyes.

"Jackson is my only son," John stated in a soft tone, "I left the service to be with him and protect him. When all this happened, I didn't know who to call. I didn't trust the police. And well," John paused for a moment, "Alex and Jim have always been there for me when I needed them, so I called them."

"OK, so where does that leave us?" Jenny said.

"Well, ma'am," John continued, "I believe in my brothers, and I believe they will solve anything that comes their way. If they trust this Michael, I do as well, because it is a simple motto for us all, never to fail our friends, our platoon, our comrades. I was not sure where to go, and I knew Jim and Alex would never fail me. They never will," John paused. "Now I have to admit, Jim is a little funny. He was in trouble a lot, and Alex too strict. I never worked with Rachel or Ronnie, but they are here for me, and I appreciate them and their friendship and honor every day."

"How can we know we will be safe?" Jenny said.

"Because Jim and Alex are Rangers or were Rangers. There are no better trained men in the world," John said.

"Well said, John," Jim said. "Can I have another Pop-Tart now?"

Jenny picked up the box, walked to where Jim was sitting at the table, and handed the box to him, "I'm trusting you." Jenny shook the box, "These are bad for you."

Jim looked deep into Jenny's eyes. "Bad for me? Really?"

"Bad for you," Jenny repeated and walked towards the room that she and Kira shared.

Jim pouted for a second and put the box down, "Bad for me?" he said in a mock sad tone. He looked up at Rachel, who was behind him slightly and grabbed another pack of Pop-Tarts. "Nawwww," he said and started eating again.

Chapter 38

Michael and Abby walked to their room at a steady pace. They held hands as Michael talked about how much fun he had at the range, drawing patterns on the targets. Abby smiled and walked with him. Listening, then she spoke of her shopping trip with Jenny, and the three boys that approached the car.

Michael interjected in that discussion and noted how proud he was of her for not backing down. "Too many people become victims, and it lets bullies, like those, have free reign when they shouldn't."

"Aren't you the one saying never jump the gun on an opponent? Aren't you the one who says assess, adapt, attack?"

"Yep," Michael replied. "In this case, you didn't have time. And how many people could stand against those heels?" Michael laughed.

Abby held her leg to the side and looked down at the heels, "And they are a good price, not even Prada."

They both laughed as they reached the door. Michael picked her up as the door opened and swung her around as they entered the room. "I love you."

"I love you too, Michael," Abby replied.

Michael flipped on the light. The room was in pristine condition. Their bags were on the stand to the left, while the bed was on the right, perfectly made by the maid. As a habit, Michael always packed before he left a room in case he had to leave suddenly. Traveling together, Abby had picked up that habit as well. In the end, it made their lives easier as they always knew where everything was and could leave at a moment's notice if plans changed.

"All packed and ready to go or stay Michael. What are we going to do?" Abby asked.

"I should stay for a day or two," Michael replied, "It will clear my name, and nothing will be hanging over my head. It will also keep these guys from getting in the middle of something bigger than they are."

"You mean they are in danger?" Abby asked.

"Hard to say," Michael said, "They are good at what they do, but the corporation has a lot of members, and deep pockets. I know I don't like being on the fringe. I'm not sure even your dad's pull could come out on top, but who knows, he is pretty well-connected too. It's not like them to make mistakes and not like them to run into the issues they are having here."

Michael retrieved his small case of cell phones. He took the first one, turned it on, and waited for it to come online. He dialed a number and waited. While he did, he put the phone on speaker and sat down next to Abby so she could hear.

"Mainstream Travel," came a voice.

"God I could use a cruise, maybe for two," Michael said.

"They have been waiting for you, a little impatiently. Let me put you through," came the voice.

There was a different ring and a click. "Good afternoon," came the familiar voice. "You are on speakerphone. A few gentlemen have joined me. We have been discussing some recent developments and how to resolve them. Your call comes at an opportune time."

"I thought it might," Michael replied. "Seems to be some activity in the area, and I am betting cleanup is near impossible. You had stated cleanup was not authorized, and this is a rogue customer service engagement."

"First to business, Michael, we will not share anything further unless we know your decision," the CEO stated. "Are you available to resolve the customer service issues in Indianapolis?"

"With a few conditions," Michael stated.

There was murmuring in the background. He heard the CEO state in a quiet voice, "Yes, yes, let him talk." There was another pause. "Go ahead, Michael," the CEO boomed.

"First, I appreciate the generous offer of the board and for the good of the group. On that note, I will do the job for only twice my normal payment. This will be an act of goodwill from me to you, and I have no other items tied to that. Second, I am, as you know, cursorily involved with Tarkington's group. I know they make you nervous, but I trust a few of them as much as I trust you. They will press to be involved. I would rather have them active with me than tripping over me. It just makes sense. Third, and this is important, something must be done for the damages. I think you could consider the leftover from my fee as a generous offering. I have respect for the organization I once did work for, but this was beneath them." Michael paused and waited.

Another voice spoke up, "Is this all you request, Michael?"

"This is all," Michael said, "I will need a list of potential targets and their acceptable resolutions. I assume this will not be a complete burn, but I know it could be."

There was some discussion on the line, then silence as Michael knew they had muted the line. He knew these men were considering a much larger picture than just Indianapolis.

The line came back on. "Michael, your solution is acceptable. It appears you have come into the situation accidentally. Do you need any type of assistance or equipment?"

"No, I am prepared at all times," Michael said.

The CEO laughed. "This one, I told you he would be ready. Michael, it is always a pleasure. You have always been the most professional customer service representative I have known. Is there anything else we can do for you?"

"No, but there is something I can do for you," Michael replied. "An agent, Tyrel Tennison, is very interested in your group. He wants information and wants to get deeper and deeper into this. We have set him aside, but I want to know how you want him handled."

The CEO chuffed and then coughed only a little. "Thank you for your candor, Michael. You need not concern yourself with Mister Tennison. We keep a very close eye on him. He has been watching us for some time, and we keep him at arm's length fairly easily." The CEO paused, and Michael could hear a glass, perhaps a glass of water. "Michael, the customer service department is in the warehouse district where the shooting took place. One of our issues is we no longer have a clear idea of the number of customer service representatives in the location. With that in mind, our first cleanup team was sent and unfortunately was less than successful. This means the current team is potentially servicing other customers and not working within the boundaries set up by our strict customer service charter."

"I see," said Michael.

"You will need to determine the depth of the customer service issue and eliminate any customer service issues that could eventually cause the corporation trouble," the CEO continued. "We will cover expenses as this could be a costly endeavor. We will also verify the outcome independently and upon completion you will be immediately paid your fee. We will also ensure that the injured parties by our poor customer service decisions will be resolved in a satisfactory manner."

"How satisfactory?" Michael asked.

"Michael, you wound us," the CEO replied. "Are we not fair?"

"My apologies, sir," Michael stated. "You have always been fair, but the board is involved after all."

"I drive the board, and my decision will be final in this item," the CEO said. "There will be no customer service issues on my watch."

"Understood, sir," Michael said. "I will assume if something happens to me, but the job is completed, our standard contract will be honored."

"As you set up years ago, Michael. You are always such a pleasure," the CEO stated.

"Thank you, sir," Michael said. "Anything else?"

"Yes, Michael," the CEO said, "I will be sending you the layout of the facility in question for your review. It is quite a facility and a den of iniquity, at the moment. It would be nice to save the facility, but it is not mandatory," the CEO paused. "I can only say I am not sure who should be more concerned, the hyenas in the den waiting to be eaten or the jaguar walking into their lair."

"I think you know, sir," Michael said and hung up the phone.

Michael stared at the phone for a moment. He then took the chip out and put it in the case.

"Michael, what is your standard contract?" Abby asked.

"Hmm," Michael was distracted. "Oh, if I should ever die but complete a task, any payments would be sent to you."

"How long have you had that?" Abby asked.

"Since we first started dating," Michael replied. "It seemed to make sense. You are the only family I have in the world anymore. I would much rather see you enjoy life from where I will be than to ever have to see you struggle or go back to your father. I know I keep our finances separate, but I hope you know I will, somehow, always take care of you."

"What now?" Abby asked.

"We go down the hall, we see if Alex is back, then I get ready and go take care of a big problem," Michael replied.

"Ok, and I am going too," Abby said.

"I thought I could convince you to stay and take care of Jackson, Kira, and Jenny," Michael replied.

"You know I would rather be with you," Abby said.

"I know. You know I will fight by your side any time," Michael replied. "I want, actually, I need to focus this time as I am walking into an unknown number of assailants with unknown abilities and an unknown field of engagement. I think that is enough random variables. With you safe, I can focus on the problem at hand and not be concerned."

"That is almost an insult," Abby said and then smiled, "but it is sweet. Wanting to keep me safe and all."

Michael stood up and pulled Abby to her feet too. He hugged her close. "I know you can fight better than anyone else here," Michael began, "but I need you safe."

"I understand," Abby said, reaching up to kiss Michael, "and you are right. I am a better fighter than most here."

"Not sure about that Rachel one," Michael smiled, "and well, Jim is a bit of a challenge."

Abby punched Michael and he pulled her closer, kissing her more deeply. As he pulled back, she opened her eyes, "Abby, there is no one I would rather have by my side than you."

"I am going to get a shower and change," Michael said. "Looks like it will be a long night."

Abby slowly unbuttoned her blouse. "I think a shower sounds great," she said. Michael kissed her again, deeply, as clothes dropped to

Fateful Friend

the floor.

Chapter 39

Alex stood at the mall with the three boys still on the ground, zip-tied down by the officers upon their arrival. An EMT was working with the boys and cleaning up their bruises and cuts. One of the boys had a large gouge on his cheek that was bandaged up. The area was covered with police when Tyrel Tennison and Walter Franks finally arrived.

Franks walked over to Alex, red from frustration, "Do you wanna tell me what is going on?"

"Sure," Alex said, "We found your three would-be rapists accidentally, and thought we would gift-wrap them for you."

Tyrel looked at the boys, "This has nothing to do with our conversation, does it?"

"No, it does not," Alex replied. "In fact, the only thing it has to do with is some stupid boys trying to get kicks by hurting people."

Franks looked down, "I know this kid, Jimmy," he said. "He is captain of a small college team here. I don't know the others."

"I'm betting they are part of his team. I am sure they will enjoy talking about it," Alex said.

Jimmy looked up at Alex, "My dad will be talking to you. Just wait until my dad takes care of this. You will be sorry. And so will that little bitch with the car."

Alex looked down and smiled then turned to Franks, "So is his dad connected?"

"You bet he is," Jimmy yelled. "You are done."

Alex looked down at the other boys who were quiet and looking away, "You guys connected to?"

"No, sir," one of the boys said. "No, sir, we are sorry, we just..."

"Shut up, you two," Jimmy growled.

A black Cadillac pulled up to the mall area. A man in a three-piece, black, pinstriped suit got out of the driver's side of the door. His bright red tie glared at everyone who looked at them. The passenger side door opened, and a woman got out of the car. She was in a beautiful red dress that came just passed her knees. The pearls around her neck looked out of place with the red dress, but she looked stunning, nonetheless. Tyrel, Franks, and Alex stared straight at the pair as they walked up to them.

"Well, I guess it is showtime," Franks said.

"Who is in charge here?" the man asked.

"I am," Walter Franks said. "How can I help you?"

"This is my son," the man said. "Your dispatch called me. My name is James Alexander the third." The man pulled a card from his wallet and handed it to Franks. "Can you tell me what the charges are?"

"We aren't at liberty to discuss it at this moment," Franks said. "May I introduce Tyrel Tennyson and Alex Brown. Tennison is in charge of an FBI task force that is looking into several violent crimes across the country. Your son and his friends have fallen into the crosshairs of his investigation. Brown oversees a special government task force that was assigned to our request for help solving a series of violent issues in this area. It appears your son has become involved in several things of an extremely violent nature. We have several witnesses that are currently being interviewed. We will be compiling a list of charges for these three boys to face."

"I see," Alexander replied.

"Dad, we didn't do anything," Jimmy said in a childish voice.

The woman knelt beside Jimmy and looked at his face. "Where did he get this beating?" she asked in an accusatory manner.

"Actually," Franks replied, "your son and his two friends attempted to assault two women in this parking lot, who had been trained in multiple self-defense tactics. Apparently, he was not quite as tough as he thought when he threatened to steal their car and have his way with them."

"You mean that he tried to rape a woman?" the woman asked as she stood and returned to her husband's side.

"Yes, ma'am," Franks replied. "We have multiple witnesses who were shopping at the mall and saw the entire altercation. We also have several video clips from cell phones that show the young lady first being attacked and then turning the tables on her attackers."

Alexander looked down upon his son and then looked at the woman standing next to him. He put his arm around her. A tear seemed to form in his eye, but he choked it back and said simply, "Thank you for the information, officer. We will cooperate in any way possible to make certain our son is prosecuted as is necessary under the law."

The woman in the red dress spoke immediately after, "Yes, thank you, gentlemen. We will help as necessary. Neither of us can condone this type of behavior or even implied behavior. It is apparent we failed somewhere and probably should have sent him to West Point last year."

"Thank you, sir and ma'am," Franks said. "I have to say I expected a confrontation from you."

"To be honest," Alexander started, "I came here with the intent of having a confrontation, but I never expected my son to have stooped so low. I cannot in any way defend what he has done and I'm certain that his sister will feel the same way. My daughter had a similar issue in the recent past. Jimmy even remotely acting this way is completely unacceptable." Alexander was obviously angry, "Suffice it to say that even if you do not have sufficient evidence to show his involvement or his guilt that I will review this thoroughly and he will be punished accordingly in our home. This just is not acceptable."

"Dad," Jimmy was in tears, "I didn't mean it! We were just having fun and it got out of hand. Please Dad! Please help us."

"You three are on your own," Alexander said, turning from Jimmy. He and his wife walked away. They got into the big Cadillac and left.

"Ouch," Franks said. "I'd bet that was scary. How do you think you're going to do in jail, Jimmy?"

Jimmy put his head on his knees and began to cry.

"Only a father could break down a son so easily," Tyrel said.

"I thought the mother did a good job as well," Alex said.

"It will be good to close this part of the case," Tyrel replied. "How are we doing on the other side? And are you ready to tell me where the witnesses are?"

"All in good time," Alex said.

"You know, I'm not sure what a good time is right now," Tyrel lamented. "Apparently, my team has been delayed again, and it is just me out here with you. We need to get this solved so I can take it straight to these people. I got a call from my superiors, telling me to back off and I don't think I can do that. I'm heading to my hotel. I expect to hear from you quickly Alex," Tyrel stated, walking toward his car.

Officers came over to collect the three boys. The EMTs had completed their tasks, and the boys were deposited in the back of a squad car. They were no longer filled with any bravado but instead looked as though they wore the weight of the world. Jimmy glanced over at Alex and Franks talking then simply bowed his head.

The squad car drove off, and Alex smiled for just a moment. "He really picked the wrong mark today," Alex said.

"So, who was this girl?" Franks asked.

"You wouldn't believe me if I told you," Alex laughed, "but I can actually say that Jimmy was probably the luckiest man in the world today to be alive."

"That bad?" Franks asked.

"I'm pretty sure that with her training she could take out a dozen people without working up a sweat. This boy walked upon her expecting a win," Alex said.

"I would really like to meet this girl since I just said that she is in the process of being interviewed," Franks laughed.

"I'll see what I can do for you," Alex smiled.

The last few officers were removing the caution tape and soon all that was left was Alex and Franks.

"I will see you later," Alex said, walking towards the mall.

"Shopping to do?" Franks asked.

"Something like that," Alex said.

"I hope I hear from you soon. The other side of this is a little scary," Franks said.

"You will," Alex said and walked through the mall door, leaving Franks behind.

Franks stood there for a moment before he walked over to his car, got in, then drove off the lot.

The parking lot was quiet. No one would have known the chaos that was there just a short time ago.

Chapter 40

"General Tarkington," Sarah said as she opened the door to his office, "Mister Vance is on the phone for you."

"Vance, what can I do for you?" Tarkington asked.

"Well, we seem to have ourselves a little problem," Vance replied. "It seems that there are a series of events going on in Indianapolis that I can't quite confirm. It appears I have an agent down, but I still haven't been able to verify everything going on with that agent. It appears I have an agent on the ground, but I have not been able to verify that agent as engaging anything. It appears that your people are doing most of the work, but I cannot verify that either. Do you understand how a person, like me, would feel if I had no information coming in?"

"I know exactly how you would feel," Tarkington replied.

"I can appreciate that, Mister Tarkington," Vance said. "I was wondering if you have sufficient information to give me some type of status, or if you are in the dark as much as I am?"

"The last status I have, Mister Vance, is that my people were unsure of who to trust and were engaging on multiple fronts," Tarkington stated. "They believe that all sides may be compromised, and as such, they have taken precautions to protect the victims. Now, I'm not sure whether that is including your group, but I am sure that my people are completely trustworthy. They will engage with me as necessary or reply to me immediately if I request status. Would you like me to request status from my team or would you like to wait to follow up with your own team member? I am more than happy to make the call and give you a callback. Or if you would like I can attempt to get them now, and you can explain your frustrations. They will be able to confirm your frustrations, disprove your frustrations, or ignore your frustrations, depending upon the information they have currently. Would you like me to do that right now for you? Or would you like to follow up one more time?"

There was a pause at the other end of the line. The thick Texas accent replied after about thirty seconds. "Why don't y'all hold off for a few. I don't wanna be a bother to your team, but I appreciate your willingness to assist."

"You know I am always at your service," Sam Tarkington stated. "I look forward to hearing from you if you need us."

"I really do appreciate that, Sam," Vance said, "and I really appreciate how hard you are keeping up with the President's order. It takes a big man to make such a massive change. I will follow up with you as soon as I know if I need more information. An' I appreciate both you and your team and the fine work they're doing to solve this Indianapolis issue."

"I appreciate your positivity. Let me know how I can help," Tarkington said and hung up the phone.

Tarkington stared at the phone for a minute. He tried to decode what had just been said to him. There were a lot of possibilities. Some of them could make his day easier, but some of them could have some serious side effects.

"Sarah, come in here for a moment," Tarkington said in a loud voice.

Sarah walked into the room and stood close to Tarkington's desk. "Yes, sir?"

"Sarah let's assume things are being watched quite closely, and I need to speak to Alex. How would you go about doing that?" Tarkington asked.

"Well Sir, I have a series of phones, that are outside of our normal pathways, that would give you a direct line to him," Sarah stated.

"Why don't you reach out to Alex on one of these external pathways and get an idea of when he is available for a short discussion,"

Tarkington said.

"I will do so right away, Sir. If I find him available, would you like to speak to him immediately?" Sarah asked.

"Yes, I need to speak to him immediately. It appears we have a wrench in our works," Tarkington replied.

"On it, Sir. Just give me a few minutes," Sarah stated.

"I appreciate your willingness to assist here," Tarkington said. "I'd also appreciate if you would keep this quiet between us."

"I always do, Sir," Sarah said.

Sarah left the office, and the room was quiet. Tarkington looked out across the room and considered all the possibilities that could have been implied by the seemingly simple phone call. It would behoove him to be on top of the situation in case it got out of control. Tarkington considered the meaning of the call with so many simple statements that were not simple at all. Tarkington knew that there was some type of external interference right now and that his group was somehow involved. However, he also knew that Alex would do the right thing in the face of any adversary and would keep him up to date as necessary.

"Sir, I have Alex on the line," Sarah said as she walked in.

Tarkington took a deep breath then picked up the phone, "Alex, where are you?" he asked.

"Believe it or not, sir, I'm at the mall trying to shake a tail," Alex said.

"Is your line secure?" Tarkington asked.

"Yes, Sir, the line is secure and showing scrambled. I am in a public place, but there is nothing near me," Alex stated.

"The stakes have just been raised," Tarkington said. "At this point, it has been stated, unofficially, that this investigation has gone rogue."

"Sir," Alex interrupted, "I have just met with all of the key players, and we have resolved the minor portion of the case. I am uncertain how it could have gone rogue when both representatives from the FBI and the local police were just here. Is there any way to confirm this?"

"I'm not at liberty to discuss it at this time," Tarkington said. "I don't have enough information from my source to really know what the..." Tarkington paused, "what the heck is going on."

"How should we proceed?" Alex asked.

"My advice is to follow what Rachel would normally do and deal with the problem," Tarkington said. "It is hard to say what is going on, and in this case, in spite of everything, I think John owes us."

"Understood, Sir," Alex stated. "We will keep our eyes open and follow your advice."

"Alex, be careful on this one. Make sure you know who you can trust," Tarkington stated.

"Sir, I believe I know who I can trust. I believe this will be resolved tonight," Alex replied. "There is a lot going on right now, and I know it is all going to happen very, very fast."

"I'm going to go out of my comfort zone here, a little, Alex and say something you likely won't hear again," Tarkington said. "At this point, I think further communications could compromise you or me or both. You have my trust in this, and I expect it to be well deserved. The complications on both a personal and professional level make any further communication a risk at best, so I don't want to hear from you until this is done. Do you get me?"

"Yes, Sir, I understand. You need to know that your old friend and family are involved as well, and I am certain they are safe," Alex stated. "Signing off until this situation is resolved."

The phone went dead, and Tarkington lowered the receiver to the cradle. He considered the words carefully that Alex had just said. Involvement, as it has been noted, had always meant potential chaos but always solutions. Tarkington thought for a moment and tried to determine how Michael and Abby had become involved. In the end, he wasn't as worried about that as he was about making sure that the team as a whole was successful. Tarkington put his hands on his desk and looked at the wall in front of him. He knew that, with the players involved, Alex was probably right. This was going to be resolved quickly and efficiently. But he also considered how it was going to be resolved.

Chapter 41

Tyrel Tennison sat in his car. He was not sure how everything was going to unfold. As he sat, he considered the Quality Castings office and how direct they had been. His phone rang, and he looked down to see that, once again, Vance was calling him. He wanted to take the call but didn't have a sufficient understanding of how he would explain the situation to his superior.

Then there were the other things he had to consider. He reached into his jacket and pulled out his Glock 23. He inspected the weapon and pulled the magazine from the handle, the 40 caliber bullets looking clean and crisp. In his mind, he even considered them hungry. He put the magazine back in place and pulled back the slide, only a little, to see that there was still a bullet in the chamber.

Putting the pistol back in his holster, he reached below and found that the two magazines were where they should be. He was amused that in all the time of carrying a weapon, he quickly forgot it was there but could draw in an instant when he needed to.

Tyrel sat for a moment and looked at the dash of the rental car. The Impala was almost new, and he was impressed with the sleek lines of the vehicle. Tyrel never really needed a vehicle at home because he was always on the road, always solving someone else's problems, always trying to make a difference.

Once again, the phone rang. It was Vance. This time, Tyrel put on his headset, and the phone instantly answered.

"Tyrel," Tyrel said.

"It would be really nice if you would pick up your phone from time to time," Vance stated. "As you expected, we got some pushback from the department of the Navy. Apparently, Quality Castings is making some type of valve for their big ships, and the Navy is concerned about our involvement."

"I expected as much," Tyrel said. "I still have no idea where the witnesses are, and I still have no way of ensuring the Quality Castings office is the correct target as far as the evidence goes."

"I am sure you will find the necessary evidence," Vance said. "But you need to keep in touch with me right now, and I will need constant status reports. Tarkington's team isn't going to back off, and if some of the stories are true, they will likely react quicker than we can."

"I'm sure Tarkington's team is taking care of the witnesses and beating up would-be rapists," Tyrel said. "I just left the scene where they caught the three young men who caused this whole mess."

"Do you really think that's what caused this mess?" Vance said. "This mess has been around for a long time, and you just never seem to solve it in time."

"Thanks for the vote of confidence, Sir," Tyrel said. "I am sure I will be able to resolve this, one way or another, in the very near future."

"I am sure you better resolve this in the very near future," Vance said. "There appears to be a lot riding on this. Keep me informed. Period."

The phone went dead. Tyrel sat in the car and thought about how this was just one more complication in a situation that never should have existed. Tyrel considered his next move carefully and put the car in drive, heading to the warehouse district.

Chapter 42

Jim open the door cautiously. Michael and Abby walked into the large hotel room. The group was sitting around the table. All of the food, clothing, and sundries that Jenny and Abby had purchased were put away Ronnie sat to one side of the table with a laptop in front of him. The laptop was a little larger than many and where some people would see an Apple or an HP logo, instead, there was a large army sticker in the center of the back of the laptop. Ronnie glanced up for a moment and then looked back down, unconcerned with the presence of Michael and Abby.

Rachel looked away from Ronnie's screen for a moment. She stopped, turned and again paid close attention to what Ronnie was doing. Jim sat down at the end of the table, waiting for Michael and Abby to sit down. Kira and Jenny were playing cards at the other end of the table.

No one had spoken.

As Michael and Abby sat down at the table, John came out of the far room and nodded at both of them. John said, "Welcome back," breaking the silence in a pleasant voice.

Abby asked John, "How is Jackson?"

"Jackson is doing just fine right now, Miss Abby. He has been sleeping quite a bit. But he is also eating well, and his stitches are just fine. This whole thing has gone so fast, but I know my boy is strong, and he will be fine when this is all done."

"Good to hear," Abby said. "I am sure he will be just fine."

"Is Alex back yet?" Michael asked.

"He called. He's on his way now," Jim said.

"I've been given permission to deal with the issue at Quality Castings," Michael started, "I would rather do this alone, Jim. Do you think Alex will allow that or will I have to be forceful about it?"

"Nice way to start a conversation. You sure it is them?" Jim asked.

"Yes, and I want to make sure this is taken care of correctly," Michael stated.

"Let's wait for Alex," Jim said.

As if on cue the door beeped, and Alex walked into the room. He scanned the room, noting Michael and Abby and his team scattered throughout. Alex made sure the door was locked and put the latch on, then took a deep breath.

"Well that was fun," Alex said. Alex turned at Kira, "The boys who attacked you are now safely behind bars. They were apparently local boys who did this type of thing often. I talked to Franks and he confirmed that it looked like more people were coming forward so it should be a pretty easy case for him to close."

"What took you so long?" Jim asked.

"I guess none of you remembered that I was over there without a car," Alex said. "I had to shake a tail, walk through the mall, and act like I was shopping, find a taxi, take it to a hotel across the street, find another taxi, take it back to the mall, then take a taxi to here."

"Did any of the taxi drivers speak English?" Rachel asked.

"Every taxi driver in the world speaks English, Rachel. Where have you been?" Jim said.

"I'm glad you're back," Michael stated. "We need to talk, and Jim wanted to wait for you."

"Of course, he did," Alex said while looking at Jim with a shrug. "What are we talking about today?"

"I am going into Quality Castings to resolve the issue," Michael began. "I stopped by to let you know and was trying to explain to Jim that

I was going to go alone. I had a conversation with certain people who have given me permission to eliminate this problem. For full transparency, I have been commissioned to eliminate this problem."

"We are sure it is them?" Alex asked.

"I asked that too," Jim laughed.

Everyone in the room stopped doing what they were doing. All eyes were on Michael now and it was obvious that as he spoke his next words it would have everyone trying to decide how they fit in. Jenny and Kira put down their game and were as attentive as everyone else. Alex looked around the room and looked at John, Kira, and Jenny in particular.

"I know this involves you, but I have to say right now that anything leaving this room could be really bad. If you want to go to your rooms and avoid this do it now but if you stay you will be involved as well and normally I wouldn't allow it," Alex said, "Seeing how this involves you more than a little I am giving you the option of being involved. Don't make me regret my decision."

John looked at Alex his big hands held together. "Sir you know I'm staying," he said in a soft voice. "I am also yours, if necessary, to help out. The person who did this to Jackson and Kira and Kira's father needs to be held accountable just like anyone else."

"I think you all need to understand right now that this will not be a matter of justice it will be a matter of elimination. I am only talking to you because I have some respect for you," Michael said. "We will not be bringing anyone to justice. We will be dealing out justice."

"What makes you think you can be judge, jury, and executioner all at the same time, Michael," Alex asked.

"I am neither judge nor jury. But in order to protect myself and the people around me, I made the decision to be executioner," Michael said.

Rachel looked around the room at the solemn faces either staring at the table, staring at Alex, or staring at Michael and said, "I don't know about the rest of you but I'm in. I'm ready to go back to the base and you know how much I hate base. I'm tired of this babysitting and I assume that we can cut loose."

Jenny spoke up, "Aren't you worried about anybody that is innocent?"

Michael turned and looked at Jenny "No one is innocent that works at that factory. Every single person there is either aware or involved somehow. If they are not involved, they have likely been sent home. Other teams have already tried what I am going to do."

Jim broke out laughing, "You know, I missed that level of arrogance that I thought only I had. The funny thing is I'm betting that you have a good chance of doing it alone. That being said, I wouldn't want to miss this for the world because either I'm going to see one of the greatest fights on the face of this planet that no one will ever be able to talk about or I'm gonna see you get knocked down a peg or two. Either way, I didn't have anyone on my dance card right now anyway."

Michael looked over at Jim. "I want to repeat that none of you have to go. I am fully prepared to do this on my own, and the only reason I am here is out of courtesy."

"I appreciate your courtesy, Michael," Alex said. "Since I have met you, you have always been fair, even when you probably shouldn't have been, but courtesy is something new."

"I'm not sure that this is the best idea in the world," Ronnie said. The team swiveled and looked at Ronnie. "By my account, looking at the records I've been looking at here with Rachel, there are almost sixty people in that plant on a normal day. Of that sixty, fifty of them have military records that are either very intense or very redacted. Pretty much we will be walking into a fire fight with an eight to one advantage on us."

"I understand your caution, Ronnie," Michael said, "but I have to go in."

"Alex, I will follow you wherever you want me to go," Ronnie said. "This looks like it would be the most difficult thing we have ever done, and we would be seriously outgunned. All we have with us are sidearms. Where can we get reasonable weapons?"

Abby looked up at Michael, "I believe in you, Michael. I believe you could go sixty to one and am betting you have already done something very similar. If you want to go alone, I trust you, but these people are willing to help you. They have helped you before."

Michael sighed, "If you're gonna go with me, we will need to arm you. I'm not carrying much with me, but it should be enough."

Michael looked over at Alex, "Abby will stay here with the civilians. She is more than qualified to eliminate any threats that may come. The rest of you meet me down at my car in fifteen minutes. Alex, I am assuming we can take that church van and use it as necessary."

"We have a Suburban across the street," Alex said.

"I think the church van would give us an edge for not being seen. After all nobody pays attention to the church van except people going to church," Michael said.

John spoke up, "Sir, if it's acceptable I will go as well. This is my fight more than any of yours."

"Fifteen minutes. Back of my car," Michael said. "I will see you then."

Michael turned as he held Abby's hand. He opened the door, and he and Abby stepped out. Michael let the door close, and the spring pulled it back with a resounding thud. A few moments later, everyone in the room got up and sprung to action to get ready. Fifteen minutes can seem like a long time until you realize how short it really is.

Chapter 43

Tyrel Tennison watched with his binoculars from a distance. Quality Castings was 300 yards from him, and anyone looking could see him easily if they were trying. Parked with several other cars in front of a warehouse that looked like it was being refurbished, he hoped the cars hid his presence enough for a good stakeout. As he watched, he soon became aware that either he wasn't important enough to worry about or that the people in the factory just didn't care. This made him feel a little more comfortable until he saw a glint near one of the top windows.

Tyrel adjusted his binoculars and looked where the glint was near the top of the building. It was a light of some type, or a reflection, but it was evident, and as he worked to zoom and focus, he saw the light shift. It was out there, he just had to get it in focus. It took a few minutes, but there it was, someone was on top of the building, there was a thin series of slots on the roof that were probably for drainage in the event of too much water, or just for looks. Tyrel didn't know. There, in one of the horizontal slots in the brick, was a scope, slowly scanning from side to side across the horizon.

Tyrel slowly slid down in the car. He obviously had not been spotted, but he would be a clear target if he was seen with binoculars looking at a man with a scope. It just seemed a little suspicious. He was not sure what to do now. He watched carefully as he slumped in the seat, and as the scope swung towards him, he put the binoculars down and hoped he would look asleep or at least not a threat. Tyrel waited a short time, then checked the binoculars again, looking for the movement.

He noted the slots in the bricks were patterned to look as though they were part of the decoration, but he also noted the vantage point the spot gave was more than enough to take the time necessary for long distance shots. It was actually perfect for defense, or even some level of offense.

Tyrel looked more closely at the building and it seemed to be built for a siege. There were minimal windows, and those that were apparent seems to have decorations at key areas making Tyrel wonder if those windows were reinforced. All in all, it seemed as though it was a pretty tidy fortress.

Tyrel reached into the back seat and brought out a Pendaflex file. He worked the nylon cord off the file and opened it carefully revealing a great many papers inside. He started at the top, looking over the plans for the building. He noticed at several junctures that the superstructure of the building had been reinforced. The area he had met with Stephanie Wise in was very plain, and also, according to his files, very well protected as well. It seemed each area was protected by an area deeper in the building forming a virtual citadel around the manufacturing area.

Tyrel wondered how many items they were able to manufacture in a building that gave up a significant amount of space to what seemed like an air barrier to the inner building.

Tyrel opened his folder further to a stack of papers. On top was Stephanie Wise. Her file from the service was near perfect. She had been an MP. Tyrel sat and read about how tenacious she had been. She was sent to a desk because she had balked at an order from one of her superiors, when a man was set free on a technicality. The man had pushed Stephanie, and she had pushed him back, off a balcony. He suffered a broken wrist. She got desk duty for two years.

Tyrel began reviewing the employees they were aware of at this time. Each appeared to have been well trained in some discipline and each not exactly a typical factory worker. Tyrel grabbed another file and began looking through Sarena's notes. As he did, he realized she had an insight into the location, and she had ruled out every other angle. He also noted the location was a "no weapons" zone, and he thought that was odd. No weapon statements were common among many businesses, but to have this type of personnel and a no weapons statement was a little counter intuitive.

Tyrel scanned again and watched the scope swing from side to side. He wondered what was at the end of that scope and laughed to himself about what he had read about the no weapons policy. Someone wasn't listening.

Tyrel noticed people getting into their cars next to him. The shift must be changing. He started his car and waited. As others began to leave, Tyrel backed out and left the warehouse as well.

Tapping his headset, he waited as the phone rang multiple times before it answered.

"Hello," the voice came.

"Sir," Tyrel said, "I need of backup and it can't wait."

"Tyrel?" Vance asked.

"Yes, sir," Tyrel stated. "There is a gunman on top of the Quality Casting location. I believe that is the source of this whole mess. I would like to get backup and go in."

"Send me your report," Vance said. "I will look it over in the morning."

"I am not sure this will wait until morning," Tyrel stated.

"You have your orders. Send me the report and let me review it," Vance said. "No more wild goose chases. No more shots in the dark. No more rushing in and finding it has nothing to do with the FBI. I am not sending in another group of people, creating media chaos, and then finding out it was a few radicals. I know you think this is a national ring, and I know you have some supporters, but this has to stop Tennison."

"Sir," Tyrel stated, "We are one team, and this is a visible case. How do you want me to proceed?"

"Send me your report," Vance said with vigor. "I will look it over in the morning."

"Will do, sir," Tyrel said as he hung up the phone. He pondered his situation for a moment, looked back at Quality Castings, then smiled and headed for his hotel.

Chapter 44

The small group was around Michael's car as he opened the trunk. The trunk seemed empty except for the near perfect grey carpet lining the bottom. Abby and Michael grabbed the small clips on either side of the car and lifted the carpet. Instead of a spare tire, there were weapons, several weapons.

It was obvious the entire insert had been cut to specification as each weapon fit perfectly. The trunk now seemed divided for two people and an imaginary line in the center made the trunk look like two mirror images of a weapon store.

Along the front edge of the trunk were two P90s with three magazines each beneath them. This created a single line of three hundred rounds of 5.7x28 ammunition. Beneath those on either side were two FN 5.7 pistols with ten magazines between the two pistols. The weapons were spaced so two people could pull them out and not interfere with each other.

Under the FN 5.7 pistols were a series of other pistols with two magazines each. Each side had a Glock 17 Gen 4, a standard 9mm pistol that was pure meat and potatoes. The Glock 17 was a staple for many law enforcement offices and was reliable to the nth degree. Eight magazines were in place for the Glock 17s.

Between the Glock 17s were two 1911 colt 45s with four magazines each. The black frames of the colt were polished and well oiled. These had stopping power and were accurate, another staple from many service groups.

Beneath the line of pistols, the mirror image split a little. On one side, a Nemesis Vanquish was disassembled and ready for use. Under the Vanquish were a series of throwing knives with Kunai ends.

On the other side was a Glock 18 and six 33 round magazines. The Glock 18 was the big brother to the Glock 17. A standard observer probably could not tell the difference between the two, but the Glock 18 was a full auto weapon and could empty a 33-round magazine in seconds. The Glock boasted a speed of about 1200 rounds per minute.

Jim was the first to utter a sound. "Sheeit, Michael, were you expecting trouble?"

"I always expect trouble," Michael stated. "I bought ten boxes of 5.7 while I was at the range, but it would be better not to be put in a situation to reload." Michael was strictly business now. "I will take the Vanquish and one of the FN 5.7 pistols. Abby, are you OK with the Glock 18 to protect Kira and Jackson?"

Abby smiled and grabbed the Glock 18, "This will be fine, I doubt we will have visitors." Abby paused and took two magazines. "You take the rest."

Rachel chimed in, "I have my M9 and six mags with me. It should be enough. Ronnie is upstairs watchin' the crew, but I know he has his M9 with him as well. He usually carries five or six mags as well. We can work off each other if we need to."

"I have my 1911 with me," Jim said. Alex looked at Jim with a glance, "Yeah, I know I don't have my M9, but the 1911 is a little more my size. I have eight mags with me."

A car drove by, but it just looked to a casual bystander like a group of people around the car. The car drove and parked, a lone occupant got out and walked to the hotel.

"I have my M9 and an M16 broke down in my bag. I have eight mags with the M9 and eight 30-round M16 mags," Alex said.

"Wow," Jim said. "Aren't we the prepared one?"

"Like all of you should have been," Alex said. "We knew we would be coming into something. What did you think we would fight with?"

"Harsh language," Jim said.

"Rose petals and butterflies," Rachel retorted.

Michael cleared his throat as he unfolded a large bag from the top of the trunk. The bag was easily long enough for most long rifles and was made of nylon. Michael loaded the rest of the weapons in the bag and set it on the ground. He folded down the hidden trunk latch and the trunk once again looked empty.

"Question for you, Michael," Jim asked. "What if you have a flat?"

"Self-sealing tires," Michael replied. "If I have a flat, it will be with something a spare won't help."

Michael lifted the bag and put it in the trunk. "Quality Castings is a fortress," he explained. "There is a citadel-like structure with concentric walls going to the casting area. The frame of the building is bulletproof. We will have to get in and work our way to the center."

Michael pulled out a small tablet and a view of the facility came up. "At the top of the building, there are alternating ports for snipers. I will assume they shot Jackson from there." Michael flipped through the pictures for a moment and pulled up a blueprint. "This blueprint shows the structure. We have to assume everyone inside is hostile and will try to kill us on sight."

"How do we get in?" Jim asked.

"Easy, we drive," Michael said. "The bottom floor has a reception area. The double doors are not reinforced. We can drive the vehicles in, and from that point we fight our way further."

"Vehicles?" Alex asked.

"I am assuming we will take your Suburban or the Church Van and my DB9. The DB9 is bulletproof," Michael began.

"Shotgun," Jim said.

"Ass," Rachel laughed.

Michael glared at the two. "You will follow me in. I am hoping they will not see you as a threat until I am in."

"The big black thing behind you is not a threat?" Alex said.

"I will have the lights pointed up, it should make it harder for them to see," Michael stated.

"OK, so we blind them, and I follow in the dark. When do we go?" Alex asked.

"It's midnight now," Michael said. "I suggest we leave here at 2:00 AM. Hit them at 3:00 AM then get out as we can. Thirty minutes maximum."

"What about the police?" Alex asked.

"We will have to be quick, because they will come. I don't relish the idea of them getting in the middle of it, but it can't be avoided." Michael replied. "I am betting it won't be reported initially, but once someone sees something Indianapolis has a superb response time. Less than five minutes."

Alex paced for a moment in the dark parking garage, "I will call Franks and see if he can buy us some time."

Michael frowned, "More people mean more points of failure." Michael paused for a moment. "I should have done this alone."

"Don't get your panties in a wad," Jim giggled. "We do this for a living too. We can handle it."

"Your baggage then," Michael said obviously not amused. "If he comes it may easily be a complication. If he can keep them off of us, all the better. If not, well, again, your baggage."

"I will handle it," Alex said. "Two hours then, down here."

"Two hours," Michael said, "I will leave if you are not here."

"Michael," Alex sad, "this was not your fight. You do not have to be involved at all. Why now?"

"I have committed my word to this. It is on me if we miss, and I won't miss," Michael said. "Besides, I would hate for Abby's dear old dad to be saddened by the loss of his prize team."

Alex was indignant, "You know, we are good at what we do."

"Alex," Michael began, "I have great respect for you and your group. You have built a very good team and they have accomplished a lot. I have fought alongside you. I have fought against you. I have watched you from afar. You will hold your own because you believe in each other and what you are doing. This was my job, plain and simple. I believe in myself because I know my limits and will not exceed them. But my limits are well above yours."

"Are you so sure?" Alex asked.

"I seem to remember having you zip-tied on my property at one time," Michael said with a wry smile.

"Touché," Alex said, "We will be here, 1:55 sharp."

Michael looked at Alex directly in the eyes, his blue eyes seemed to twinkle in the LED lighting of the parking garage. "Alex, I do appreciate you and your team, but I don't like to make mistakes. You are one mistake I didn't regret making."

"Mistake?" Alex asked.

"I didn't kill you and Mark when you approached my home," Michael replied dryly.

"I guess that is that," said Jim.

Fateful Friend

Michael closed the trunk, and the team left for their rooms.

Chapter 45

"Franks," Alex said in the phone, "I need to see you."

"Do you have any idea what time it is?" Franks replied.

"It is just after 12:00 AM," Alex stated in a dry tone.

"It was rhetorical you know," Franks said. "I just laid down not ten minutes ago."

"It's time to get up," Alex said. "Meet me at the mall."

"Nothing is open you know," Franks replied. "Weird time to want to get some Reeboks. Can't this wait until morning?"

"This will all be over in the morning," Alex said.

"What will all be over?" Franks asked, suddenly clear.

"Everything," Alex replied.

"Can't you explain?" Franks began.

"No," Alex said. "This is not a phone conversation."

"Tyrel?" Franks asked.

"No part of the equation," Alex said. "I need to see you, are you coming or not?"

"Twenty minutes," Franks said.

"Bring your tac gear," Alex said.

"What?" Franks asked as the phone went dead.

A short time later, Alex and Jim stood in the mall parking lot next to the black Suburban. Franks pulled up in his black Taurus and stepped out, holding a cup of coffee in one hand and a black bag in the other.

"Want to tell me what is going on?" Franks asked.

Alex looked around. It was almost 12:45 AM now. "You're late."

"I know you won't believe traffic. I needed coffee, they had to brew a pot. And, well... does any of this matter? I'm here. What is going on Brown?" Franks said.

"Quality Castings is the spot," Alex began. "We are going in at 2:00 AM."

"Let me get backup," Franks said, moving toward his car.

"No," Alex said. "No backup."

Franks turned back to look at Alex, "What is it you are saying here?"

"I am saying we don't want backup. In fact, I was hoping you could keep everyone off us until this is done," Alex stated.

"Let me get this straight. You called me in the dead of night to go attack some place you don't know is bad, but you think is bad. And you want me to put my ass on the line to keep everyone out?" Franks said in an incredulous tone.

"That pretty much covers it," Jim said. "But we want you to come with us and play in the bullets too. Didn't want to leave you out."

Alex looked at Jim for only a moment, "We have more intel than we need right now. The police will only make this worse."

"I am the police," Franks jumped in.

"I am hoping I am right about you, and we will have a little leeway there," Alex said.

Franks looked at the two men in a cautious manner, his eyes scanned from one to the other. "Why are we going in?"

"Things are out of hand. If we are going to keep the two kids safe that were witnesses, it is time for this to come to an end," Alex stated.

A wry grin crossed Jim's face. "Well, you know we just want to go shoot up a perfectly good factory."

Alex glared for a second, but Franks looked at Jim and then started laughing.

"What is the plan, and why am I here?" Franks asked.

"In a little over an hour, we are going to storm what can only be described as a fortress to put a stop to all of this," Alex said. "The police probably normally shouldn't be involved. We will go in as a fighting force, not as an arresting group or to negotiate. We have reason to believe the people in Quality Castings are all or mostly in on this. We will verify that as quickly as possible."

"What about innocents?" Franks said. "You just said you didn't know."

"It is a risk, but we are more than certain there are no innocents involved," Alex said in a monotone. "In this case, this will all be over in a few minutes, but we need you to keep the police out of the situation. It will only complicate it."

"The department here is top notch they can handle anything," Franks began.

"Sure," Alex said, "You are right, but there is another gear in this watch. This is going to be over tonight, with or without us."

Franks looked at Alex for only a moment, "Why is that?"

"There is someone else here that will solve this, and we are merely collateral if we are not involved. Personally, I would rather be in the middle of it than off snoring while these guys go down." Alex stated. A car with green flashing lights drove the parking lot and was slowly lumbering their way. "In or out Franks."

"I am in," Franks said as he started to get into the Suburban.

"Umm, you can follow us over," Jim said, "No need to leave your car here."

"You let me stand holding this when I could have left it in the car?" Franks questioned.

"Could have been a new workout thing," Jim laughed. "Don't you feel stronger?"

"I need stronger coffee," Franks replied, "to deal with this crap."

"Scotch works better," Jim said, "but Alex won't let me have any."

"Let's go," Alex said as he got into the driver's seat. Jim walked to the passenger side of the suburban and jumped into the vehicle.

Franks got into his car and followed the Suburban out of the parking lot.

The car with green lights turned and began patrolling the other side of the mall, oblivious to all that had happened.

Chapter 46

"Stay safe," Abby whispered to Michael as he held her close.

"I am always safe," Michael replied as he kissed Abby's neck ever so softly.

Abby shivered and grabbed Michael tighter still. "This will be over today, and we can keep driving?"

"I am sure we have a giant ball of string to find somewhere for the bull to play with," Michael replied as he kissed her neck.

"Michael," Abby said. "I'm serious."

"I am too," Michael said, "I know there is a giant ball of string out there."

Abby pulled back and looked at Michael with a terse grin, "You know what I mean. You have been taken unaware before, what makes you think you have all the angles figured out." Abby posed to him.

Michael laughed, "I was taken unaware, coming out of the shower after hanging my towel up. I was stark naked and still found a way out." Michael saw the concern on Abby's face. "Abby," he said, "I will be OK."

"I know you will," Abby sighed. "I just wish I was going with you."

"How many other couples have this conversation?" Michael laughed. "Honey, I really want to go with you. I know you are walking into a highly fortified area with 100-150 armed and well-trained commandos, either ex-military or at least highly trained, but it would be nice to share this experience."

"That should make me mad, but it makes me want to giggle," Abby said.

"Exactly," Michael said, "that is why I love you so much." He picked Abby up with no effort and twirled her for a moment as she giggled. "We have nothing to fear. How could we? We are made for each other."

Abby held Michael close as he lowered her to the ground. "I love you, Michael. I will babysit tonight, but tomorrow I get to drive."

"Deal," Michael replied.

Michael busied himself for a moment and put on a thin vest. It was woven Kevlar that would resist most small arms fire. In the pockets, he had put small titanium plates. They were light and would provide protection from most fire not absorbed by the Kevlar. The Kevlar would provide protection against most rounds, while the titanium could stop larger rounds but it would still hurt like hell. The combination offered more than reasonable protection if someone could hit you. Michael preferred stealth and to avoid being in a position to be shot, but this would be a different approach.

"Your car may take a few hits, but I will get it fixed," Michael said.

"I know you will," Abby said with mock indignation.

Michael finished putting gloves, glasses and a set of earplugs in a front pocket. Michael always laughed at the movies because most people shooting had no hearing protection. In a gunfight, everyone in a movie would likely be deaf even if they survived. Michael used mini noise cancelling earbuds that were great at what they did but could interface with his radio set or cell phones if necessary.

As he finished Michael looked at the time. 1:30 AM.

"Ready?" Michael asked.

"To babysit?" Abby smiled, "Sure, I can't wait."

Michael laughed, "I would rather it was just us enjoying the evening somewhere."

"Me too," Abby said.

"How do I look?" Michael grinned.

Dressed all in black, Michael could have been a modernized angel of death. His black flak pants and black shirt were covered by the Kevlar vest with empty pockets waiting for weapons. Only his FN5.7 was in its holster. He had topped it off with a black pair of running shoes that did not seem to match the normal boots but were much more Michael.

Abby laughed. "Lookin' good," she said.

"Oh, I forgot," Michael said as he pulled out a pair of dark sunglasses, "this finishes it off." He put the glasses on and nodded his head with a goofy grin.

Abby melted and jumped on him, "You know you are awesome."

Michael caught Abby easily with one arm and picked her up again, "It was the glasses, right?"

Abby kissed him again as he set her down. "Time to go." Michael said.

"Yeah," Abby said as she opened the door.

Abby slid the Glock 17 into the back of her jeans and pulled her shirt down over it.

Michael patted the weapon, "Nice."

Abby looked at him and raised an eyebrow as she stepped into the hallway.

The gunshots were deafening. Michael pulled Abby by her jeans back into the room. The shots ceased. Michael pulled a mirror from his pocket and leaned low to the door, edging it out into the hallway. Two men were at the end of the hall and alarms began to sound. They were advancing towards Michael's door. Each carried an M16 or a similar variant that he could not discern in the small mirror. Each was wearing vests and were helmeted but had no face shields.

Michael looked back at Abby, "Are you ok?" She was already standing and had the Glock in her hand ready.

"Yeah, thanks," Abby said.

"Let me borrow your Glock," Michael whispered, reaching for the weapon. "The FN will go through the walls here. The Glock has LPs in it."

Abby handed Michael the weapon. He pulled back on the slide a fraction of an inch to see the chambered round. Michael took the mirror again and put it low to the ground. The two men were a few rooms down, about twenty-four feet away. He looked closely and noted both had their weapons in ready position, but both had their fingers on the trigger guard, a taught safety hold. Michael stood without a sound, rolled around the corner and fired twice.

Before either man could move their fingers to fire, they were falling backwards. The shells reaching their mark at the bridge of their noses, avoiding their bulletproof vests and the helmets. The LP ammo went in as a small dot, but Michael knew it did not exit as cleanly. With both men down, Michael turned to Abby and handed her the Glock before grabbing his bag. "I think we will be checking out now."

"Should we fill out the comment card?" Abby said as she grabbed her bag, headed out the door, following Michael down the hall.

As they approached the three rooms occupied by Alex and his group, the door swung open and three guns over each other appeared facing them. Jim, Alex and Rachel had weapons trained down the hall and upon seeing Michael, pulled back in.

"I guess someone knows where we are now," Michael said. "Time to go."

John stepped around the corner. "I can carry Jackson to the bus."

Michael and Abby stepped into the room, and Michael left the door open, straddling the entryway. "We need to go now." Michael continued to glance both ways down the hall.

"We stick with the plan," Michael said. "The hotel is compromised, but I doubt they know where you are, and this will soon be swarming with police. Play it cool, let them come in, there will be too much going on here and it will actually work in our favor. John and Abby should stay with Kira and Jackson."

"How do you think they found us?" Alex said glancing out the door next to Michael.

"Who knows. Phone call? Your new friend," Michael nodded at Franks.

"Not me," Franks said. "I am clean."

Jenny starting crying.

"Source found," Michael said.

Alex moved from the door to Jenny. "Who did you call?"

Jenny looked at Alex through tears. "I just called my friend at home and told her I would be a little longer. I didn't mean any harm."

"No one ever does," Michael said. "Then someone interrupts my drive and makes a mess out of things."

Walter, Rachel, Ronnie, Jim and Alex lined up behind Michael. Michael looked back at Abby. "I Love you, lock it up." He smiled at her and ducked out the door as the others followed.

Patrons were starting to come out of their rooms. They tentatively glanced down the hallway at the carnage, then at the five people walking to the broken flashing red exit sign.

"Sorry, folks," Jim said. "Just go back to your rooms and try to sleep. It's all over now."

"Who are you?" an older man asked in his white robe and white slippers.

"Police," Franks said, Showing his badge.

People began going back into their rooms.

"Badge works pretty good." Jim laughed. "Maybe I should get one." He paused and spoke in a country accent, "Sheriff Jim at yer service."

Michael turned and whispered, "Eyes open." He scanned in front of them, "Just two? You really believe that?"

Alex glanced at the team and at Franks, "Eyes open, guys."

They walked down the hall without incident. As they reached the exit door, Michael stepped to the side and slid it open. The hinges were quiet. Looking into the plain grey concrete stairwell, there was nothing. Michael pulled the mirror from his pocket and looked over the painted iron rail.

"Seems clear," Michael whispered., "I will go first. Spread out as we descend, cover all the doors and work our way down."

The group nodded. Michael, FN 5.7 in hand, began the descent.

As they all reached the bottom of the stairs, the sirens became evident. Michael opened the door and walked out into the lobby area, FN behind his back. The lobby was empty. The group was spread wide and quiet. Michael peered over the counter. Seeing a young woman tied up on the floor, Michael looked at Franks and pointed, then kept scanning the area.

Franks went around the counter and took the tape off her mouth. "Owwww," the girl said, and Franks put his finger to his lips. She quieted in a moment.

She was a small thing, maybe 5'4, but obviously athletic with tattoos down her right arm, depicting a dragon coiled on her. Her tight-fitting t-shirt was covered by a larger short sleeve blue smock with the hotel name on it. Franks could not help but appreciate the young woman.

"How many?" Franks asked.

"I don't know," the woman said in a normal voice that seemed to echo in the room.

Franks put his finger to his lips. "How many did you see?" Franks whispered.

"Two men," the girl now whispered. "They went upstairs after they looked up some rooms on the computer."

"What's your name?" Franks asked.

"Anne Marie," the girl replied.

"Anne Marie," Franks repeated. "Are you OK?"

"I am fine," Anne Marie stated. "Just tired of getting tied up. We were robbed a few weeks ago, and I was tied up and left in almost the same place."

Michael had been listening as he scanned the rest of the room, weapon still behind his back. "We need to go. We are out of time. Franks can you cover this and join us when possible. Try to keep them away from-," he paused, "-from where we are going." He nodded at the girl.

"Yeah," Franks said, "I can do that."

Franks reached down and untied the simple square knot, holding Anne Marie's hands together. The extra rope fell away, and she was free.

"Let's go," Michael stated.

The rest of the team headed out the door to the parking structure. As they left the view of the front desk, Anne Marie rubbed her hands together where the ropes had been mere moments ago. Franks pulled out his cell phone and called dispatch.

Chapter 47

Kira, Jenny and Jackson were all in Jackson's room. Jackson was wide awake after the gunfight in the hallway and Jenny was obviously shaken knowing she may have been a cause for the hotel being compromised. Her hair was mussed and her eyes puffy. Kira and Jackson were calm and collected, the situation seemingly becoming more normal to them.

John walked into the room. "Everything will be OK, now."

"Dad," Jackson said, "how can you say that?"

"I just know," John said. "It will all be over soon. We can go back to our lives. You can go to school. Graduate. Make something of yourself."

Kira squeezed Jackson's hand.

"What's going on with this?" John asked.

Jackson eyed his father. "Nothing Dad. We are just holding hands."

Kira realized what was happening and let go of Jackson's hand. Jackson looked over at her then back at his father.

"Jackson," John said. "Stay focused."

Abby walked to the doorway. "John, we should clean this area up just in case."

John turned to her. Abby was small compared to John. His massive frame was incongruous to her diminutive features. John could tell she was in shape and saw the Glock tucked tight in a holster in her pants. The dark pants and grey shirt seemed military. John knew who she was by reputation only but knew she had not been in the service. After all, he had worked for her father. "What are you expecting?" John asked as he rubbed his hands together.

"Everything and nothing. I know the police will be here, at a minimum. Michael texted that Franks was downstairs cleaning up. Who knows, maybe this is over, maybe not. We can prep the room for visitors and make sure we are ready to defend it if we need to, ok?"

John looked back at Jackson, Jenny, and Kira, "I'll help."

The two busied themselves going over the main room. Cleaning the conference tables of anything out of the ordinary, and also working to make certain that lines of fire could be curtailed from any point of entrance. They moved the conference table so it could be pushed over and would block the room where Kira, Jackson and Jenny were. They set up the couch so it would be a good hiding spot. Working in silence, they each walked to the door, surveying the area, then walking to different spots to see how it might play out.

Abby looked at John. "I remember you."

John glanced at her as he moved a TV closer to the wall. "I remember you, too," he said. "You were younger, maybe even a teen. Much younger than Jackson now. I met you when you were at your father's office. You sat so quietly as he spoke."

Abby chuckled, "What else could anyone do around my dad?"

"I guess you're right," John said. "I always wondered how you would turn out. With your dad I mean."

"So how did I turn out?" Abby asked.

"Better than I thought," John said. "I expected you to be dead."

Abby stood and looked over John. "Why would you think that?"

"I know what we did was the right thing to do, but your Dad was not so nice to a lot of people," John said. "Things happen."

Abby regarded John, "I suppose that's true, John. I am happy now, and rarely see my Dad."

"He is still your dad," John said. "Someone will try to use you someday to get to him."

"They have tried," Abby agreed. "I am sure it will be hard to find us. I am more certain that we will be more prepared for them than they are for us."

"I know your Michael only by reputation," John said, "but he seems to take care of things."

"That is one way to put it," Abby said as they stood and looked around the room.

There was a knock at the door.

Abby moved to the far side of the door while John moved back to the door of the room with Jackson, Kira, and Jenny in it. "Yes," Abby said.

"It's Franks," she heard the voice say. "Team is on the way. Michael said he forgot something."

Abby unlocked the door but held her position to the right side she motioned to John to move back into the room. The door burst open and Franks fell forward to the carpet. Anne Marie stepped into the room brandishing a Micro Uzi. The Uzi was outstretched in the woman's arm as she leaned in and aimed at Franks. Abby stepped in, pushing the weapon up as Anne Marie squeezed the trigger. The twenty-one shells in the weapon burst into the ceiling in an instant, deafening everyone in the room.

Abby slammed the weapon down and brought her knee up to the elbow of the woman, causing her to drop it on the floor. Anne Marie was already swinging at her, but Abby stepped into the swing, grabbing her arm. With a simple Jiu Jitsu move, she used the woman's weight to bring her over Abby's shoulder and land hard on the carpeted floor while Abby moved back to a defensive position between Anne Marie and the Uzi.

Anne Marie landed with an audible, "Oof".

Franks was trying to get up, but his hands were tied behind his back with a handcuff knot. The knot would be hard to remove without assistance.

Anne Marie was already back on her feet and surveilling the area. She moved toward the room housing Jackson and the small group, but as she reached the room John stepped out. Anne Marie bounced off his imposing frame then fell back as he reached for her.

John swung again, but Anne Marie kicked hard and caught John in the groin, knocking him to his knees. As she started towards the door, she pulled a 6-inch knife from a small sheath and moved up. Abby caught her from behind and swung her into the room. The knife clattered to the floor at Abby's feet.

There was a glint in the hallway and Anne Marie grinned slightly. Abby was catlike as she reached down, grabbed the knife and flung it towards the door just as she saw the tip of the AK-47 enter the room.

The man holding the gun fell to the ground with no sound. His body twitched several times like butter dancing on a hot skillet.

As Abby was distracted for an instant Anne Marie grabbed her from behind and yanked her long blonde hair. Abby tried to turn but her ponytail held her fast as Anne Marie pulled her into a hammerlock.

Abby kicked her instep, but Anne Marie held fast. Abby swung her arms backwards but missed. Anne Marie smiled and said, "Good night, bitch."

Two giant hands grabbed Anne Marie by the back of the neck and lifted her like a child. Anne Marie dropped Abby and reached for her neck, she was two feet off the ground and could gain no purchase. Her legs kicked back and forth trying to find a target, but John held her fast and far enough away she could not reach. To anyone else it would be like a man held a ragdoll in the air. As Anne Marie's struggles began to slow, John raised her higher and slammed her bottom first on the ground. Anne Marie yelped in pain, certain her tailbone was either bruised or broken by the hard fall on carpet covered concrete.

Anne Marie was not done and winced through obvious pain. She began to jump up from the floor, although not as fast. She stopped cold when she saw the Glock 18 with a 33-round magazine staring her in the face.

"Wanna see how fast this one empties compared to that Uzi?" Abby asked.

"Might as well," Anne Marie said as she continued to jump towards Abby.

The Glock 18 trigger was pulled before Anne Marie moved a fraction of an inch. A one second burst put twenty rounds into Anne Marie's head, leaving very little left except fragments of bone, brain, and skin on the floor.

"You killed her," John said.

"God, I hope so," Abby replied as she coughed a little. "She was a real pain in the ass. If she gets up from that, I will not be happy."

Abby stepped over the body and to Franks a few feet away. She made sure she had missed him and pulled out a spring assisted Kershaw knife. It was razor thin and razor sharp and cut through the ropes on his hands with ease.

"Thanks for the heads up," Abby said. "Michael does not forget things."

"You got that?" Franks said, "I was suspicious but careless. She took me by surprise downstairs. I think these two are the last of them." Franks walked to the door and the other man with the AK47 lay on his stomach with his head tilted to the side. The knife used by Anne Marie minutes before was embedded in the center of his forehead, and his eyes were locked open in astonishment. "Nice throw," Franks said as he pulled the body into the room and closed the door.

"Thanks, I practice every day," Abby said.

"I go to the gym once a week," Franks replied.

Abby didn't know what to say. She turned to looked at John, still sweating from the kick he had taken a few minutes ago. "Thanks, John."

"No problem, ma'am," John said.

"I better get downstairs. I am sure there are going to be a lot of questions," Franks said. Walking out the door, he closed it behind him.

Jenny and Kira looked around the corner. Kira saw the bodies on the ground and asked, "Are you ok?"

Jackson moved to the door, obviously limping but holding a vase ready to throw.

Abby closed the Kershaw knife. "Yep, we are fine. Shouldn't you be in bed Jackson?"

Jenny saw the bodies, then focused on Anne Marie's remains and the mangled head. A split second later, she fainted.

Chapter 48

"What do you mean you are on your way to attack a fortress?" Tarkington asked with obvious frustration. "I did not approve you going in and destroying a building and I told you not to call me."

"No sir, but you did say to help in any way possible," Alex said. "We are solving the problem.

"What the f..." Tarkington stopped. "Why did you choose this course of action?" Tarkington said in a quiet voice.

"We really had no choice," Alex replied. "Michael was going in with or without us."

"What is your plan?" Tarkington asked.

"We are following Michael in. He has briefed us on the facility," Alex stated. "We are not involving other agencies for fear of them being compromised or worse. We have one FBI agent missing, we will attempt to determine the outcome of her disappearance, but it may not be connected."

"We both know that is unlikely. She is in the middle of this somewhere," Tarkington stated. "My daughter?"

"Not in the line of fire, sir. She has stayed at the hotel," Alex replied.

"Stayed doing what?" Tarkington asked.

"Protecting the witness, John and his son," Alex replied.

"Keep me apprised," Tarkington said. "I will call Vance after you are complete. Try to protect Masterson, but not at the cost of the team."

"Understood," Alex said as the phone clicked.

"What did he have to say?" Jim asked.

"For us to take care of it, in not so many words," Alex said.

"I bet that is exactly what he said," Jim laughed. "I am sure it was laced with colorful metaphors."

"No," Alex replied as he focused on the DB9 in front of him, "He has been uncommonly clean when talking to me. He almost slips sometimes, but he is not the General I have dealt with recently."

"Really?" Jim said in an incredulous tone.

"Really," Alex said. "I told you this was getting weird."

They were less than 5 minutes away from the warehouse, the city was quiet. It was a beautiful city, with building that came up and stretched across the skyline. Even the warehouse district they were entering was clean and though void, quite nice.

Alex grabbed his cell phone as it rang, "Yes"

"Follow me in," Michael said. "We will take it slow unless we are fired upon. Right into the doors."

"Will do," Alex said.

The phone went dead.

"He is all business when he is in the mode," Alex said.

"Aren't you a little glad?" Jim replied. "I mean, he is a bit of a character, but he gets the job done."

"Yes, he does," Alex replied.

"So, do we," Rachel's voice came from the backseat.

"Yeah, but it is ok to let someone else take the heat sometimes," Jim stated, looking back at Rachel.

"Sure, whatever," Rachel said. "I would rather pound a few

people myself."

"I am pretty sure you are about to get your chance," Alex said.

"Me too," Jim chimed in.

Ronnie was silent in the back seat, watching the car in front of him and the looming factory they now approached. Ronnie checked his weapon, then slid it back in the cross holster. "Alex, how do you feel about this engagement? I am concerned we do not have enough intel."

"Engagement?" Rachel asked, turning to Ronnie. "We are not going to marry them."

"Ronnie has a point. This will not be an easy incursion, stay tight, I want us all out alive," Alex stated, "I will take point and follow Michael in. Jim and Rachel will follow. Ronnie, you cover our butts."

"No looking at mine," Rachel laughed.

"I would have preferred a lot more planning. Maybe we should have just stayed on the sidelines and let Michael do his thing, but this just seems wrong. And we have an obligation to right wrongs." Alex stated.

"I don't remember seeing that in the manual anywhere," Jim jumped in. "Alex, you know I am in, but we are not some team of supermen trying to solve the world's problems. We are a team trying to right a few things that come up. We could be cleaning up covert loose ends for a long time. This, well," Jim searched for the right words, "this is a bit out of our normal playing field."

The building was getting closer. Michael's DB9 suddenly lit the building up completely as they entered the drive with Alex following close behind the small car, in the Suburban. No bullets were fired, no contact, nothing.

"You know, you really should have said things earlier if you had concerns," Alex said. "But it doesn't matter. We are going in now.

Committed."

"We should be committed," Jim laughed.

The lights went out on the DB9 in front of them. The warehouse was quiet. Michael got out of the car and crouched behind the door. The four in the suburban waited a moment, then their doors opened.

"Stay inside, just hold," Alex said.

The breeze was cool and glided through the big Suburban. There was a silence in the area with sounds of distant workers and machines, but nothing else.

"Earpieces," Alex said. All four put in their headsets.

"I don't like this," they heard the voice of Michael say. "The plant seems dead."

"Maybe they bugged out," Rachel aid over the communication device.

"Let's find out," Michael replied. The DB9 began flashing bright strobes in the air, and they could see Michael heading to the door of the plant. The strobe gave an effect making Michael look as though he was jumping from spot to spot with no clear direction. Suddenly he was at the door.

The lights stopped and there was relative darkness except the few overhead lights in the area.

"Door's open," Michael said, "checking for booby traps. All lights are very low, almost out. It seems like emergency lighting."

In emergencies, it was common for some areas to be left more easily accessible so that security measures could direct the line of entry, in this case in or out.

"Clear," Michael said. "I am going in."

"Did you check for an old-fashioned trap door?" Jim said.

Alex, Jim, Ronnie, and Rachel got out of the car and stood behind the doors of the suburban as Michael went inside.

It was quiet. A pin could easily be heard dropping.

"Lobby is all clear. The hanging art is worrisome, but I will push through," Michael stated. "I am of the mind it has been moved for cover and confusion. I am also certain we are expected."

"Ya think?" Jim whispered. "I am pretty sure that we are probably not the first here. I bet they are waiting with cake and candles."

"Moving up," Alex said, and the group walked carefully to the door in pairs. Alex was in the front, his M16 was trained high to the top of the building. Rachel and Jim each had a P90 and walked slowly scanning each side of the building. Ronnie had packed his M16, as well, and scanned side to side, turning behind them, just in case.

The four reached the door and walked in. The scene was as Michael had described it. There were metal sculptures at ground level all over the large lobby. Alex walked to the nearest which was shaped like a tree. The steel was cut well but thick and would withstand most arms' fire. Alex guessed each piece of art weighed hundreds of pounds. He followed the heavy aircraft cables up and lost the cable in the rafters. Taking out a small flashlight he flashed the ceiling and saw that each piece of art was on its own motorized lift, allowing them to be raised and lowered at will.

"Feel like we are back on a tactical course?" Alex asked.

"Yeah," Jim said, "I hate those damn things. They always flip the little girl at me, and I shoot her."

"I wouldn't expect a little girl in this one," Alex said. "I am looking for something out of a bad horror movie."

Michael was oblivious to the group that had just entered the lobby. Since they were in house Michael reviewed the cameras in the room. There appeared to be three. Paying no attention to the four people behind him he took three knives from his wrist sheath and methodically threw each one directly into the lens of the cameras that were evident. As he threw the knives in a rapid manner, they all heard the tinkle of glass breaking. The room was silent again.

Michael walked back to the small group, "Four doors. According to plans, two are conference rooms, one bathroom and one a hallway to the core of the plant."

"Jim and Rachel will clear the conference rooms. Ronnie will check the bathroom. I will stay here to back you up and wait for this room to be clear. We will than take the hall together," Alex whispered.

Michael looked to Jim and Rachel and pointed to the two doors on the left side of the room. He nodded to Ronnie and pointed to the door on the left, near the reception area. Rachel and Jim moved forward in a careful manner. They moved in and out of the steel sculptures which obscured their view of Alex for seconds at a time. As they reached the first door, they split to either side of the door. Jim reached down to the handle and slowly opened the door. There was no movement, no sound, and the room was dark as the outside night. Jim and Rachel each had a P90 in one hand and Jim pulled a flashlight from his vest with his left hand. Rachel looked at him with wide eyes. She reached around the corner from the left side of the door that she was on and flipped on the light switch.

There was a hum of lights coming on and the bright white light of LEDs casting a long glean into the reception area. Jim put his flashlight back. Rachel glanced in the room, it appeared empty. She glanced again, it still appeared empty so she entered the room and looked around. The room was clear, and crisp, obviously comfortable. A cherry credenza was in the corner and there were numerous televisions and a whiteboard, perfectly cleaned as though they had been purchased yesterday. Rachel stepped back out one foot at a time, flipped off the light and closed the door.

"Next," Rachel whispered.

"Want my flashlight?" Jim asked.

The next room was equally as sterile and equally as empty. Michael had his Vanquish trained on the warehouse door the entire time. The sleek rifle seemed to drip with anticipation.

Rachel and Jim nodded to Ronnie who had waited at the edge of the bathroom door. Like Rachel he opened the door from the left side, then flipped on the light switch. The bathroom was as sterile as a hospital room. Ronnie scanned the room several times and noted the shower stall with towels as well as a bidet style toilet. Far nicer than anything he had seen at any warehouse he had ever been in. Ronnie turned off the light and closed the door.

Michael moved forward to the final door.

"Is this like one of those old Scooby-Doo episodes where people run in and out of doors?" Jim asked.

"Quiet," Alex said as Michael reached the door.

Jim laughed in his mic, and Alex glared for a minute. Jim made a face then acted as though he was locking his mouth with a key.

The silence was deafening as the door opened and the hallway beckoned them in. The door creaked ominously the last few inches of its path. Michael looked at the walls and the art everywhere, then saw one camera at the end of the hall. Another knife was thrown, and the camera shattered as the knife penetrated the outer cover. Michael then proceeded down the hall. Alex followed a few steps behind. The end of the hallway the path turned left into the warehouse and they had no view for that distance. The walls were nondescript but covered with metallic figures and artistry. They came to the end of the hall with no incident. The corner loomed to the left. Michael looked back at Alex, then pulled a small mirror from his pocket. Leaning low he put it out past the edge only to see a short empty hallway, then a turn to the left again. Michael moved into this short hall and moved his mirror to see the hallway that doubled back. The hall went the length of the previous hall this time with a door at the end to the right.

Michael looked at the door in the mirror. The steel frame and card lock should be easy to enter, but now they would be down almost 200 feet of hallway to defend. It was as though they were in a maze. Michael consider for a moment, looked up and counted the ceiling tiles, then doubled back getting a side look from Alex who soon followed. Ronnie was at the rear of the group and still by the lobby. Michael stopped there. He looked back at the long hall and counted. Michael then looked at Ronnie and whispered, "Cover the hall."

Ronnie knelt with his M16 pointed down the hall.

Michael walked past the closed bathroom to the middle conference room and entered it. He looked at the walls carefully then pulled one of the Kunai throwing knives from his sheath. He put the knife to the plasterboard wall and pushed with minimal force, turning the blade as he did so, soon the blade was deep in the wall. He twisted it slightly.

Alex and Jim joined him in the room. Michael turned and put his finger to his lips. He pulled the knife from the wall and looked into the small hole. Through the wall there was another room, inside at least fifteen men were standing pointing their weapons at the door.

Michael stepped to the side and whispered to Alex, Jim, and now Rachel. "There are at least fifteen men behind this wall. It is at the end of the two hallways. The room is enclosed. We can open fire from here and surprise them as long as we take them quickly. We are just as vulnerable if there are any left standing. I have the two FN 5.7s, you have my P90s, and one m16. If we lay down fire that will be 170 shells in nothing flat. It should clear the room. We just have to each spray a different area to ensure no one gets by."

Alex spoke into his mic. "Ronnie, keep things covered."

"Done," came the reply.

"Once we are done firing, we need to push through this wall. No idea why people don't reinforce walls more," Michael said.

"Let's do this," Rachel said.

Michael pulled out the two FN 5.7 pistols, one in each hand, Rachel and Jim both aimed at the wall, and Alex put up three fingers, then counted down, two, one.

If all of them did not have some type of hearing suppression in it would have been deafening. As it was each could feel the onslaught in their skin as the two p90s and the m16 unloaded. The two 5.7 pistols created a series of blasts and were nearly as rapid. The wall was littered with holes and Michael rushed into it where a mass of rounds had hit smashing through insulation and splintered wood.

He could not push through but there was now a large opening and a clear view into the room. It was a chaotic scene with men laying all over the floor in various states. A few stirred and Michael fired at their helmets quieting them with minimal effort.

The door at the other side of the room was cracked slightly and Michael saw the grenade fall into it.

"Down," he said as he dropped flay to the floor. The explosion shook the room, but enough of the wall remained and to protect them from the blast even though shrapnel was now all over the conference room as well the grenade was behind multiple bodies, which absorbed the lower trajectories.

Michael turned and took the Vanquish from his back and chambered a round, aiming through the smoke he shot the door handle which split in the center. The door stayed closed. Michael chambered a second round and fired at the lock and the door shuttered and slipped only slightly ajar.

Michael was about to push through the room when they heard Ronnie begin firing. Alex and Michael exchanged glances, and Michael said, "You three help him, I am betting they are pushing the walls."

"You?" Alex asked.

"I will cover this side," Michael said as he dropped the magazines from the FN 5.7s and slapped up two new magazines.

Rachel, Alex and Jim went back through the lobby to the hallway.

Ronnie was reloading.

"There are about 10 coming down the hall, I got about half of them, but they came out of the far wall sir," Ronnie said.

Alex glanced down the hall. Several men lay on the floor and one of the pieces of art lay partially open to another area. Alex spoke into his mic, "Watch out for the art, a door behind one piece here."

"Roger," Michael said as he worked with steady hands and a sharp knife to make the hole in the drywall bigger. Michael watched the room and noted no one else was coming in.

Michael heard the shots from the hallway and waited. There was movement on the other side of the door, then the door swung open. Michael stayed low and watched as several men came into the room and checked the bodies on the floor. It was a grisly sight as Michael watched them turn the bodies. Michael looked down at the 2 FN 57 pistols, then walked through the slats into the room firing at each man once. Each man slumped onto the floor with the other bodies.

Michael moved forward into the room and pushed the door open. Another hallway beckoned, a formidable looking door at the end. No one remained in the hallway beyond. Michael took two steps into the hallway and pressed his knife through the wall again. He peered in and there was a lot of activity in the room. Men moving around, forklifts moving crates to the walls, and a woman in the center tied to a chair.

Michael looked down at the bodies beneath him and considered his options. He heard gunfire again from the first hallway.

Michael moved back, "Alex, status."

"Holding hallway," Alex replied.

"Spare anyone?" Michael asked.

"On their way," Alex replied.

A few moments later, Jim and Rachel showed up at the room.

"Been busy I see," Jim stated.

"We have a problem," Michael said. "They have a hostage."

"Probably that FBI agent," Rachel whispered. "Tall woman?"

"Hard to tell, she is tied to the chair," Michael said. "We have been here ten minutes, police will be coming, we need to make this quicker."

Jim looked at the men lying on the floor. "I see lots of smoke grenades, and some gas masks, we could even the odds."

Michael looked down, "Good idea." Michael paused, "I don't suppose I can convince you all to stay here and let me take care of this?"

Rachel looked at him in a cross manner, "And miss out on the fun. Hell no."

Jim and Alex looked at each other, "We are in this, for John, and for solving another problem."

"Let's do this," Michael stated as they began picking up all the smoke grenades.

Chapter 49

Abby and John tried to clean the room, but the room was winning. Kira helped where she could and kept going back to spend time with Jackson. Inevitably the knock at the door came.

"It's Walter Franks," the voice came.

Abby pulled the Glock 18 and pointed it at the door while John waited at the left side. Abby nodded at John and he opened the door in one rapid motion and found Franks on the other side.

Franks stepped in the door, looked at Abby and put up his hands halfway.

Abby slowly lowered the Glock 18 with the 33 round magazine tucked in the bottom.

"Watch where you point that thing," Franks said, "Might put my eye out."

"Already did someone else's. You brought company last time," Abby stated. "Have you heard anything?"

"Nothing," Franks said. "Think they were late?"

"Late?" Abby asked, "No, not Michael. They were not late. Something else must be going on."

"I am getting ready to head to Quality Castings," Franks said, "I will let you know what is going on. I will mark this room clear. They are still walking the rooms and a lot of guests have left. This floor may need some renovation. Keep the two bodies in the other room for now. We will sort that out when I return."

"I am sure it will, we'll leave the maid a tip," Abby smirked.

"Might be nice, not sure that brain stains are in normal maid duty," Franks said as he began to close the door.

"Franks," Abby chuffed.

Franks cracked the door back open, "Yeah"

"Thanks for not being one of the bad guys," Abby said.

"I'm having a hard time telling who is good and who is bad without a playbook," Franks said.

"Yeah," Abby replied, "Well, the lines are drawn with a strange marker sometimes."

"Never realized how much until I got involved in all this," Franks stated.

"You never do until you are in the middle of it all," Abby replied. "Michael has said many times that good and bad are useless unless you see the bigger picture. Best to shoot from a distance so you can see everything."

Franks look confused, "Uh, I will try to figure that one out," the door closed.

Abby went to Jackson's room where Jenny had a gallon Ziplock bag full of ice on her head. "You better?" Abby asked.

"I think so," Jenny replied. "I don't think I am ready for your world."

Jackson looked at Abby, "Are there really pieces of brain everywhere?"

Abby made a strange look on her face, "Umm, yeah."

"Could I see one?" he asked. "After all this, I may go to med school."

Kira laughed, "I think I want to learn how to throw a knife, like Abby."

Abby turned not knowing how to respond to the conversation at the moment and went back to the main room. John was on his knees cleaning up the best he could. He had found a large pan under the sink of the kitchen area and was filling it with pieces of Anne Marie's head.

"You know, they will get that," Abby asked.

"I know, Miss Abby, but I've cleaned up a lot of messes in my life. One more won't hurt."

Abby looked around the room. Much of the room was straight now. The holes in the ceiling were superficial since the ceiling was concrete. What remained was the blood on the floor, the bullet holes in various walls, and pieces of Anne Marie's head. Abby knelt down and began helping John, one piece at a time.

Chapter 50

Jim, Michael, and Rachel collected ten smoke grenades and ten tear gas grenades. Each of them took what they could carry. The trick was to open the drywall and get the smoke in before anyone was aware of the threat. Michael had solved that with one of his Kunai throwing knives and cut a good-sized rectangle on their side and started a cut on the opposing wall. It was likely nothing could be seen from the other side, but the access hatch was now complete. All they needed to do was punch the rectangle out and deposit the smoke grenades.

They had taken the conference room table and put it on one side of the hole to offer some protection against return fire, but not much.

"Alex," Michael said in his mic, "you and Ronnie provide a small diversion. Some small arms fire will have them looking your way when we open this."

Michael looked through the small hole he had created, watching the room and wondered how an elite team had not reinforced these walls, or even considered a non-standard approach. He set the thought aside as the gunfire started. The group in the room turned toward the access hall and Michael look back at Jim and Rachel, "Pull your pins and be ready."

Rachel and Jim did so, and Michael looked back, pushing the makeshift access door open. The rectangle was about 2 feet by 4 feet tall and the first two smoke grenades went off quick. Michael, Jim, and Rachel had gas masks on in seconds and began throwing more smoke grenades. Gunfire erupted in the room and Michael pushed through the hole he had created, FN5.7s in hand he began taking out targets, one by one.

Michael saw men began to spray their weapons at hip length. Eyes watering, they could not see much. Michael dropped to the ground and as he could see each target, he shot them between the eyes. He could see the woman in the center of the room jumping back and forth as gunfire erupted around her. Michael's noise cancelling earplug headset kept him from hearing too much, but he could feel the rumble of multiple firing all around him.

Michael turned to see Jim and Rachel taking shots from the door and moved further into the room. Gunmen were turning at the sound of Jim and Rachel firing, and Michael would fire one shot and they would fall. Michael crawled over bodies as he worked his way further. One man saw him and swung down. Michael grabbed the tip of his rifle and pulled forward before the man could get his finger in the trigger guard. Michael put his weapon under the man's chin and fired once. The man slumped over as Michael wiped the blood off of his gasmask. As Michael reached the center of the room, he realized he was covered with blood now, a result of the growing river caused by the bodies all over the floor.

It was quiet except for robotic cutters and other various systems running in the background. Rachel and Jim walked into the room, Michael stood up and walked to the woman in the center.

"Who are you?" Michael asked as he ripped the tape from her mouth.

"Oww," Sarena coughed, "Sarena Prince. You FBI or local?"

"Neither," Michael said as he walked past her. "They will let you go."

Michael walked towards the central area of the warehouse. According to the maps, it was an office area, and most likely where they would make a stand.

"Michael, wait for us," Jim said as he cut the ropes from Sarena's hands.

Michael kept walking.

Jim called out on their com channel. "Alex, entrance is clear, move up as possible. Michael is heading towards the central office area. Rachel is moving up with him."

"On it," Alex replied.

Michael crept forward past whirring blades and plasma cutters. They continued to do their job with no operators. Unknown parts fell to bins and lights flashed in an impressive lightshow. As Michael walked by a large machine extruding thin metal a man stepped out behind him. Raising a knife, he was about to put it in Michael's back when he gasped. Michael turned and fired one shot into the man's head as he fell only to see a knife deep in the man's back. Rachel behind him moving up.

"Might be a good idea to wait for backup, Superman," Rachel said as she got close.

Michael nodded and continued forward.

Rachel fell in behind watching side to side as they progressed. It was only a few more feet to the center when Michael and Rachel saw the door swing open. A spray of bullets hit everywhere tinkling off of machines like windchimes. Michael and Rachel ducked behind a large system that seemed to just bend metal into thinner and thinner pieces.

The bullets stopped. Michael pulled a mirror from his pocket and looked around the edge, the door was closed again. He fumbled for a second and pulled out a smoke grenade. Pulling the pin, he threw it near the door.

Smoke sprayed into the room and soon it was hard to see the remaining few feet. Michael could barely see the door. He rolled onto the floor and pulled the Vanquish from his back. He chambered one round, lined up and shot the lock.

The lock shattered and the door slipped open slightly.

Michael crawled forward one inch at a time until he was next to the door. Rachel had followed. Each was on a side of the door now. As Michael looked back, he saw Alex, Jim and Ronnie aiming at the door.

Michal motioned to them and slid a little further from the door.

Rachel saw what was about to happen and slid a few feet to the other side. Michael nodded to Alex and closed his eyes.

Fire erupted in the room as two M16s and one P90 emptied their magazines. The resulting smoke and massive fireball would have been impressive anywhere, but it did not end. As Ronnie and Alex dropped magazines and reloaded after a mere 3 seconds, they began firing again as Alex ran out of shots on the slightly faster but larger capacity P90. Each of them emptied 2 magazines into the door. After less than ten seconds 320 rounds had been fired into the door and the room beyond, the high velocity bullets would have raked the room completely. Michael and Rachel stood, and Michael pushed the door open.

Behind it was a scene out of an "Expendables" movie. Bodies littered the floor. The room was in disarray and no less than 30 people lay fallen before them. In the far corner, one woman lay gasping. Rachel and Michael walked to her.

Stephanie lay gasping with blood on her face. "Who are you?"

Michael looked down and saw the gun she held in her right hand. He grabbed her hand and pulled the gun away, discarding it.

"You deviated from the job," Michael said to her.

Her eyes squinted, "I know you. You deviated from the job too. Why?"

"I had to do the right thing," Michael said, thinking about the shot he had taken years ago.

"We did too," Stephanie said. "We did too. We got the call, we did what we had to do."

"We'll see how that plays out in court," Rachel said to her.

Stephanie looked at her and smiled. "You must not be with him."

Michael stood while Rachel looked at Stephanie's wounds. "It's not too bad," she said.

The single shot to Stephanie's head splattered very little. Rachel jumped up and away from the body.

"What are you doing?" Rachel said.

"She didn't survive the firefight," Michael said in a stoic voice as he looked at the room. "No one did."

"But she could have," Rachel began.

"She could have done nothing. She was dead when she shot Jackson. She just didn't know it until a few seconds ago," Michael said, walking out of the room.

Alex walked to him, "Anyone left?"

"No, no one," Michael said. "We had better get out of here."

The six moved in a rapid manner out the maze they came in, and into a silent night. Sarena limped a little from being tied up so long but made it out fine. Another car waited for them in the parking lot. When they emerged, Tyrel Tennison stepped out of his car. He remained behind the door of the car watching them approach.

"Is it done?" Tyrel asked.

"What?" Alex replied.

"Anyone left alive?" Tyrel asked.

"No," Michael said with sudden realization of the situation.

"Stephanie?" Tyrel asked.

"Done," Michael said.

Alex and Jim looked at each other and realized what Michael

already knew.

"You'll have your money within the hour," Tyrel said to Michael.

Michael nodded, "What about Sarena.?"

Sarena looked at Tyrel and to Michael, "What about me?"

"I will explain it to her," Tyrel said. "Either way there is no evidence of much. It will be done." Tyrel looked at Alex and Jim. "Sorry you got dragged into all this."

"Me too I think," said Jim, "What just happened.?"

"How do you make an organization disappear? Easy, by investigating it. I keep the investigation at arm's length from the people that matter. I go through the motions, and in this case, I was not up to speed until it was almost over. I am not always trusted with info. Looks better if I fumble around."

"Were we just pawns in this whole thing?" Alex asked.

"To be honest, I never expected you to stay. I didn't expect Michael. There was so much wrong with this, I can't begin to understand how it worked out. If your friend hadn't sealed your fate by calling you, we would never have met," Tyrel stated. "In the end, I had no idea how to get Sarena out, and you provided that solution and all the work."

"What now?" Alex asked.

"First, we get out of here. When we are a little bit of a distance away, I press the detonator on the charges that I planted behind you while you were in the building. They do a lot of work with magnesium here. The whole thing will be consumed by fire that the fire department will not try to put out. Nothing will remain but a memory of Quality Castings," Tyrel said. "Sarena, come with me, we will talk it out."

Michael looked at Tyrel, then at Sarena. "She can ride with me."

"I'm afraid I have to insist," Tyrel said. Sarena began to walk towards Tyrel. A gunshot rang out and Tyrel slumped over the door.

"He would have killed her," Michael said. "Didn't seem right to me."

"I thought I liked to hurt people," Rachel quipped.

Michael walked to Tyrel's car. Putting Tyrel's body in the driver's seat, he started the car. In the passenger seat was the detonator as described. Michael put the car in gear and walked with it, aiming for the lobby. The car moved forward until it hit the lobby and went partially inside.

Michael pressed the detonator button and the building exploded inside and windows shattered outwards. Each of them covered their eyes for a moment, then watched the fire.

"Time to go," Michael said.

Michael left alone in the DB9 while the rest got in the Suburban and drove away. As they drove down the warehouse road, they saw Franks pass them, heading towards the Quality Castings building.

In the Suburban, it was Rachel who spoke first. "You guys run into any more 'old friends', leave me out."

Jim laughed. "Whatsamatter?" he asked, "Not enough action?"

"Hell no!" Rachel said. "I mean, action sure." Rachel thought for a few seconds, "but I don't know who is good, who is bad, and who is neutral in this one. I could go to court and would be telling the truth that I have no idea what just happened."

Sarena chimed in, "I just wish someone would explain what just happened to me."

Alex stared ahead as they drove back to the hotel. "I think we all could testify we had no idea of what just happened."

Epilogue

As the returning group with Sarena entered the hotel room, Abby jumped on Michael with her arms around his neck.

He kissed her and she him for a moment, then slid down off his body.

"Is everyone ok?" Abby asked.

"I think I need a kiss too," Jim said.

Abby winked at him. "Maybe next time."

Kira, Jackson, and John walked in from Jackson's room. Jenny followed a few moments later.

"Is it over?" John asked.

"It's over," Alex said. "There is no one left to come after you."

John wrung his hands together, "Thank you, sir."

"John," Alex began, "You're our friend. What else could we have done?"

"I still owe you a thank you," John said. "I still owe you."

"Let's call it even," Jim said. "If we can get a hamburger somewhere."

"A hamburger sounds good," Rachel chimed in. "I could use some fries too."

"It's five in the morning. Where are you going to get a hamburger?" Jenny asked.

"Waffle House," Jim and Rachel said in unison.

Michael held Abby, "Want to drive?" he asked her.

"Sure," Abby said. "Where to?"

"Ivel," Michael said. "We're done here."

"I have some great places to stop along the way," Abby said.

Michael rolled his eyes.

Alex walked over to Michael and held out his hand. "Thanks, Michael." Alex looked at the man for a second, "I think."

Michael studied Alex, then took his hand. "You're welcome." A grin crossed his face, "I know."

"If you need anything, just ask," Alex said.

"Peace would be nice," Michael replied. "Peace and quiet, and of course Abby."

Jim stepped over to Michael, "We'll have to spar soon."

"Michael will spar?" Rachel said. "Hell, I'm in."

"I would like to spar with a cheeseburger now. Y'all got me hungry with all the talk about food," Ronnie said.

"Let's go get a cheeseburger," Jim said. "John, you and Jenny can stay with the kids? We will bring you back a few."

John nodded. The room emptied and John wrung his hands together a last time.

"Dad," Jackson said from behind him. John turned to his son. "Dad, make sure they get extra fries."

John smiled then laughed. Kira ran to Jackson and hugged him.

Jackson laughed with them as they waited for their breakfast.

About the Author

Andrew Allen Smith was born in Anderson, Indiana. Until the age of fifteen, he moved at least once per year and finally settled in Lexington, Kentucky. Andrew spent a significant amount of his teenage years reading and writing short stories, attempts at novels, and poetry. He published his first book, "A Slice of Passion," in 2005. It was a book of poetry compiled from dozens of years of work.

In 2015, Andrew published "The Theft and Other Short Stories" as a collection of some of his favorite portions of his writings after he was challenged to self-publish a book. Challenged and excited about his success, he published his first novel, "Vengeful Son," in 2016 and began building a franchise with that book. "The Masterson Files" (the series containing "Vengeful Son") now includes six books and has fifteen in outline form. The story follows an ex-assassin that is reluctantly engaged in helping others while trying to retire.

In 2020, after a tragic event, Andrew co-wrote "What NOT to Say to People Who Are Grieving." This book showcased emotions and an approach to helping others be more mindful of their words during grief.

2021 gave us "A Slice of Fear" followed by "Another Slice of Fear" in 2022 with short stories focusing on fears of all types. "Another Slice of Fear" won Andrew a Literary Titan Award and has been reviewed positively for several stories in the genre.

In 2023 Andrew released "Yet Another Slice of Fear" that showcased even more horror and thriller stories followed by a diametric opposite with "Another Slice of Passion", poetry focused on passion.

As Quality Leader and System Architect, Andrew's work gave him credit for a series of instructional manuals for site relationship management systems, various quality documents, and development lifecycles. In Andrew's spare time, he has a passion for many hobbies and his family, which he considers paramount. For more information about

Andrew, please visit **andrewallensmith.com**.

Books by Andrew Allen Smith

Fiction

A Slice of Passion

Another Slice of Passion

A Slice of Fear

Another Slice of Fear

Yet Another Slice of Fear

The Theft and Other Short Stories

The Masterson Files Series

Vengeful Son

Sinful Father

Deadly Daughter

Fateful Friend

Silent Sister

Curious Cousin

The Eternal Forever Series

Adam

Non-Fiction

What NOT to say to People Who are Grieving

Books Containing Andrew Allen Smith's prose

Monster Hunter Intern and Other Tales

The Gift and Other Stories

Simple Things: Moments of Isolated Gratitude

The Portrait of Herbert Losh and Other Stories

The Drifter and Other Unusual Tales

Quire

Coming Soon

Burial Ground

Stealth Drive
The Eternal Forever Book 2 – Morgan